Stories That Need to Be Told 2024

Stories That Need to be Told 2024

edited by

Jennifer Top

TULIPTREE
PUBLISHING, LLC

Contents

I Love You. I Promise

Mike Rosen

*I want to tell you this story without having to
be in it.*   —Richard Siken

It's simple really. When my father died he died completely, my mother died a lot, and I—well, I told you, I just wish I could tell you this story and not be in it.

It's Saturday. I'm 10. My dad wakes me at 4 in the morning. My hockey pads are already on from the night before. He gets the car while I have breakfast, and I meet him downstairs in the brilliant hush of New York City at dawn. In those moments, before even the newspapers arrive, it feels like the city is ours. Me and the greatest dad in the greatest city in the world. We admire the sunrise over the train yards as we search for music on the radio.

"Do you even know whose song you just skipped?" he says.

"No," I say.

"Michael, that was the Beatles. The greatest—"

"This is Ja Rule featuring Jennifer Lopez."

Ja sings, *"Straight loving, I ain't doing this shit for nothing."*

J Lo sings, *"I can't go on without you."*

Ja sings, *"Is this as good as it gets?"*

And I ask him.

"Dad, when *do* garbage men sleep?"

He turns down the radio.

"I don't know, but I bet they wish they could be taking their kids to hockey right now."

I haven't opened the windows for days. There are pints of ice cream and juice glasses scattered around my childhood room. A few days earlier, Tasha got drunk and started hooking up with her roommates. I wasn't there. She came over the day after. She told me casually. Like it was just another Tuesday. I went straight to my parents' house.

Four days later, and I am the furthest thing from comfortable. My dad comes into my room, which smells like a college kid who hasn't bathed in half a week because that is 100 percent the situation, and he sits at the end of the bed.

"You know what old Billy Shakespeare would say?"

My dad loves Shakespeare, reads it by the volume, even on the beach.

"He would say that now is simply the winter of your discontent."

"Dad, what does that even mean?"

"I have no idea."

We're laughing.

It's been months since I saw her. We split. We travel. We miss each other. We make plans.

When we finally meet up in Vietnam, it is obvious: her smile is so soft I think it could keep an egg from breaking. I love her completely. She's in my whole head at once. She greets me at the door of the hotel on a side street in Hanoi. We hold each other in the big white bed. Looking back, I should've ended things then, before the storm, before we lost our keys, but stories are worth holding on to. Besides, love is why you become a person.

We fall asleep.

We wake up.

We're in her little Brooklyn apartment with the wooden window frames and sea-green cabinets. She leaves for work, and I feel like a guest in someone else's life. I've got no job, no money, and nothing to do today. My phone rings.

"Hey, Dad."

My dad is a businessman. My dad *has* things to do today. I don't know business, but I know good businessmen don't make calls in the middle of the workday unless it's about business.

"I'm not sure, probably around nine. You need any . . . Is every . . . When did you . . . Why didn't you . . . I'll be home for dinner. Dad, I'll be there."

This bit about coming home for dinner is the only thing I actually remember saying. The rest is just how I hope it went, or assume, or I don't know. I just don't know. I just know it happened. The way you know a storm happens by looking at the sidewalk after it passes. Or the way losing your keys happens. If you remembered how, then you wouldn't have lost your keys in the first place, would you?

All I remember is that at some point in this conversation my dad tells me there has been a storm. He says we have lost our keys.

"We have to paint the key."

"Okay."

"Michael, we have to do it right."

"It's just a line."

"We have to do it right."

We disagree a lot. I like hockey. He likes basketball. Worse, he's an uncloseted New York Knicks fan. Of any franchise in any league my father chooses the single greatest shitshow in professional sports. He plays, too. In a 60+ league up at the public school on 104th Street there are more knee braces than shots made, but it's ball. His doctor tells him to stop like once every three months, but he'd rather have his fourth surgery than give up that game.

We all have things we hold on to.

Right now, business is good for him. So he pulls out the swing set at the side of our house, and pours concrete on the ground to make our own court. We wait for the asphalt to settle. We argue over where the hoop should go.

"It needs to go here."

"Why would you put it on the long side, you got to put it on the short side so people can shoot threes from deep."

"I want to practice my side hooks."

"Dad, it's not 1970, no one shoots side hooks."

"It's my money so it's my choice."

At 12, I find that a difficult cognitive model to work around. So, under protest, I help paint the key on the wrong side of the court. It takes us three hours to paint three straight white lines. But when we finish, it is perfect. It is just a 15- by 20-foot morsel of crooked blacktop, but it is our Madison Square Garden. It is beautiful.

It is beautiful as I walk to the park near her house. Sometimes in Brooklyn the weather itself is hopeful, like the air got a fresh coat of paint. It feels obnoxious.

I want to text her, but what the fuck do you say . . .

~~hi babe!~~

hey darling!

~~can.~~

c

c

c

can you talk?

hey darling! can you talk?

She calls.

"Did I bother you?"

"My dad called . . . He says . . . He has . . ."

I pause.

It's not that I don't know how to tell her. It's that I don't know if I can.

I pull the word from my gut. It comes up soft as gravel inside my mouth.

"I don't know."

"I love you, too."

We're breathing.

Which feels like a miracle. I tell myself how good it is that in that moment I'm not panicking. Not yet, at least. That happens later.

It's a 10-minute affair—getting him out of bed and back again. He grabs onto the bed bar, and then the walker, and then the side of the door. He's got his arm around my waist, and I have my arm across his shoulders as if I was trying to hold a cape around him.

"One step at a time."

"I'm sorry."

"Nothing to be sorry about."

"My robe is opening."

"I got you."

We do a little shuffle. It's kind of adorable the way we sway together on the way to the giant hospital bathroom. I close the door. He likes his privacy, which is a totally okay boundary for me. But then,

"Michael, I— I need to sit. Can you—"

He's got one hand on the wall. He's trying to turn around, and his robe is open again. I grab him under the armpit as I lower him to the toilet.

I watch him go to the bathroom. It's disgusting. Still, I would rather see him like this than see his side of the bed still made in the morning.

It's absurd: 27 years ago my father created cells and it gave me life; today my father creates cells and it's taking his.

I take hold of his hand.

"I'm right here, Dad. I know it hurts, I'm sorry, but this is going to help, just a little longer. It's going to help, I promise."

I'm lying.

In fact, it's the greatest lie I have ever told. It's reassurance I am wholly unqualified to give. In all my other lies, the difference between the truth and the lie is clear, but right now I have no idea what the truth really is. I have no idea how bad it can get. So I stand there and watch the night nurses try and fail, try and fail, try and fail, try and fail, try and fail to install the catheter into my father's urethra, and then

"Enough. ENOUGH."

I'm yelling.

They're doing their best, but their best just failed five times.

"You are torturing him. Get out. Just *get out*."

They pack their gear, hang their heads, and leave. For a moment, the hospital is as quiet as it can be, which means the world sounds like a refrigerator left open in the night.

I sit my father up. He's had tubes up his nose and down his throat. He's had a tube punched through his side. And now this. He sits with his feet over the side of his bed. If his body was doing anything he wanted it to right now he would cry, but he can't. It's absurd: a man can spend a whole life trying to control the world around him, but in the end it's the world inside him that's out of control.

I wrap a warm blanket around his shoulders like a cape. He is so thin I can see the alive under his skin. He looks at me. It's a tired look, but it's deep, all the way to the bottom.

"I can't do this anymore. I tried. I can't. I just want to be comfortable."

"I know. I'm so sorry, Dad. We're all trying to make you comfortable."

"No."

"What can I do to make you more comfortable?"

"Michael, I just want to be comfortable. Just comfortable."

A man goes his entire life without ever asking for anything. And,

"I need you to tell them. Please. You have to tell them to stop trying to keep me alive."

The cancer wing of the hospital is set up like a giant number 8. He's dying. But he's also been staring at the same wall for 10 days. I don't know which one is worse, so I strap him into the wheelchair and push him around the floor so he can look through other windows. It feels like we're getting ready to go somewhere, to do something together, like we have a plan.

I promise you: I could have pushed that wheelchair for the rest of my life.

We're walking around the Upper East Side. Five blocks behind us, my dad lies under the fluorescent light. I'm trying to decide what's worth telling her and what's already obvious. We all know it's going to happen, but we don't know what it means, or where the story goes after that. Death is imaginable. It's the life without the person that's not.

"How about this place?" Tasha says. She's nervous.

There is a white light above us, an emblem of hope: Chipotle Mexican Grill.

"Yeah, sure that sounds good."

She holds the door open. She urges me to order extra things: chips and guacamole, Mexican Coke, extra cheese. We clean the place out like a wound. She spreads the containers out like a banquet. She is smiles. I am not. I am hospital.

"Babe, why are we here?"

"Hun, it's . . ."

She looks at me, and I have no clue.

"Oh, Mike,   baby,   it's your birthday."

She is close to me.

"Maybe that doesn't seem important right now. But it *is* important. You know that, right?"

She made a hand-drawn card, and wrapped a gift, and bought a slice of cake, and this is how I celebrate my 27th birthday: in the glow of a Chipotle on 2nd Avenue.

It is the nicest thing. It is just the nicest thing.

When true love runs its course, the whole world knows but you.

So we kiss. And we keep busy. The year after he dies we get an apartment. We talk about getting a dog. We talk about getting a couch. We host dinner parties on the floor because she doesn't think it's time to invest in furniture. We try date night. We try therapy. We try reading the books people read when they can no longer hear the music. We drift through the new grocery store looking for the person we fell in love with in the old grocery store. She drinks too much. I go to early yoga. We open the windows until we run out of windows. A fly comes through the window, and buzzes for days. A sparrow comes through the window, and loses its voice immediately. We rearrange the little furniture we have like we're expecting company. We're not. We promise to change. We promise we love each other.

She cheats, and she comes back. I know, and I let her. We sleep on the same mattress. But we're not sharing a bed. We're just next to each other—like strangers on an overbooked flight.

We wake up. She goes to work. I feel like a guest in someone else's life.

Why do people fear death so much when it's the living that's hard?

It is 6 p.m. now. I am on a Brooklyn-bound D train, and as we climb over the Manhattan Bridge the light that enters into the car looks like a thing alive. It is fat, the light. And buttery. And it bathes the whole car—about half a dozen passengers, all of whom have rent to pay and mothers to call back—in the flame of an East River sunset.

Somewhere inside the car my anxiety, too, is alive, and like the anxiety it is spilling over. It starts to speed, and spin, and spiral until it shoots down the track.

I didn't panic when the call came.

I didn't panic at the sight of a catheter.

I didn't panic when she finally left. But I panic now.

The panic leaps from the car. It catches flight, the flight she promised not to take back to Minneapolis, it lands at a hospital, a basketball court, a hockey rink, a graveyard. I'm at a bedside, I'm in Vietnam, I'm in Brooklyn. I'm trying to get to New Jersey where my father's bones remain. I imagine his teeth. I imagine he's wondering when his one son will get a real job. I try to imagine lists of things I know for certain. I am kissing her in a ballfield. I am lying to my father. I am arguing with my father. I am putting a cape on my father. My father keeps losing his cape. I shake some nights. I wake up in sweats some mornings. There are days when the grief is so dark and black that I think it will swallow me from the inside.

Honestly, am I the only one who thinks the truth is more reassuring than reassurance is? Am I the only one who takes the long walk home just to avoid seeing the people who love me when all I want is to see the people who love me?

There's another memory.

It's me and my dad, but you knew that already.

It's me and my dad and the 1999 New York Knicks.

And if you were alive in the year 1999, and you were watching basketball, and you were in New York City: then you know. You know exactly what it's like to watch an entire city rise like a wave that will never break as Larry Johnson bobbles an inbound pass, slides to the left, and drains a three-point shot he never should've been the one to take.

As the shot falls, my father and I leap from the couch like we are on the team, like I had sent the pass to Larry myself, like we have blue and orange blazed across our chest. We high five so loud that it shakes the block. And he holds my hand.

And years later, in a hospital bed cold as moonlight, and brighter than a wound dressed in sequins I hold his hand, which by now is the very opposite of fat, and his breath is the very opposite of buttery, and his body is nearly the opposite of alive, and my sister is on the other side of the bed, and my mom is by his feet, and we ask him,

"Dad, can you tell us about your life?"

and he breathes, which feels like a miracle, and he says,

"The word 'movie reel' comes to mind."

"Dad, that's two words."

We're smiling.

"Dad, do you believe in god?"

He looks up.

He points to me.

I am in this story.

It's okay.

If love is why you become a person, then healing is how.

Floaters

Ross Berger

Francine Hucker, a ginger-haired beauty with freckles to boot, captured the world by storm at age 28 when she, on a lark, auditioned for an animated television pilot directed by two graduate students from the University of Southern California. It was her first time doing a voice-over, and it was only her third audition as an actress. Los Angeles, her childhood dream, had been her home for only two months. The pilot, *The Misadventures of Dinnie Dorphin*, was a space Western starring a high-pitched desperado (Dinnie) who travels from celestial body to the next to save its inhabitants from the evil Garbon the Fattie, a contemptuous marauder who swallows carbs and planets whole. The pilot became an instant hit on the internet, and soon the Fox Network bought it for an embarrassing sum to develop it for a full 22-episode season. The show premiered to massive ratings and quickly cemented itself as a mainstay on the Fox primetime schedule for years to come. Francine's voice, squeaky and unsure but always warm and with bouts of pip and vim, found itself in press-button toys and video games and made the actress a millionaire ten times over in just a few years. The voice-over job was steady, and while the novelty had long worn away, Francine treated every session in the VO booth as if it were her first time—excitedly, clumsily, and boundlessly.

Outside of the booth, however, life was less collaborative. Francine was now 45, divorced, and had a beautiful home in the Silverlake section of Los Angeles. It was all to herself, as evidenced by her sprawling closets overflowing with Tom Ford silk satin shirts and Manolo Blahniks and by an interminably messy bed with a comforter that folded over to the left every morning and stayed that way until the evening, when she went under it to form shapes with her restless legs, outstretched arms, and hands that had nothing or no one to hold on to.

Work defined Francine, and, as such, she never took time off or traveled for weekend getaways. She remodeled her home to fabricate that "everyday vacation feel." She did, however, look forward to attending the various fandom conventions across the country, and always took part in a highly anticipated panel at the San Diego Comicon every year. "Women in Voice-Over" invited packed crowds held in 200-person meeting rooms that accommodated over-capacity. She was one of three "trailblazing women" in the field and always provided her audience with a sobering education on how to break in, often beginning her remarks with a few impressions to break the ice.

This year, Francine was joined by several unwanted visitors.

Floaters. Retinal jelly that dripped from the iris and drifted across her eyes like satellites lost in orbit. From what she remembered from 10th-grade biology, these floaters resembled paramecia and comprised stacked tubes on a single strand. One floater. Two floaters. Dozens of floaters. Infestation.

She administered eye drops to clear away these little buggers. But they returned and were followed by punctuated light, as if pierced through a flimsy sheet of white fabric, focused on just one corner of her left eye. Something was wrong, yet she signed autographs in the hallway before her panel began and gave every fan a warm hug. The handiwork of denial.

She wore sunglasses during her panel and smiled and answered questions superficially, agreeing with the consensus so as to move the event along, so as not to show panic. She failed to answer questions from the audience cogently. Retinal creepy crawlers and glare from unforgiving overhead lights arrogated her attention. She taxied it to the emergency room at the UC San Diego Medical Center, all the while cupping her right eye and refusing to remove her hand. A doctor, who recognized Francine from online interviews, overpowered her grasp and held open her lids and drew his own flashing light into her pupil. She let out a scream, a familiar one, one of Dinnie Dorphin oomph. The doctor laughed and said, "You sound just like her! My kid loves that show." When Francine couldn't bear it, she fainted, vasovagal-style.

"You have a tear in your retina," said the attending nurse, who checked Francine's pulse after she came to. "We can refer you to a retinal specialist in Los Angeles, someone in your network. It's a quick fix these days. Simple laser surgery that welds the torn tissue together."

"I'm sorry, did you say 'welds'?"

"Very common. Probably won't last more than fifteen minutes. The specialists have these handheld devices nowadays, and all they do is prop open your eyelids—"

Francine waved her off. No more opening of eyelids, be it talk or action, or else another fainting spell was imminent. Years ago, she adopted the self-help approach to health, opting for holistic remedies instead, and when in doubt, the Postponement Strategy. As in, *If I don't see a retinal specialist, what will happen in, say, two weeks, two months, two years from now?*

"Well, it's likely to lead to a detached retina, which means you could go blind in less than twenty-four hours in that eye."

Likely, thought Francine. *Likely, but not certainly.*

"By then, an eye surgeon will perform a pneumatic retinopexy, where they'll inject a gas bubble into your eye, which pushes the affected tissue back into place. And then they'll seal the retina against the wall of an eye with this."

The nurse brought up an image of a metal probe on her iPhone: a golden tube with a bulbous tip measured no more than two inches in length, slightly angled midway, as thin as an ink filler for a pen. All Francine could think about was the doctor tripping over his shoelace and bludgeoning her eyeball like a lychee nut.

Such thoughts incited tingling in her calf muscles, sweating, and shortness of breath. Warning, Warning! Vasovagal response in 5 . . . 4 . . . 3 . . .

Her ex-husband Bennie, a voice-over director whom she met during a recording session of *Dinnie Dorphin* when they were both in their early 30s, drove from Silverlake to San Diego that evening. While they hadn't seen each other in a month, Francine was too tired to question him as to why. When does the lease expire on the tenancy of exes? Two years? Three years? What did it matter; he was here for her now.

Bennie escorted her from the edges of the hospital exit to his Mercedes, belted her in the passenger side, blasted the air conditioning immediately, and played Christopher Cross's "Sailing." They, at one time, loved yacht rock as a couple. Yacht rock was there go-to soundtrack, at home, in the car, everywhere, and dictated the emotions of every simple act around the house, be it opening up a jar, flushing the toilet, or watering the plants. They'd frequent mediocre restaurants that would only play that kind of music, just to sit there and listen. Bertie Higgins, Kenny Loggins, Air Supply, Jimmy Buffett, Michael McDonald . . . it was a euphonious distraction to a one-sided marriage. Francine had little interest in Bennie, nothing to talk to him about after nearly a decade and a half of marriage, but the music . . . the music seemed to make her forget all about that. She was shipped away at sea, sailing on a mariner in Key Largo, sipping piña coladas, and cutting footloose. This dependable man, both boxy and too eager, miraculously morphed into Her Captain and Steward.

She was nice to him, or so he first thought. She wielded a powerful alchemy over successful, lonely men. Chubby, good-hearted men. Men who couldn't stop chasing. Acolytes. Anxious boys in grown-up bodies. She fell for them. They were an easy audience, always returned the next day. Francine was attracted to attendance. That and thick forearms.

Her relationship with Bennie was one of safe love. No glamour, no rocking the boat. A paint by numbers romance, of which there was no romance for her. For him, this, all of this—sunshine or rain, happiness or sadness, abuse or misuse—he could not get enough of. He was consumed by her avoidance of him, of her dismissiveness; he was enraptured by her smell, foul and fragrant, but mostly foul. He wanted to absorb all her pain, make it his own, no matter how jagged or frequent. He never tired of her. Never would. Even divorced, he longed for her terribly and refused love and affection from Aphrodites of gentler worlds.

"So, are you going blind?" asked Bennie.

"We'll see. Get it? 'See'?"

Bennie broke away from the focus of the highway and shot her an earnest stare. Francine added, "They referred me to a retinal specialist in North Hollywood. Some guy named Kaminski. I'm calling him first thing Monday."

"How's your vision now?"

She swerved her neck and head, rhythmically, left to right, aimed upward, in the signature style of Stevie Wonder.

"My cherie amour, lovely as a summer day . . ."

"Seriously."

She stopped the routine, curled her upper lip, and shook her head.

"Hello?" he asked.

"It's fine, Bennie, it's fine. Now can you just fuckin drive?"

He rolled down the windows and didn't say a word for the next two and a half hours, for 15 years of drama had trained him not to interrupt moments of intense disquiet.

He steered onto her driveway around midnight and helped her scale the three-part stone walkway, each part rising by two feet, two steps per incline, 100 percent Silverlake opulence. Francine gripped her ex-husband. "Easy," he said, tapping her talons to let up just a bit. They did not. He led her to her bedroom, turned on the light, and walked the ginger gingerly to the edge of her bed, which hadn't been made in weeks.

"Love what you did with the place," he said, deadpan.

The muscles around her eyes slackened. She inspected her ex-husband up and down, down and up, and smirked at the various sweat stains upon his shirt.

"What now?" he asked defensively.

"Are we working out?" She gestured to his belly, to 20 pounds of midsection excess, flimsily disguised by a blueberry-colored, extra-large Polo shirt.

"Are we being an asshole?"

"Shnookums," she said, "you don't have to eat every single donut in the shop."

He matted his shirt down with both hands sharply.

"I can't see you," she said. "Come to the light."

He entered the spotlight from her lamp, an unforgiving light that made soft angles harsh and reduced one's physiognomy to a vague rendering of a child's drawing.

"Take off your shirt," she said.

"Absolutely not."

"But I miss you."

"Then be kinder."

"Kinder?? I should be demanding that of *you*. I'm the one who might be going blind."

She reached for him—an aimless throwing out of her right arm. She didn't know what she wanted to touch, but settled for grazing his lower belly.

"Why won't you hug me?"

"Because you know what that leads to."

"I do." She put her index finger down her lower lip, sultrily.

"And I don't think that's something we should do right now."

"Come on, Bennie. Don't be such a killjoy. Let's take off that shirt so I can see your tits."

"Making fun of my weight, once again, shouldn't be the cornerstone of your sales pitch."

"Let me rephrase. Please doff thou shirt so that I may press mine digits upon thy mammaries . . ." When she attempted to unzip his fly, Bennie lightly pushed her away. Outrage took hold of her face.

"Where've you been the last month, Bennie?"

He was pacing. And sweating. These nerves, she's seen before. Right after their divorce, he fell in love with a cashier at Trader Joe's. He went there every day before he mustered the courage to ask her out. Till then, he amounted a collection of bagged cashews that rivaled a nut shop. The cashier agreed to a date; courtship ensued, but whenever he stopped by Francine's, he could not look his ex-wife in the eye. Then after six weeks, after the cashier dumped his ass for a man half his age and half his weight, the eye contact resumed. The jig was up; Bennie confessed. And today, he would do the same.

"Who is she?"

"Just a girl I met through work."

"Another actress?"

"Yeah, actually."

"Someone I know?"

"No, she's just starting out."

"Oh god, don't tell me she's a teenager."

"No, she's our age."

"And she's just starting out? Did you tell her how merciless this town is? Especially to women? Especially to older women?"

"She knows."

"So she's crazy then. Right? You know I'm right—"

"Okay, Francine. I'm gonna go—"

"Waitwaitwait. I wanna meet her."

"Yeah, I don't think so."

"Well, I'm gonna have to meet her eventually, right? Holidays, birthdays . . . ?"

"Right." The eye contact scattered again.

"Does she know I exist?"

"She knows I have an ex-wife."

"That you sleep with from time to time?"

"*Slept with*," he corrected. Francine arched her left eyebrow. "That bit of information," he continued, "I neglected to share."

"An ex-wife that you drive to doctors' appointments? Help with groceries occasionally?"

"Additional bits of information I neglected to share."

"How do you expect to get away with this, Bennie?"

"I haven't thought that far in advance yet. We're just having fun."

Francine reached out her hand and indicated for him to do likewise. His clench was slight and pro forma.

"I need you to get the fuck outta here. Okay, Bennie?"

"Okay, Francine. I'll call you tomorrow."

She attempted to lie back, but she held her neck an inch or two away from the headboard. The inability to find comfort looked nothing more than an awkward yoga pose. When the headlights to Bennie's car turned on and he backed out of her driveway, she did not feel relief, but loss—and not of a lover, ex or current, but of a limb.

She remembered a different ending, one from a month ago, before the radio silence. It was the night where she was battling the flu and could not get out of bed. Bennie heeded the call. He brought her eight cans of organic pea soup and spoon-fed her some Nyquil. Even in her stuffed-up state, she could still catch a whiff of his sweat and other mammalian residue. She reddened and reached for his inner thigh. He lightly rebuffed her. A fight ensued with common refrains: how he always takes care of her and they're not even married anymore; how she's too old to be taken care of; how she's a child, or—in Bennie's words—"A 45. Year-old. *Fucking*. Child"; and, his favorite, how she's too close to her father.

She wanted to throw a vase at him, but there were no flowers in the house. A sock—a frayed, white tube sock, bundled up into an orb-like malformation—launched toward his chin, hitting it unremarkably.

"Call him now," dared Bennie. "It's, what, three o'clock in the morning over there? He'll pick up for you. Want me to dial?"

"What I want is for you to get the fuck outta here."

He stared her down and then headed out.

"BENNIE! YOU FUCKING ASSHOLE! GET BACK HERE!"

When the door slammed, she knew her charms had worked. Years of countless fights indicated that she would only have to wait five minutes before he would return, often with wet eyes and an erection, craving to devour, to apologize, and to be healed. To be forgiven of a sorrow he thought he committed, but never did. He was forgiven anyway, always. He whimpered when he held her body. He did not ever want to push away such beauty, such fragility. He kissed every inch, every freckle, every sinew, every wrinkle, and every harsh bit. After years of rejection, Bennie knew these moments were not about love, but about luck, and he savored every moment, dreamt of its happening, and always prayed so that dreams would come true. *I'm sorry,* he said over and over again. She closed her eyes when she kissed him, and after Bennie said his last "sorry," she hushed him, pressed her lips upon his forehead, and held onto his sturdy ballast as if it were the last raft in the sea.

Hugging Alder

Laura E. Garrard

Many humans visit my point on the edge of Lake Crescent at the mouth of Barnes Creek, which flows more like a river, I think. They pose for cameras, throw rocks across the water's calming surface as the sun begins to set behind what's called Aurora Ridge. Sometimes they sit, lean against me, or the little ones hang from my lower limbs. But there is one, a woman comparable to my age in human years, who presses one foot against an offshoot at my base and carefully lifts herself to perch on my level branch. She rubs the ribs of my wrinkled bark, picks at my lichen, and pats me with her hand, her love. I can feel it, you know, the light releasing into my marrow. I think we share a beginning story. I feel the water in her well, we all carry similar ruminating material in our cells. We share golden moments in sun's setting warmth until the ball of flame hides behind the range. One day, she spots one carving in particular, humans like to knife their marks, make me weep until I slowly scab. She traces a finger over the letters a man and woman created together. She whispers, "I'm sorry that they've done this to you." I've healed those cuts yet her words soothe something deep, which speaks of human loss that's rubbed off on me, like the lichen. Later, one of the couple returns and notches these numbers next to their lines: '81–'23. I can't wait to show the woman. Sure enough, she notices, and I feel her joy dim. She says, "It has ended, a life or a marriage perhaps." She hugs herself closer to my trunk. We weep together for the couple, for loss, for time passing. We cry into the growing dark and cold. We hold the water and scars of one another.

The Blink of an Eye

Terry Hartley

I should have ripped that paper bib from around my neck and made a run for it the moment I spotted that chipped tooth of his. A dentist with a chipped front tooth; a red flag if ever there was one.

But I did not run.

Instead, like a fool, I chose to sit there and take my chances.

"Let's get you numbed up; it's not a very large cavity," he said as he pushed the needle halfway through my head. "We should have you out of here in no time." As he spun around and left the room, he added, "Let's give that a little time to work."

Cindy, his dental assistant, patted me on the shoulder. "We should have you out of here in no time."

It could not have been more than three minutes when he returned and began getting the drill ready.

I thought, "Whoa, he's back way too soon, I'm not feeling a bit numb yet. But, well, he is the dentist, surely he knows what he's doing."

Sadly he did not. I wasn't even close to being numb.

"AARRGGOG!!" I yelled the second the drill touched my tooth.

"I don't believe he's quite numb," the "dentist" calmly said as I landed back in the chair.

"I'd better give him another shot; it doesn't look like the first one took."

Cindy nodded. "He's gonna give you another shot."

After getting the needle ready he said, "Open wide."

I hesitated. My mind was screaming, "You didn't wait long enough!"

I obstinately refused and remained tight-lipped.

Glancing first at one another, then back to me, they appeared bewildered and didn't seem to know what to do next. Apparently, no one had ever ignored a direct order to open wide.

Cindy took matters into her own hands, offering a professional visual of precisely what was expected of me. She opened wide, then proceeded to point at her mouth. "Like this," she said.

I knew without a doubt that he didn't give the first shot enough time to work and I started to say as much, but with pressure mounting, I reconsidered, asking myself, "What do I have to lose? When it comes to dentists, is it remotely possible to be too numb?"

I said nothing and did as I was told. I opened wide.

Less than three minutes after receiving the second shot I was vindicated. As I had predicted, my jaw was now dead as a doornail from the first shot.

I began formulating a way, without sounding too arrogant, to let him know that he had screwed up.

Cindy broke my train of thought when she popped in to ask if we were beginning to feel numb yet.

I blurted out, "He rewey trewed up!"

She gave me a patronizing smile, wiped the drool from my chin, and said, "The doctor will be with you shortly."

I thought it might be best to wait until I could articulate a little better before confronting him.

As I was finally beginning to relax I noticed a burning sensation in my eye. I felt around on my forehead and eventually located my eye directly below my eyebrow. My eyelid was stuck open. I pushed the eyelid closed and it wouldn't open. I pulled it open and it wouldn't close. All at once it hit me, a staggering realization! Oh my God, my eye won't blink!

"Thindy!" I bellowed.

Cindy rushed in to find me blinking one eye by hand while the other eye darted around confused, panic-stricken, and looking for answers.

Apparently a pro at deciphering incoherent babble, she immediately understood my ranting. "Let me try," she said. She closed my eye, it wouldn't open. She opened my eye, it wouldn't close. "Wow, that's wild, your eye won't blink. This has never happened before."

That seemed to imply that just about everything else had happened before!

"Just calm down and relax," she said as she gave me a reassuring smile. "I'll be right back."

I could hear whispering in the hallway followed by what sounded like hushed snickering. Within a couple of minutes, they were hovering over me. It was obvious they were doing their best to maintain a straight face.

"So, Cindy tells me the ol' eye won't blink. Let's have a look."

Pretending to be the professional dentist that he wished he was, he knew that it wouldn't be prudent to simply concur with Cindy's diagnosis without conducting a thorough examination himself. "Um-hum, um-hum," he said as he opened and closed my eye with the concentration of a doctor performing brain surgery. "Uh, yeah, well, I suppose it's safe to say you're numb, haha. I would prescribe something for you but there is nothing on the market to help treat a non-blinking eye, haha."

I didn't crack a smile, and I wouldn't have even if I could. Instead, with my one remaining eye, I gave him the most intimidating evil eye that I could muster.

"We're going to leave your eye closed while I work on your tooth. Blinking is what keeps the eyeball moist. Your eyeball will begin to dry out and you will feel a burning sensation if we leave it open. A little Novocain probably worked its way up into the facial muscles that control eye movement. Your eye should begin blinking just fine again after the Novocain wears off."

Cindy chimed in, "You should be blinking just fine in a little while."

Right. Excuse me if I don't appear to have much confidence in your reassurance.

I began wondering if perhaps I should have been more like my dad. He had no use for dentists. He ignored his cleaning and checkup appointments even though they warned him that he would eventually lose *all* of his teeth if he didn't take his dental health more seriously. He dismissed their warning, simply saying, "That's how they get you."

In the months before he died, despite his neglect, he still managed to have four teeth left in his head and he considered that a triumph. "Reckon I showed them!" he would boast.

I too have never had much use for dentists but, unlike Dad, I rather enjoy having teeth. So here I now sat, more or less second-guessing that decision.

When he finished with my tooth Cindy wiped the drool from my mouth, removed the bib, and to my relief, they handed me a couple of goodie bags and turned me loose.

I marched straight through the empty waiting room toward the exit. The receptionist was on the phone. She was telling someone, "I'm not exactly sure what happened, but something got screwed up and this dude's eye wouldn't blink; kinda creepy huh?"

I was blinking my eye by hand and mumbling to myself as I drove out of the parking lot. "The nerve of them, trying to pacify me with that extra free toothbrush!" Naturally, the words didn't come out like that at all. I couldn't understand even one syllable of what I had just said, which infuriated me even more. So I drove along in silence, thinking, "I can't blink, I can't mumble; what the hell has this man done to me!?"

I had one more errand that I had to run before I could go home, relax, and let the Novocain wear off. I had to stop by the post office to mail a small package and a couple of bills.

I had no illusions, I knew things could get ugly if this were not handled properly, so I devised a plan, a simple plan. I would speak only when absolutely necessary and shield my eye with the palm of my hand, blinking it as necessary with my index finger. Get in and get out in mere moments without ever losing my composure, credibility still intact.

A good sign as I entered the post office, the line was short. I quietly assumed my place at the rear of the line, package and envelopes in one hand, nonchalantly blinking my eye with the other.

Looking around, I suddenly realized that I would do poorly if, God forbid, I were indeed handicapped. I couldn't help feeling guilty and didn't like the person that I was becoming, but resentful thoughts were floating around in my head whether I liked it or not. It had been less than an hour and already I found myself envious of everyone who had two eyes that blinked unassisted.

When it came my turn I stepped forward and placed the package on the counter. Without looking up, the postal clerk put it on the scale and asked, "When would you like this to arrive?"

"Thaderday," I answered.

I gave it another shot. "Thaderdayth good."

Now he did look up. Peering over the top of his glasses, he eyed me suspiciously as he gave me the once-over. Then he casually tried to act like I was his average everyday customer and said, "To get it there by Saturday we'll need to send it first class. That would be thirteen dollars and eighty-nine cents. Will that be okay?"

I nodded yes, then slid the envelopes toward him and pointed to the corners of both.

This time he spoke a little bit louder. "Do you need stamps for these?"

Again I nodded, but by now he had spotted my index finger moving and knew I was up to something. He tore off a couple of stamps then shuffled a little to one side so he could sneak a peek.

"That will be a total of fourteen dollars and fifty-one cents. If you like, you could just put the stamps on them now and I'll just drop them in the box here."

I handed him fifteen dollars and took the stamps. The pressure was building. I could sense that the customers in line behind me were also getting suspicious, so I knew that this could be the last chance I would have to prove myself.

I knew it was risky, but I had no choice, I was forced to leave my eye in the open position to free up both of my hands. I stood a bit sideways next to the counter to demonstrate to the skeptics that I was perfectly capable of handling the task at hand.

To the surprise of all onlookers, affixing the preglued stamps on the envelopes went off without a hitch.

One final hurdle remained. With a tongue that felt like it was the size of a grapefruit, licking the envelopes should be a snap; how could I possibly miss? I stuck my tongue out, and with a smug confidence, that in hindsight was unjustified, I completely missed my tongue and casually tried to lick the envelope with my chin.

The charade was over . . . the jig was up! Sure, I made a quick rebound. I found my tongue and held it with one hand while the other hand successfully guided the envelope across my tongue until the licking process was complete.

But it was too little too late, the damage had been done, and disappointed pity was written all over their faces.

Unfortunately, they hadn't seen anything yet; the bottom was about to drop out big time.

My eye was beginning to burn so I was forced to blink it once again by hand. I was beginning to feel panicky so I tried to muster up a pleasant reassuring smile to relieve the tension. From the horrified look on their faces, I gathered that my crooked contorted smile was neither pleasant nor reassuring.

At that point, I should have just cut my losses and got the hell out of there, but I desperately wanted to explain my situation to salvage a little dignity. That little voice in the back of my head was begging, "Don't do it, please don't do it!" But the portion of my brain that should have insisted that I heed the warning of that rational little voice was apparently still numb, so like a half-wit, I pointed to my head and cried out, "Denesht, I jush leff da denesht!"

The postal clerk cleared his throat and patiently began counting my change back to me, "Now here's your change, two quarters and one penny."

I handed him the envelopes, grabbed my change, and slinked away toward the exit. Out of the corner of my good eye, I could see the well-intended looks of pity, and as I walked out the door, I heard the distinct sound of coins dropping into the "support the handicapped" can that sat on the counter.

As luck would have it my eye began blinking normally about the time that I returned home. When my wife greeted me at the door I launched into a tirade against the dentist and told her every gut-wrenching detail of my awkward experience at the post office. Any normal, caring wife would have been in tears after hearing such a heartbreaking story.

But instead of receiving some much-needed sympathy, she thought the entire ordeal was hilarious and even had the nerve to imply that I was a big baby. Me! A big baby!

"That's the last time I'll ever come to you with my problems!" I yelled as I grabbed a beer and flopped down in my easy chair.

After I calmed down, I conceded that I may not have presented the magnitude of my heart-wrenching ordeal suitably, but now was probably not the proper time to readdress the situation. Instead, as I sat there blinking my eyes, I couldn't help but marvel at this underrated bodily function and concluded that few things in life can compare with the pure, unadulterated, bliss of having two eyes that blink unassisted.

Flinching

Cass Peterson

To be fair, she did always warn you to *Never Talk Back To Her*
but on this day you did anyway, when she barked an order at you
and you said, *No I Won't Do It*, and she said *What Did You Just
Say To Me?* And then you added, *I Don't Care What You Think
Anymore* and with that, her small lean muscled body snapped to
attention while she quickly swiveled onto the balls of her feet like
a boxer, locking eyes with you with a predatory precision, before
lurching forward, her hands in fists that were rising up toward
your chest and then your head like they always did, but this time
instead of stepping back and desperately shielding your body
from her blows, you leaned forward onto your toes, surprised to
see your own hands balled up tightly and your chest puffed out
and you weren't hiding or running away and you could feel all
the ways that you were taller now, bigger than her, and you could
see her also seeing this with your newly dilated pupils because
you kept them all the way open, and before her hands could land
anywhere on your body something in her stopped as if in the
middle of a sentence and her arms came back down to her side,
sharply deflated like popped balloons, landing back into herself
with a heavy, resigned thud and she looked at you with a raised
eyebrow and a snarl before she quickly turned and left the room,
and left you alone, stunned, with fearsweat running down the
back of your neck and pooling under your armpits and you were
silent and still until your body finally remembered to breathe,
maybe 20 years later, and you took a breath and found the door
to the old dirt road by the house and you just kept walking

walking walking along it, not knowing where you were going but pretty sure about where you had just been, feeling your heart pound inside of your own chest for perhaps the very first time and knowing deeply, *Oh that's where this belongs.*

And then there you are in his small twin bed, reading him a bedtime story about school-aged-children-and-their-magical-pet-unicorns while he is lying softly in your armpit, scanning the words on the page for the one-day-real-soon when he might understand what they say, when suddenly one of the children in the story *flinches* and he stops you immediately from reading to ask, *But What Does Flinch Mean?* Because he likes it when you explain all the words he doesn't understand and so you say, *Hmmm, Okay, Well, Flinch Is When You Think Someone Is Going To Hit You, So You Move Out Of The Way Before It Happens*, and you feel that your explanation is pretty straight forward, but he looks at you, even more confused and says, *What Do You Mean? Why Would Anyone Think Someone Else Was Going To Hit Them?* And with this, you look over at his childbody lying vulnerably in the bed beside you and you scan his face, his belly, his legs, his feet, the way his head, swarmed by long blonde soft curls is resting on your shoulder and you are suddenly made aware that he has never ever flinched before and that he doesn't know the feeling or even the word—*He Doesn't Even Know The Fucking Word!* You will think, before flashing to all of the past flinching and the unnecessary future flinching, the flinching that happens when people get up from the couch just to make more tea, the flinching when teachers used to walk up behind you to look at your work, all the flinching into your young adulthood, dodging entirely imagined attacks from your lovers, in bed, at the breakfast table, getting into the car, the popcorn line at the movie theater, that time she was just reaching for a book on a shelf near your head, and all of this flinching makes you feel so far away from him now, and nauseous in the face of his unbearable innocence, and you are quickly drowning in your own reservoir of grief, so you jump out of the bed and tell him that you need to open the window before you can continue reading, because you *Just Need Some Air*, and you really do feel happy for him and proud of yourself for providing him with an unflinching life, but you also feel so much envy and so much hate at his nonchalant, baked-in sense of safety and then he shivers a little bit, maybe because of the open window but probably not, and he looks at you like he is reading an ancient text and he says, *Did A Cannonball Just Shoot Through Your Whole Body?* And all you can say is *Yes, Yes It Did, A Cannonball Just Ripped Through Time And Space And It's Okay And I Am Sorry And Where Were We, What Page Are We On Again?*

Patrick Gets Schooled
Patrick Watts

Headed for School

John, John the Leprechaun

Went to school with nothing on.

"Wait for me, Patrick." Momma scurried down the hallway putting on her cotton cardigan.

"It's all right, Momma. I know where the bus stop is." I opened up the front door putting on my brave front.

"I wanna make sure. Plus, I wanna see what kinda stuff's on the way."

"Please, Momma. Let me go by myself." Not even out the door yet and already mortified.

"Sorry. Just this once. This is all new to both of us. I feel kinda responsible for doing this to you."

"Don't be that way. I understand. I. I'm actually lookin' forward to public school."

"Thanks, kiddo. But I am going to the bus stop with you. No more arguments." Momma marched past me and out the door in a way that made it clear the argument was over.

The bus stop was only two blocks away, where our street ran into Sheila Street. Just before crossing Angela Street halfway there, Momma brushed her hand against my arm. "Give me your hand."

"What?"

"Give me your hand."

"No. Why?"

"We're about to cross this street."

"So?" I grabbed the straps of my backpack, loaded with only my sack lunch, and adjusted the imaginary weight in a way that made it clear this argument was over.

"Oh, okay, then."

I did not care at all that she used her tone that made it clear that her feelings were hurt.

We made it across Angela Street alive and scurried the rest of the way to Sheila Street. The farther away we got from our house, the more agitated Momma got.

She rushed right up to the pod of kids at the corner. "Hi, guys. Is this the bus stop for Patton Middle School?"

One of the girls nodded without looking up from her phone.

"Geez, Mom." I turned to run back home.

Momma grabbed the hand loop at the top of my backpack and pulled me around to face the others. "Well, this is Patrick, everybody. He's new to public school. I homeschooled him for six years. But that's as far as I could take him. He qualified for seventh grade, so here we are. And you know what? He's never ridden a school bus before. Isn't that something? Please make him feel welcome and help him fit in." As she spoke, she held me in place with her hands pressing hard against my chest.

I squirmed and tried to move her hands. "Mom," I whispered. All the time she had been talking, I had been looking at my new bus mates. They were all dressed in T-shirts, faded jeans with rips across the knees, and high-top canvas sneakers. The two boys were vaping and playing a game with each other on their phones. The two girls were texting.

I was wearing a red, white, and blue plaid collared short-sleeve shirt, khaki pants, and moccasin-style loafers. My Sunday school clothes. Boy, was I ever glad no one was paying any attention to us.

The whoosh and squeal of school bus air brakes were harsh but welcome. Bus 13. Great.

All four veterans bunched up at the door and elbowed each other for the privilege of being first to board the rusty, smelly pride of the school district.

Momma finally let me go. "Be good. Everything will be just fine. I love you."

I was already on board by the time I heard "love you." I stood there looking at the driver, waiting to fill out a form or sign something.

She was the oldest woman I had ever met. I don't think she had any teeth. She had plenty of hair, though. Mostly on her chin. Without looking at me, she released the hand brake and lithped, "Get behind the line. I got a thchedule to keep."

I searched the depths of the bus for an empty seat.

In the dim morning light, ogres glared back at me.

The bus jerked into first gear, and everyone settled into a ruckus much like what I had imagined when Momma taught me about Bethlehem Royal Hospital.

I pulled my pack off my back, hugged it in front of me, and lurched to a seat three rows deeper into the din.

The girl by the window caught a big, wet sneeze with her bare left hand and continued texting with her right without stopping.

I couldn't decide if I was sad or glad about my very first encounter with the public school community. I gulped and sat, hanging half off the edge of the seat with one leg in the aisle. I wanted that advantage in case I had to bug out. I said nothing. I couldn't. Terror sat on the lid of my voice box. All I did the whole way to the school was stiffen up and listen to the chaos behind me, expecting just about anything to hit me in the back of the head.

Heigh ho, heigh ho.
It's off to school we go,
With razor blades
And hand grenades.
Heigh ho, heigh ho.

Classroom

Now I lay me down to rest,

    A pile of books upon my chest.

    If I should die before I wake,

    That's one less test I'll have to take.

    My history teacher, Mr. Hall, always talked in a loud, angry voice. I never got over being nervous in his classroom. After this year with him, I decided that the only thing he was angry about was having to teach seventh graders. Today he shouted, "By then the New Babylonian Empire controlled the entire Fertile Crescent."

    My bladder shouted, "Gotta pee. Gotta pee. Gotta pee."

    I squirmed and reasoned, "Two more minutes. Two more minutes. Two more minutes." I deeply regretted drinking that juice box at the ten o'clock break.

    "Now, who remembers who Palestine was named for?"

    I thought I heard Mr. Hall ask a question about something Momma had taught me at home. Before I could suppress it, my right hand shot up into the air. I looked around at everyone staring at me and felt my bladder surge. I forced my hand back into my crotch.

    "Patrick?"

    "Um. The Philistines?"

    "Right. Good, Patrick. I'm glad someone in here is paying attention." Mr. Hall looked straight at Rodney.

    Becoming aware of an overall silence in the room, Rodney pulled his pinky finger out of his nose and looked around.

    Everyone, except me, Mr. Hall, and Rodney, laughed.

    Rodney bent over to pull up a sock (wipe off his fingertips), glaring at me the entire time.

    Rodney's friend and intellectual equal, Gary, called out,

    I am going to see my honey.

    Her nose is cold and runny.

    You may think that's funny,

    But it' snot.

Everyone, except me, Mr. Hall, and Rodney, roared. I did catch the corners of Mr. Hall's mouth twitch upward a bit.

"Enough. Get out of here and go to lunch."

School's out, school's out.

Teacher's let the monkeys out.

One went east; one went west.

One went up the teacher's dress.

Hallway

Hickory, dickory, dock.

Three mice ran up the clock.

The clock struck one.

The rest escaped without injury

Regardless of the fact that everyone in the classroom was up and jostling around at once, I made it out the door before anyone else. Ever notice how when you're desperate, time slows down? And why was everybody shuffling down the hall in the opposite direction as I? I hopped to one side, flattened myself against the wall, and sidestepped toward the bathroom, shoulder blades rattling locker handles. I could hear Rodney and Gary behind me.

I see England.

I see France.

I see Shirley's underpants.

After that I lost them. Shirley was flouncing down the hall in her cheerleader outfit, arm in arm with her JV tackle boyfriend, Greg.

Boys' Room

In days of old

When knights were bold

And toilets weren't invented,

They laid their load

Beside the road

And walked away contented.

The boys' room was empty, thank God.

The urinal was one six-foot-long porcelain trough. At the end by the sinks, a spigot dribbled water. The water splashed onto a rust stain in the bottom of the trough and trickled down into a green drain at the other end under the windows. Beside the drain lay this godawful-smelling orange piece of plastic shaped like a daisy.

I pressed against the wall as far as I could get from the door and proceeded to water the daisy.

The relief was blessed, but it was short-lived.

The door to the bathroom banged wide open and crashed against the steel trash can behind it.

My pecker dried up and retreated into the cul-de-my-ball-sac.

The school bully, Avery, had kicked the door open.

I know, right? With a name like Avery, you about have to be the school bully. He was half muscle and half fat. His skin was so pale, it looked a little pink. Or that could have been all his pimples. His big lips, upturned nose, pudgy cheeks, and low forehead made his eyes look small. Those were almost black. His unwashed hair covered his ears, so I couldn't tell if they lopped over.

He strode in with his two disciples, Douche and Doofus. That's all I ever heard him call them. "Man, I cannot believe Caitlin's gettin' away with those jeans today. She's showing off her camel toe on purpose."

Douche and Doofus guffawed.

I didn't know what they were talking about but still didn't think it was that funny. You know how minions are.

All three advanced to the urinal, pulling out their tallywackers halfway there, and began to douse the back of the urinal with strong streams.

Toilet splash invaded my personal space.

"Harold needs to get in here and scrub this piece a shit." Doofus was referring to the school's janitor and the urinal, but he started up another topic of loud derision.

Comet. It makes your teeth so clean.

Comet. It tastes like gasoline.

Comet. Will make you vomit.

So, get some Comet, and vomit, today.

I continued to stare at the rancid daisy, stretching what I could find of my pecker out away from my pants and concentrating with all my might to restart any amount of flow. Hopeless. By then the whole bathroom was filled with boisterous boys. I gave it up, zipped it up, and retreated.

"Hey. You never peed." Avery's tone portended devilry.

"Uh. Uh. No. I, uh, realized I needed to take a shit." I retreated further across the room to the stalls. All were filled, so I again concentrated hard to look nonchalant standing outside of one.

Now, I had never ever said the word *shit* out loud before. I had only said *poop* at worst. It felt really wrong. But it also felt absolutely like the right thing to say under the circumstances. And you know what? Saying it out loud actually made me feel a little more like I was beginning to belong here.

"You're Patrick, aren't you?"

"*Oh, shit,*" I thought. Avery's question scared me. I knew him, of course. I had already seen how he welcomed seventh graders. How could he know my name? So much for gliding under the radar. I'd never be able to pee in this building. "Um. Yeah."

"Peeless Patty."

I expected the volume of laughter from everyone in there to loosen the tile on the walls.

Everyone began to chant, "Peeless Patty, Peeless Patty, Peeless Patty."

The guy in the stall I was waiting outside of laughed so hard he farted.

The stall served as a megaphone to the false-starting lawnmower. The noise and the odor blossomed over the top of the stall and pervaded the entire room. That diverted everyone's attention away from me. Never thought I'd thank a fart for anything.

The first marine found the bean, *parlez vous*.
The second marine cooked the bean, *parlez vous*.
The third marine ate the bean;
Blew a hole in the submarine.
Inky, dinky, *parlez vous*.

Cafeteria

Nobody loves me.

Everybody hates me.

I'm gonna eat worms and die.

My lunches were usually sliced deli chicken, sliced white cheese, and romaine lettuce within two slices of multigrain bread soggy with brown mustard. Sides were usually raw carrots or celery stalks and an apple or pear. Momma always fixed them. She might be able to tolerate public school education; she drew the line at public school lunches. I didn't mind at all. It was a little connection to home within this alien land. Also, I had seen the oily mystery meat and faded green beans firsthand.

Kids who brought their lunch lined up on one side of the hallway outside the cafeteria, and kids who bought their lunch lined up on the other side. Kids bringing their lunch only needed to buy a carton of milk. There was a separate station for that.

Today, while slouching along in my line, I became aware that someone ahead of me in the other line was looking at me. I mean she was staring right at me, arms crossed and leaning against the wall. Having to face backward in her line to look at me, for goodness sakes. I looked away and began reading faded names on the back of the T-shirt the guy ahead of me was wearing. A Hornsby family reunion on July 4, 2010. After about ten names I peeked around.

She was still staring at me, still leaning against the wall, arms still crossed. Now she was directly across from me. She smiled.

My heart exploded.

My lungs imploded.

My nose dribbled.

I wiped it with my bare arm, then went back to the T-shirt. I read only five more names. I just had to look again.

Yeah. She was still staring at me. Since her line was slower, she was behind me now. But she was still looking at me. She smiled again. I'm sure it was innocent enough, but it scared the tweet outta me. Way too much attention from a complete stranger.

"*Oh, great. Now I'm on the radar of a girl bully.*" I turned toward the cafeteria door and double-checked the contents of my lunch bag. I kept my head down all the way through buying the room-temperature milk to laying out my lunch on an empty table in the far corner of the cafeteria.

The girl stalked me. She and two companions settled themselves at the table next to mine. She sat on the far side so she could see me.

I took a deep breath and began to eat my sandwich. I ate a whole lot faster than usual. I gulped lots of sips of warm milk. I kept choking myself. I focused on the squiggly lines of the design in the tabletop, but every time I took a sip of milk, I'd peek up through my eyebrows to reconnoiter.

She spent half her time whispering to her companions and half her time glancing at me. A couple of times when our eyes met, she'd smile. She was absolutely nothing like the fair blonds and brunettes in my Sunday school class. Her skin was light brown. Darker-brown freckles covered her round face. Her hair was super curly and bronzy-colored. It was all braided in about a dozen narrow rows tight to her scalp. Those continued out from the nape of her neck in pigtails reaching halfway down her back. All were dyed an emerald green that matched the color of her eyes. Each ended with several fluorescent yellow beads.

I became aware that I was staring right back at her with my mouth half open and half full of chicken sandwich.

Momma had told me at the bus stop on the first day that everything would be fine. I remember thinking she was horribly mistaken. At best, it would be a full year, when seventh grade was over, before everything would be fine. Now it seemed like everything had become fine in one spectacular cosmic event.

A fatty hand lunged over my shoulder and snatched my apple.

It took a moment for me to return to Earth. I whirled around and saw the school troll, Avery, taking a massive bite.

"Good apple, Peeless."

My whole head got hot. I'm sure my face was redder than my apple. I didn't care about Avery's thievery. I was sure his critique was loud enough for the brown girl to hear. I lost all reason. "Hey, asshole. Gimme back my frickin' apple!" I reached up and grabbed the wrist of his offending hand. As I yelled, I sprayed his shirt with chewed-up chicken sandwich.

The whole cafeteria got silent.

Avery grabbed my wrist with his free hand and twisted until he broke my grip on him. He continued to twist until he nearly popped my elbow out of joint. He smashed my half-eaten apple right down into my half-eaten sandwich lying on the wax paper on the table. His face became placid. "One day, Peeless. Soon. You won't know when or where." He brushed the chicken pulp off his shirt into my face, slapped my ear, and shuffled away toward a herd of guys that looked like his own personal sounder.

I looked down at my mangled lunch. No matter. No point in trying to eat any more. I was about to barf. I left the remains on the table and trotted to the cafeteria bathroom. I would have passed my number-one fan, but, frankly, I didn't notice if she was still there or not.

In the bathroom I took several deep breaths and several swallows of lead-flavored water to try to calm down. I did not barf. I did not leave either. I decided to stay there until Avery and his cloven-hooved brethren had drifted off. While there I rubbed my aching elbow and listened out for them with my throbbing ear. I conceded that that cosmic event was nothing more than a little swamp gas. I did remember to congratulate myself for standing up to Avery. That should boost my standing around here a little bit, right?

Spider, spider, on the wall.
Ain't you got no sense at all?
Don't you know that wall's been plastered?
Get off that wall, you stupid spider.

Recess

Two lips together.
Twilight forever.
Bring back my love to me.
What is the me-eaning
Of all these flow-ow-ers?
They tell the stor-or-y.
The story of love from me to you.

I was outside after lunch. I was lonely and miserable. After a month or so, I still hadn't made any friends. I figured that if I associated with anyone who called me Peeless, then I was admitting that I was okay with what Avery had done to me. Everyone I talked to called me Peeless.

I sat alone on a steel bench bolted to the concrete walkway. I worked out arguments to give Momma for homeschooling me again. If it was just a matter of money, I'd cut grass and wash cars. I'd even babysit. I watched and listened to all the carefree kids enjoying their recess. Who was I kidding? I was watching out for Avery.

Vote, vote, vote for dear old Betsy,
Calling Amy at the door.
Amy is the one
Who's having all the fun;
So, we don't need Betsy anymore.
Shut the door, kick her out.

After a while I was feeling a little better. Those gals jumping Double Dutch had impressed the hell outa me. Then I recognized a plump one jump out from the ropes and head my way. She had light brown, freckly skin and bronze cornrows with emerald green pigtails. I caught myself rubbing my eyes to make sure of what I saw.

My heart pounded up against my throat. The closer she got, the more her aspect confounded me. Sweat chilled my armpits. I shivered. All the girls in Sunday school were so well dressed, so well composed, so, well, ordinary. This one was just too exotic. Too much, too fast.

She had not yet recovered from jumping rope. Her own sweat darkened the color of her freckles and brightened her hair. Underneath her ribbed knit top, live grapefruit shifted up and down.

I couldn't not look. I was going to hell. Worse, I was going to screw up this moment.

She saw me looking. She giggled. She strode right up to me. She smelled like a freshly sliced onion. "Hi. You're Patrick, aren't you. I'm Eefa."

The first thing I noticed was that she did not call me Peeless. The second thing I noticed was that I had a full-on boner. Welp, I had made it to hell. I covered my tent with my empty lunch bag and tried to cross my legs.

She watched me trying to hide my willy. She covered her mouth with her hands and tried to hide her giggles.

"Uh. Uh. Sorry. Gotta go to the bathroom real bad." I rolled away from her on the bench, stood, and ran to the opposite end of the playground. I plonked down onto the ground with my back against a chain link fence and watched a pair of gleeful girls clapping each other's hands. I glanced back towards the steel bench.

Eefa was gone.

Over and over I imagined myself vaulting off the top of the monkey bars head first.

Oh, little playmate,

Come out and play with me.

And bring your little dolly;

Climb up my apple tree.
Slide down my rainbow,
Into my cellar door.
And we'll be such jolly friends
Forever ever more.

Headed for Home
There's a soldier in the grass
    With a bullet in his—
    Don't be alarmed.
    It's only in his arm.
Mid-afternoon Friday. Praise Santa Claus. I was standing in the bus loading zone just as close as I could get to the number 13 painted on the concrete. I would make good and durn sure I was the first one onto the bus home. I was so excited about getting away from middle hell for a couple of days, my neck was stiff.

I began to fantasize about the snack Momma would have waiting for me. Musing over the possibilities helped me relax. A bunch of grapes. Peanut butter on celery. I crossed my fingers tight that it might be my favorite, fresh baked Toll House cookies and ice-cold milk.

Strong hands clamping hard onto my shoulders from behind crumbled all my cookies.

My neck stiffened up again. So quickly that pain shot from there, over the top of my head, and down to my eyebrows.

The hands spun me around to face their owner.

My mouth dried up. I think some of that moisture made its way out of my pecker. I clenched every muscle I had conscious control of down there. I blinked out the tears in order to see Avery more clearly.

"It's time." Avery looked down at me with his standard menacing smirk.

It didn't sound to me like he'd spoken very loudly. However, within seconds all the riders of buses 12, 13 and 14 had formed a perfect circle around us. Lots of practice, I suppose.

My stomach lurched upward, expressing something awful-tasting into my mouth. My throat closed up. That helped stop the bile but hindered my ability to speak. So what? I couldn't think of any comeback anyway. I was at panic's mercy.

Panic was unmerciful.

You know how when you're scared to death, you can't think any deep thoughts at all? Like a drowning sailor in a maelstrom who grabs at the first bit of flotsam that swirls his way, you blurt out the first thing that pops to the surface of your terrified conscious.

I see the moon; the moon sees me.

Diddling June up the apple tree.

Avery's face changed. I had seen his menacing grin so many times before that I had kinda gotten used to it. This was different. His new face was not like his typical gleefully malevolent expression. No. Avery's face now showed a genuine, deeply felt, deadly rage.

Visions of Toll House cookies and ice-cold milk came swirling back around in my mind.

I think my anus may have squirted out a little peanut butter.

I did not understand at all at the time just how much danger I was in. The following year I learned that Avery's mother's name was June.

Avery stepped back, clenched his right hand, and cocked his right arm back to smash my nose into my brain.

I think it was Douche who laughed out loud behind him.

Now, after watching these turds a number of times, I had become familiar with their silly sniggers that preceded the pounding of a seventh grader. This was different. It was more like he was laughing at Avery, or at the brilliant bit of wit I had just recited.

Avery swung around to face the traitor so fast that he lost his balance. He almost fell down.

Doofus laughed.

"What the fuck!" Avery regained his balance but not his poise.

Doofus hollered out,

Here comes Avery,
Floating down the Delaware,
Chewing on his underwear,
Doesn't have another pair.
Ten days later bit by a bear.
That's how the bear died.

All the boys in the crowd roared wholehearted approbations.
Many added their own favorite bits of middle school doggerel.

Tarzan swings; Tarzan falls.
Cheetah grabs him by the balls.
That is when he always calls,
"Aaahh-eehh-aahh-eehh-aahh-eehh aahh."

Old Mother Hubbard
Went to the cupboard
To get her poor dog a bone.
When she bent over,
Old rover drove her,
And she found he had a bone of his own.

Asshole, asshole,
A soldier went to war.
To piss, to piss,
Two pistols by his side.
Fu kyou, fu kyou,
For curiosity.
For cunt, for cunt,
For country and for king.

My name is El Pancho.
I work on el rancho.

I make-a fi'e dollah a day.
I go see my Susie;
She give me some pusie.
She take my fi'e dollah away.

I realized I was laughing my ass off. I also realized that Avery was laughing his own ass off. Everyone appeared vulnerable, so I stopped to ponder what was going on. Was I safe or not? I looked at Avery.

Avery looked at me.

All my body heat dissipated into the fall afternoon air. My fingers felt cold. Then I couldn't feel them at all.

Avery stepped toward me.

Those Toll House cookies came swirling back.

Avery laid his hands onto my shoulders.

Now I couldn't feel my legs.

Avery moved around to my side and braced me up with his semi-flaccid arm. "Hey!"

Everyone had learned a long time ago to heed his commands. Things got really quiet really quick.

Don't cuss.
Call Gus.
He'll cuss
For all us.

Everyone was pretty much laughed out by now. They managed deferential chuckles as they dispersed to their respective bus loading zones.

Avery released me. Without looking at me he slapped me hard on the back. It was that kind of slap on the back that a guy gives another guy which is meant to be sincere but which must appear to the rest of the world to be perfunctory. He returned to his drove, and they all strayed off to their own loading zones.

I watched them a moment and then checked myself for injuries. None. Neither physical nor psychological. I turned to join my bus mates streaming around me. Beyond them I saw Eefa.

She stood alone with both her hands clutching the straps of her book bag between her, uh, in front of her. She stared right at me.

Happy, happy, joy, joy. I had escaped a beating by Avery. I might even have made friends with him. Eefa had sought me out even after that excruciating meet-up on the playground weeks ago. Maybe I had licked middle school after all. I began to own my nickname. Had I been paying attention, I might have noticed Eefa's wet eyes and pooched-out lips. I raised my hand and waved. "Eefa. Did you see what I just—"

"Boys are so gross." She turned and trudged away, laden with heavy books and disappointment.

Every molecule of my body pulled apart. I thought of Crew Member Number Three on *Star Trek* who always got zapped by a phaser set on vaporize. The elation of keeping my life, mixing with the despair of losing the girl twisted my guts into mush. I wanted, no, I needed, Avery to come back and actually reset my nose into the middle of my brain. There was only one thing at that moment that I was absolutely, positively sure about. I was definitely *not* going back to home schooling.

"Get on the bus. I got a thchedule to keep."

There's no place
Like this place
'Round this place.
So, this must be
The place.

In the Cocoon

Aruna Gurumurthy

Behind the lit lamps in the Ganesh Temple,
past the sway of marigolds and bells,
devotees slurping hot tea in a roadside stall,

Viji Ma, my mother, tucks her sari in her left hip,
walks to my school like a soldier
on rubber sandals spattered by the falling rain.

She clicks the umbrella to a close,
heads straight to the fifth-grade classroom.
My teacher hands me my report card,

pats my back and says *Well done!*

My mother and I find a quiet corner to sit,
heartbeats drum my chest,
suspense oozes out of the laminated leaflet,

3rd rank!!

On the way back,

swinging hands by the pond,
we slap sloshes of wet sand
beside earthworms wriggling on lotus leaves,

to a restaurant on the main road
dressed in Warli rugs, a wooden table
enlivened by a daisy.

Get what you want, honey. It's your day.

A moth in the rainforest
hanging from twigs,
I nestle in your bright sari,

Mom, you are my cocoon.

A triangle of *dosa* into coconut chutney,
the scoop of sizzled potato fry,
my lips on the steel tumbler

tremble as I sip mango *lassi.*

I mull over my journey,
the jigsaw,
the jazzercise within.

The pain inside
from the bulging stye of hate
in the eyes of my fellow classmates

who tease me for being fat, for my cleft palate,

hide my stuffed panda in the crevices of the classroom,
turning the key, laughing
at me, the plastic duck dancing on its butt,

quacking.

Wailing, I slam the bathroom door.
The bruise on my arm, the bloody rouge in my mind,
Oh, this scar,

how my mother covers it all in layers of linen bandage,

and now, under the roof of the restaurant,
to the smear of a blue felt marker,
draws in cursive on my wrapped hand

a poem, a peony, a pomegranate.

July Fourth

Sallie Bingham

July Fourth come round and the state banned all fireworks, took down the big tent by the highway where we always sold them and said the tribal cops would be watching.

"It's this drought," Daddy Cowboy said. "We's all got the day off so let's go down to the City and look around."

More than a hundred miles south and ordinarily he wouldn't waste the diesel but I guess he didn't want us kids hanging around with nothing to do. He told us to be ready, my cousin Tara, Jimmy-James her little brother, and me they call Sure Enough if I don't stop them.

We got up early, washed, dressed, waited by the door for Daddy to come by with his big red truck. He don't live with us no more after the last fight with Mama and she was sleeping late, knowing we was off her hands. It was already fearsome hot, that dust wind starting, the sun looking like a big red blister on the east edge of the sky, getting ready to cook us all day.

Daddy come roaring up in his truck, we run out. He had Aunt Your Mean Horse riding shotgun, not my favorite of the aunties but so what.

"Never was this hot till the government started monkeying with it," Daddy said.

Tara and me knowed to stay quiet. No use asking him questions once he started down that road.

We got in the back quick before Daddy got pissed and changed his mind. He could do that if some kid was too slow

❖ 51 ❖

getting in or tried to come barefoot. We wedged Jimmy-James between us, him already squalling.

"Shut that kid up before I drop you all the side of the road," Daddy said.

Tara come prepared with a piece of gum she shoved in the kid's mouth. Took him a while to chew and swallow it.

Aunt Your Mean Horse stuck her big moon face over the seat. "Where's them seat belts?"

"I cut them out a while back, fixed that damn beep," Daddy said, pulling out onto the highway past the fireworks tent laying on its side like a big busted balloon. Not many cars this early on the holiday, only a big eighteen-wheeler hauling hay down from Colorado. Drought took all ours. "Price of hay going to kill me," Daddy said, flying by.

"You ask me it's time you got rid of all them horses," Aunt Your Mean Horse said "now you too old and busted up to ride rodeo."

"Nobody asked you," Daddy said.

Aunt kept her big face hanging over the seat, white as the moon, black eyes a pair of searchlights. "You kids better mind yourself," she said in her whiskey and cigarette voice. She's Mama's sister, not Daddy's and they never have seen eye to eye but he had to go live with her after Mama kicked him out. She was married sometime back to Uncle Thrash but then he run off and left her 'cause she never made no babies and she couldn't find nobody else. That story got around.

We parked in one of them lots with about a thousand spaces, got out and commenced to walk around the City. Daddy spied somebody he knowed from way back laying under a tree. "How you doing old man?" he said and went to sit with him and smoke.

Auntie hoisted Jimmy-James asleep on her shoulder and told Tara and me to keep close. She commenced to walk down the sidewalk. In a minute here come Daddy. "Worse drunk I know," he said. "I guess they finally threw him out back home."

Well that city's a big place, streets and streets, all kinds of shops but friendly-seeming 'cause there's more of us there than any other city between the university, the streets and the jail. We looked at everything and Tara started fussing to go in one of the jewelry shops but one look from Auntie shut her up fast. I didn't see nothing I had to look at close up.

Pretty soon it was eat time and Jimmy-James woke up fussing but Tara had a bottle in her purse and she took him and started feeding him before Daddy could say a word. Daddy turned into a place he knowed, got us out sized us up, made me tuck in my shirt tail, swiped a dried bugger off Tara's cheek. Auntie pulled herself up like she mattered too.

It was cool in there with the A.C. running and six of us sitting at the big table, a few more at the counter. I seen pie slices full of juice in the case behind the counter and some guy was frying up burghers.

Daddy made us speak to the men he knew which was most at the big table. Then he set us at another table and went up to order Green Chile Chicken Stew for everybody like he always did. "If you don't like it you can pay for something else." I like green chile but my first spoonful was so hot with chile it just about choked me and I put my napkin over my mouth so Daddy wouldn't see. Tara took one sniff of hers and pushed back from the table. Daddy was shoveling the stew down like there was no tomorrow and Auntie was making a good run at it too.

"Box it up," Daddy told the guy waiting on us. "That'll be your supper," but Tara and I knew he'd forget it by the time we got home. It'd lay in the back of his truck till it rotted.

Tara said, "Jimmy-James needs changing bad." We could smell him.

"Take him to the bathroom quick," Daddy said and Tara did.

"Why you made all these kids," Auntie said in her tired voice.

"I only made four of them so far," Daddy said. "Have to make some more since you won't."

She was heating up. "You think that's what I wanted?"

"Well, far as I know, Thrash is—"

"Nothing to do with Thrash," she cut him off. "IHS got me when I was fifteen, took everything out."

"Why you?"

"I'm a full blood, that's what they was looking for. Did more than a thousand of us, I heard."

"Thrash know that?"

"I didn't know myself for sure."

"Well, time told," he said.

"It sure did." Her voice was like sucking lemon.

Then Tara come back with Jimmy-James cleaned up and Daddy paid and we went out of there, didn't even wait for the guy with the takeout boxes.

We stopped at a coffee place so Auntie and Daddy could fill up and when he paid I saw Daddy had a sizable roll of bills in his front pocket. Never did carry a wallet, charge card or most times not even his license. "I'll look back home for it," he'd say if he got stopped. Most likely it was out of date or suspended. Tribal cops didn't make much of a fuss, state cops something different.

Daddy took us to this museum place, shelves of our old things, pots and such, so many I couldn't hardly see them all. Daddy didn't like the smell of it, said real low they was all stole. White women everywhere trying to explain the pots to us.

Auntie took out a sage smudge stick, lighted it, waved it around till a white lady said it was against the rules but by then the good sage smell was all around us. Some beeping started and Auntie had to go outside and bury the smudge stick in the dirt.

Daddy had just about had it. He hustled us out. Jimmy-James was fussing again and Tara put her finger in his mouth for him to suck on. That worked for a while.

Heading for the truck I saw a big sign nailed to a post. It read, "Site of Clifford Indian Boarding School 1879–1960."

"Was that where they sent the kids?" Tara said.

Auntie said, "They got me when I was eight. I stayed there four years. We did all the cooking and cleaning for the nuns and then they put us out to service. The boys had to cut off their hair and take care of the cattle and the barns, some of them run off fast."

"You learned reading and writing," Daddy said, wiping his sweaty face with his bandana. "The monks at my place taught me the use of tools."

Auntie didn't argue though I could see she had another opinion.

"Did the kids want to go?" Tara asked, jiggling Jimmy-James on her arm and looking up at Daddy.

"Hell no, didn't have no choice," he said. "My place was up near the Yellowstone, run by these monks. Do something wrong they beat you. Do something right they beat you. I run off the first year."

"I went right here," Auntie said. "Great big school. Learned to crochet and make biscuits. Every winter a fair number of us died. Used to be a graveyard here." We was standing in the parking lot.

"Still there only they cemented it over," Daddy said.

"Well that does seem a shame. Families never knew?"

"How they going to find out, way up on the reservation? Didn't have no phones back then, no way to get here to see."

"I knowed one of them that died," Auntie said. "My baby brother."

"That must of been way back in time," Daddy said.

"Well it was but still. It was a cold winter, he coughed all night in that freezing room with all the beds. I went and laid with him to warm him but some sister come and yanked me out. He was gone by breakfast time. They put him down in the dirt before I knowed what happened."

Daddy looked at her and I saw something you don't see too often with Daddy Cowboy. It seemed like maybe he was sorry. "You all wait here," he said and he went to his truck and opened the back and I saw the welter of his tools. He pulled out a pick ax. "Come on," he said and went to the middle of the parking lot, only a few cars baking in the sun. "Tell me where," he said to Auntie.

She commenced pacing, looking down. Stopped here, stopped there. After a while she said, "Here," pointing down.

Daddy went to where she was, pick ax hefted. She pointed, he drove the ax down hard on the spot, six times and a big piece of cement broke up. "Get them pieces out," he said and Tara and I kneeled down and started picking. We opened up a sizable hole, orange clay at the bottom of it.

"All right, go to it," he said and Auntie handed Jimmy-James to Tara and went down on her old creaking knees by the hole. She put her face right to it. That hot wind blew up her skirt and I didn't get no pleasure out of seeing her big white bloomers or her fat thighs straining.

Tara pulled her skirt down.

Auntie started to say some of the old words nobody knows no more. Sounded almost like singing or praying. Far as I could tell she said the same words over and over and Daddy was watching her with the stare he gets when he sees a flock of wild turkeys in what's left of his corn.

Auntie fished a little pot out of her pocket and let some drops fall in the hole all the time saying her words. Then she made the sign of the cross and hoisted herself up. "Fill the hole," she told us.

Tara and I scrambled the pieces back in. "How they going to breathe down there?" Tara said.

"They quit breathing a long time ago," Daddy said.

Auntie made the sign of the cross one more time and said one of the church prayers and Daddy chimed in but Tara and I don't know none of those words. Mama is against it.

Daddy said, "Tell them to rest in peace, kids like you."

Tara said, "Rest in peace" and I said it too after Tara bumped me in the side.

Then Jimmy-James went to squalling again and we all piled in the truck for the long ride home.

Aunt Your Mean Horse couldn't let it go. She come to me a week later, asked me to drive her down there again. "You got your permit?"

"Yes, ma'am," I said, which was a lie. Daddy Cowboy didn't have time or patience to take me for the test but sometimes you have to lie to get something done. I been driving everything with four wheels, ATVs, trucks, sedans, cement trucks since I turned eight.

"Well get ready to take me tomorrow early, you can drive my Chevy," she said. "I don't drive no more now I'm half blind."

I never had noticed that. Seemed to me she had eyes in the back of her head but anyway. It may be she wanted company.

"And don't you go speeding and get us stopped," she said like I was that kind of fool.

So we drove that long hot drive to the City in her old rusted out Chevy. It turned out she'd made an appointment with somebody at that museum. He was waiting for us, big fat white man in a suit and tie like the heat never bothered him. AC running full blast in his office anyway. He started out all friendly. "What can I do for you folks?" But he was looking at us like we was some spoiled piece of meat.

"They's kids buried under that parking lot of yours," Auntie said. "I want them dug up."

"Well now that may be so but all that's a long time ago, nothing left by now."

"They's bones left," she said, "and their folks want them back to bury right."

"That's government property, I don't have the authority—"

"Then who do?" Auntie was hanging her big white moon face over him and I saw him lean back to get away.

"You need to get in touch with D.C. to answer that question," he said. "And now if you'll excuse me."

I thought for sure that would stop Auntie in her tracks but no such thing. She told me, "Drive me to this here address" which turned out to be the office of the City paper. When we got there, she told me to go find somewhere to park in the shade. I took time to get me a Pepsi and some chips and when I come back for her waiting on the sidewalk, she was grinning. "Didn't want to talk to me but changed they minds fast," she told me. "Now take me home."

Few days later paper run this big story, "Where Are All the Lost Children?" It wasn't a week before somebody from DC called the fat man and he had to call Auntie and make another appointment.

"Well you sure have made enough trouble," he said when we come in the door.

"Not yet," she said. "What're they saying they'll do?"

"They ain't going to dig up my parking lot—"

"Stop right there," she said. I could feel her heat right through the sleeve of my shirt.

"Now wait a minute before you get all het up. They're going to put up a plaque."

He reached for a paper. "Solid bronze, last forever. They want you to approve the words. 'Under this parking lot untold numbers of Native children are buried. This plaque honors their lives and asks their survivors to forgive the past.'"

Then it was quiet for a while in that office with the AC roaring. Auntie said, "I'll have to think about it. My baby brother's under there."

"Well I'm sure sorry for your loss," the fat man said.

"His mama is still with us. Still cries for him. She'll want to bury him proper."

"Nobody is going to dig up my parking lot," the fat man said. "Why at times like when the balloon fiesta is going we have five hundred cars out there."

"Driving over those kids without even knowing it."

"They'll know it now with this plaque," the fat man said and I knew it was the best we was going to do.

Turned out Auntie Your Mean Horse knew that too though it took her a while. The next Native American Day she asked me to drive her down to the City again and when we got to that parking lot, she saw that piece of bronze nailed up on a thick metal post and the whole base of it was jammed with make-believe flowers.

Remembering the Farm

Bill Smoot

Why do certain days lie dormant in our memories, ready to arise so vividly that we live them again, even when they make our hearts ache? So it is with that cold, gray morning in early spring when Dad drove the two of us out to the farm. It was thirty years ago, the last year of his life, and I was visiting Kentucky from California, where I taught American history at a prep school. It was my spring break, and I had come alone. My wife, a real estate agent, had several active listings and couldn't take time off. A native Californian, she never liked visiting Kentucky anyway.

A month later the countryside would be verdant, but as Dad drove toward the farm, the land looked lifeless and bleak. Trees had yet to leaf out, and fields were soggy and unplowed. His eyes on the road ahead, Dad squinted, a habit he had when deep in thought. He did not always say what he was thinking. Trying to make conversation, I asked if his tobacco beds had been planted yet.

"No," he said. "It's been too cold and wet."

Dad was wearing a coat and tie, as he did every working day. A lawyer in town, he dressed well—not flashy, but with dedicated respect for how a professional man should look. On this morning we were going to visit the farm and then see my grandmother, recently moved into a nursing home after a fall in her kitchen.

Dad's car, a Chrysler New Yorker land barge, was new since my last visit, and I complimented him on how nice it was. I didn't always say what I was thinking, either.

"Fabulous car," he said. "Drives real smooth."

He cleared his throat.

"The farm will be yours one day," he said. "What you do with it is up to you."

His lower jaw jutted forward. "Maybe you'll just want to sell it."

I thought he was going to say something more, but he just shrugged. I noticed the space between his shirt collar and his neck, and I felt a pinch of fear. Mother had told me the night before that she was worried about Dad. He was not always finishing his meals. He had seen Dr. Stuart a couple of times and would not tell her why. One morning she walked in on him while he was shaving and he grabbed a towel to cover his chest.

"But I saw," she said. "Two large lumps. The size of peaches." She curled her fingers and pressed her knuckles to her mouth.

"Did you ask him about it?"

"Yes, and he told me it was nothing. I asked if he was sure, and he told me to get off his back. You know your father."

Well, I knew him and I didn't. Reading him was an art. I was only fair at it; Mother was better. But he'd said, "Maybe you'll just want to sell it." Why just? Did that mean selling it would be the easy way out, throwing in the towel, as in "maybe you should just quit"?

Dad had inherited the farm from his father fifteen years earlier, and he employed three men who did the work. Pete and Shorty lived in the two tenant houses. Pete was in semi-retirement after fifty years as herdsman for the dairy cows. Shorty did most of that work, and Moose, who lived with his mother a few miles down the road, farmed the crops—tobacco and feed grains.

As we drove through the dreary morning, I stole glances at Dad. He looked thin, and his face was as gray as the sky. Three months later he would be in the ground.

We parked in my grandmother's driveway as we always had, and Dad lifted his gray felt fedora from the back seat and fit it on his head. For the first time ever, my grandmother was not there to open her back door, the smell of warm cinnamon rolls wafting from the kitchen. Instead, we walked past her empty house and down the lane, dodging muddy puddles, to the tenant house where Pete and his wife Verna lived. The house had three rooms—a kitchen, a sitting room, and a bedroom. When my father took over the farm, he had a bathroom built just off of the kitchen, the first indoor bathroom Pete and Verna ever had. He said it was worth the cost of a bathroom to keep a herdsman as solid as Pete.

The cows were gathered in clumps in the pasture, chewing their cuds and watching us, the only moving objects in their sight. The dank cold seeped through my flimsy California jacket. We stepped onto the small wooden porch, the boards wet from the damp air, and knocked on the door.

Verna, in baggy blue jeans and an orange sweatshirt, greeted us. Dad removed his hat and we stepped inside. I hadn't seen Pete in a couple of years, and I was shocked at how much he had aged. Sitting in his chair, a horse blanket wrapped around his shoulders, he seemed reserved, even embarrassed—by his frail state, maybe—and he hardly looked at me. In spite of a coal oil stove in the corner, the room was cold. I kept my jacket on.

When I was a boy, Pete taught me to milk a cow. He stood by the ladder to the hayloft in case I fell, hosed the manure from my boots, and set me on his knee and let me hold the steering wheel while he drove the tractor. My grandfather was taciturn, stingy, and cold. He would no more have lifted me into his lap that he would have built Pete and Verna an indoor bathroom. Dad had resisted the worst of his father's qualities. Each generation makes what progress it can.

"Keith is visiting from California," Dad said. Verna nodded suspiciously. I wondered if she suspected Dad was ill.

Verna told Dad how Pete had spent two hours that morning using the bush hog. Even semi-retired, he worked harder than the other hands, she said. Pete looked sheepishly at the floor.

Dad turned to Pete. "I don't want you to do any more than you feel like doing," he said. "You deserve some rest. This farm would not be what it is without you."

"Well . . ." Pete said.

"You've always got this place. I've told you that."

"We earn our keep," Verna said. "You look behind the calving barn. He done all that hisself with the bush hog."

"Like I said, don't do too much," Dad said.

"I bet he done a quarter acre," Verna said.

"How's the herd?" Dad asked. "What's the story on the mastitis?"

"Six of 'em got it," Pete said.

"Six? Last week it was four," Dad said.

"It's Shorty," Verna said. "He don't wash the teats good like Pete always done."

"Did you tell him?" Dad asked Pete.

Verna answered, "He don't listen to Pete."

"Well, I'll talk to him," Dad said.

"Shorty oughta done that bush-hogging hisself," Verna said.

Dad bounced his hat on his knee. "Been a right cold spring, hasn't it?" he said.

"Dogwood winter. I feel it in my bones," Verna said, rubbing her kneecaps. "He does, too," she said, lifting her chin at Pete.

The four of us sat in uncomfortable silence for a few minutes. Dad said, "I expect we'd better get going. We're going to visit Mother."

"She coming home soon?" Verna asked.

"No, she can't stay by herself."

"We'd look after her," Verna said. "It won't discommode us none."

"I know," Dad said, "but she's better off there. She can't get around on her own."

"Don't she want to be here on the place?" Verna asked.

Dad pressed his lips together and then said, "She can't be home, Verna. I just told you that."

"I bet she wants to come home."

Dad stood up and put on his hat. Pete pushed down on the arms of his chair and struggled to stand.

Verna helped him up and said, "He's got stiff from all that bush-hogging."

Lady, a regal-looking collie, was lying outside the door to the milk house. She was my grandmother's dog, now staying with Shorty. Seeing us approach, she stood up and barked twice, pointing her slender muzzle to the sky. When we got closer, she wagged her tail. The milk company truck had just left, and Shorty was hosing out the tank. The rich, sweet-sour smell of Jersey cow's milk hung in the air.

Dad mentioned the mastitis and reminded Shorty to wash the udders well. Dad looked at the clipboard hanging on a nail and remarked that if the bacteria count got any higher, they'd have to start dumping the milk.

"That's what the driver done told me," Shorty said.

"When is Doc Riley coming again?" Dad asked.

"He said he'd try to make it this afternoon."

"I might call you this evening, then," Dad said. "It's always something on a farm."

I wondered if he said that for me to hear.

The three of us walked through the cattle barn to look at the new calves in their pens. They backed away as we passed, their heads low and their eyes shiny and wide. Lady lay down and alertly pressed her chin to the ground, as if daring one of the calves to jump out of its pen. At the end of the row stood the bull pen, built strong with four by sixes. Sam, the gentle old bull, lifted his massive head over the top board, a copper ring in his nose, his moist eyes gleaming. Sam was black through his head and massively muscled neck, lightening to mahogany through his thick body. I never visited my grandmother without strolling through the barn, and I never walked the barn without a long visit with Sam. He was over ten years old. With both hands, I scratched the sides of his large face. He met my efforts by moving his head like a giant dog. His eyes rolled upward, and I felt his wet, heaving breath on my arm. He licked my wrist with his sandpaper tongue.

"I thought I told you to take Sam to the stockyard," Dad said.

Shorty chuckled. "Pete told me to ask you again. He don't want to let that bull go."

"He's not the one not feeding him twenty-five pounds of hay a day."

I turned my back to Dad and massaged the insides of Sam's ears. Sighing loudly, he leaned forward with the look of a beast who could hardly believe his luck.

Shorty lifted a foil pouch from his shirt pocket, took a pinch of chewing tobacco and pushed it into his mouth.

"Sam sired most of the herd," Shorty said.

"I know that. But he's been out of service for over a year. You take him next week on stock day."

Shorty rubbed his chin. "Pete says he remembers the night he had to pull Sam out of his mother with a chain. Didn't think he was going make it. Went on to be one of our best breeders. Big bull like that, had a sweeter temper than most cows. Never even dehorned him—weren't no need to. Followed Pete around like a dog."

"Hell's bells, Shorty. This is a farm, not a petting zoo. I'm trying to turn a profit here. I don't want to see him when I come out next week, you hear me?"

"All right, then," Shorty said, looking at the ground. "He won't bring much."

"He'll bring something. And he won't keep eating my hay."

I hung back a minute to scratch Sam's head at the base of his horns, a little sick at what I had just heard.

As Shorty slid the barn door closed, Dad asked if Moose was around.

"He took the tractor to town to get the clutch worked on."

That's when I realized Dad's unspoken agenda for the morning was to reintroduce me to his three workers. It's also when I realized that Dad was dying and knew it.

Shorty leaned over from the waist to spit tobacco juice. "I reckon I'll take old Sam in, then."

"You do that," Dad said.

On the drive to the nursing home Dad was silent for a while, and then he snorted and said, "Hell, I can't keep feeding that bull. Shorty and Pete are good workers, but they don't know a damn thing about the business end of a farm." Then he added, "You know what I mean?"

"Yeah," I said. Trying to sound agreeable, I added, "You've been using artificial insemination anyway, right?"

"Yes. It's more economical in the long run, and you don't have to worry about injuries during the breeding. It's better all around."

I knew he was stewing. Inwardly, Dad suffered conflict like cuts that stung and were slow to heal. That's why I outwardly agreed with him. Inwardly, I was having a fantasy of shipping Sam to an animal sanctuary where he could live out his days in a peaceful pasture.

"It's real hard for medium-sized farms these days," Dad said. "Milk prices aren't good, and tobacco prices have been falling since they started letting imports in."

Maybe Dad was suggesting that my selling the farm would be prudent, not a defeat.

As we drove, I remembered what visits to my grandmother on the farm had been like. After cinnamon rolls and a glass of fresh milk from the dairy to "wash them down," she'd ask us to "sit a spell." In the summer we sat on the front porch where there was usually a soft breeze, even on the hottest days, and in the winter we sat in the parlor where she would toss a couple lumps of coal on the fire and stab them with the poker to bring up the flames. As soon as there was a lull in the conversation, she would start a story.

One of her stories was about the house burning down. It happened during World War II when Dad was in the army. Cleaning out the upstairs attic one afternoon, she smelled something burning. When she made her way out of the attic, the house was full of smoke. The furnace in the basement had started leaking coal oil, which caught fire, and the flames had moved up the wooden stairs and were roaring into the kitchen. "I grabbed the silver chest and the family bible and ran like a deer," she laughed. By the time the volunteer fire department arrived, the burning walls had sunk into a heap. My grandfather vowed he would rebuild with brick. "And so he did," my grandmother said with a sharp nod. "We're sitting in it."

She loved to tell stories from her girlhood, like the time some local Klansmen rode up on horseback and called her father onto the front porch. He had criticized them openly, and now they threatened to beat him. One held a horse whip. When they began to drag him off the porch, the screen door flung open and out marched his wife—my great grandmother—with a small American flag in one hand and the Bible in the other. She accused the men of being un-Christian and un-American. She thrust her Bible at each man, calling him by his full name and then speaking the names of his wife, his parents, and his children. "What if they could see you now?" she fumed. Reduced to chastened schoolboys, the men climbed on their horses and rode off the place. "Whenever my mother saw one of them in town," my grandmother laughed, "she starred them down until they dropped their heads."

Dad grew visibly drowsy during these stories. In the summertime the buzzing of flies and in the winter the soft crackle of the warm fire had a soporific effect, and sometimes his chin would drop to his chest then jerk abruptly up. But I was mesmerized. I wondered if she would tell us a story today.

The nursing home was a big converted farmhouse with eight first-floor rooms for the eight guests. A recently built wheelchair ramp connected the sidewalk to the wrap-around porch.

"We call them guests," Florence, the owner, said when Dad introduced us. "Because that's how we treat them."

"How's Mother doing?" Dad asked.

"She's fine," Florence said, "but she keeps asking when she's going home."

"Well, she can't do that."

"That's what I tell her."

We passed the dining room where a woman fastened in a wheelchair with a seatbelt stared at a bowl of soggy cereal. She looked up at us and groaned. Medicinal odors mixed with the acrid smell of urine hung in the air.

As we walked back the dim hallway, Florence told me that they had given my grandmother the best room. "We got her dressed since I knew her grandson was visiting," she said, winking at me.

We paused and Florence knocked on the frame of the open door. I had not seen my grandmother in a year, and it took me a moment to recognize the old woman sitting in a chair as her. She had lost weight, and she looked lifeless. "Dressed" was a beige housecoat. Dad gave her a peck on the cheek, and I gave her a half hug. She put her arm around my waist and patted my back. Florence clicked off the TV and slipped from the room. Dad and I sat in two metal folding chairs.

"Look who I brought," Dad said.

"I see," my grandmother said brightly, looking at me and smiling. The smile made her look more like herself. Then she turned to Dad and the smile slid from her face. "Have you come to take me home?"

"No, Mother. And we're not going to talk about that today."

Her room was wallpapered in patterns of cardinals in trees. The once red birds had faded to a dusty rose. The linoleum floor was asparagus green.

"Honey, please take me home."

"Now, Mother, we've been over this. Don't you remember how you fell and banged up your knee? What if you fell and broke a hip?"

The scab and bruises were visible on her knee. The doctor suspected a small stroke had made her gait unsteady.

"Well, what if I did?"

"Now don't be silly. Keith, tell her about your new job."

I told her I had been made head of the history department. On this morning, it could not have seemed less important.

Dad said, "Don't you think that's great?"

"Yes, 'tis," she said, smiling at me again. I sensed that her mind had dimmed and that she no longer had it in her to tell a story. She turned back toward Dad and said, "Please let me go home. It's all I want."

It was not her words as much as her desperate, pleading tone that nearly unhinged me.

"I never thought I'd end up this way," she said. "It's like jail."

"Now, Mother, don't talk like that," Dad said. "Florence is real nice."

"The food is just terrible," she added. "It's all out of cans." Her mouth turned down and she shivered.

Dad was right—she might fall and break a hip. She was also miserable here. She had lived on the farm for sixty-five years, the last fifteen of them by herself. She must feel like an animal snatched from its cozy den and locked in a cage. I imagined myself in her place. I would want to be home, too. If I broke a hip and shortened my life, so be it.

"Keith came all the way from California to see you. Aren't you glad to see him?"

"Yes. But I want to see him in my own home. I want to bake him cinnamon rolls." She started to cry softly. I swallowed hard.

Bouncing his hat on his knee, Dad looked around and said, "This is a nice room, Mother. You've got a TV and everything."

Her mouth formed a child's pout. "I want my own things."

"What do you want to have, Mother?" Dad said sharply. "Just tell me and I'll bring it over. Don't I do everything for you?"

That remark defeated her. She heaved a sign that seemed to expel from her chest the very will to live. I tried to think of something diverting to say, but I couldn't come up with a single thing. We sat for a while longer. Dad told her some news about people in town. When we stood up to leave, I squeezed her hands in mine. They were ice-cold.

That morning has slept like a seed in my memory for thirty years. Two days later I flew back to California, where I was swept up in the frenetic pace leading to the end of the school year. Dad declined rapidly and died just after our graduation. When I flew back for the second funeral, I stopped by the farm. Sam's pen was empty.

My grandmother passed away in her sleep several weeks later, never knowing that her son had died. I surrendered to the practical impossibility of managing a dairy farm from 2,400 miles away and put the place up for sale. My wife called it a "no-thinker." When I contacted the real estate agent, he said, "Your dad told me you'd probably sell it." I wondered how Dad had said it—with approval, disappointment, or neutral resignation? When a buyer was found, the sales contract contained a clause that Pete and Verna would be allowed to live in their little house. Mother kept active with some of her friends who were widows, and she enjoyed a good decade before her own death.

Last June I retired after thirty-five years at my school. I enjoyed the summer, but my first September without a classroom to return to left me feeling at loose ends. When I received an invitation from my college fraternity to attend October homecoming activities in Kentucky, I jumped at the chance. I got a cheaper flight by going a day early and decided to visit the farm.

So now it is a Friday morning in October, and I am driving toward the farm I have not seen in many years. Though today is sunny and crisp, and the autumn leaves are blazing yellow and red, I am reliving that cold spring morning lodged in my memory like a stone—the cold wet fields, my forlorn grandmother, and Dad with his thinning neck.

A new highway has been built, and only when I turn onto the county road to the farm does the landscape look familiar. At the junction, the country store with its single gas pump in front has been abandoned. At the crest of the hill, I recognize the big maples in the front yard and the red brick house with two dormers, familiar as a family face.

I pull into the drive, ready for the car to bounce over the cattle guard, but that has been replaced by gravel on solid ground. I step out of the car, sniffing the air for the smell of cinnamon rolls. I knock on the door and introduce myself to a stout young woman holding a baby. I ask if I can look around.

"Help yourself," she answers. She does not know of my grandparents; the property has passed through several owners over the years.

"No more dairy?" I ask. There are no cows to be seen.

"There are hardly any dairy farmers left in the whole county," she says. "Can't make a go of it. Milk companies won't pick up from a small dairy."

The lot where the cows grazed after milking is overgrown with weeds—Queen Anne's lace, pigweed, and Johnson grass. The gate I used to swing on is tangled in brambles so I worm my way through the second and third wires of the fence. I tramp through the weeds, with each step seeing more clearly the dairy's state of ruin. It's like a slow-motion kick in the stomach.

The milking barn looks smaller. Its sliding wooden door, large enough for a pickup truck, is missing, so I walk in. The cattle stanchions hang empty and still. Some of the windows are broken, others are translucent with dirt. On the walls, peeling paint curls like dry leaves. Abandoned wasp and hornet nests hang from the ceiling. A section of the roof is missing, revealing a triangle of blue sky. Shoots of dead grass lie matted against the concrete floor.

It feels as lonesome as an empty church. I sit cross-legged on the floor, rest my chin on my fists. I am again a boy, and every day is sunny and warm. Tan Jersey cows stand in their stanchions munching silage from the mangers. My grandfather in his khaki work clothes and straw hat checks the tubes that carry milk to the tank. Pete kneels beside each cow, his cheek pressed to her smooth flank. With a rag and a bucket of soapy water he washes her udder, a partnership of animal and man. He attaches the cups of the milking machine to her teats and flips the switch. I hear the gentle, rhythmic pumping of the machine, the scraping of the cows' hooves on the concrete, the plop of their manure hitting the floor, the sound of their teeth grinding their grain. I see my boyhood self, tow-headed and skinny in short pants, pushing the grain cart on its squeaky wheels. Each cow gets one scoop.

Pete calls them his girls: Rose, Jill, Bumble Bee, Lady Bug, Dancer, Hollyhocks, Crazy Sally, Jumping Bean, Sister Sue. He speaks to them in his own language: "get along now," "ease up there," "settle in." Some of the words are just sounds—musical, strongly inflected, tonal. Hup-hup he says to one coming in late, trotting just ahead of the dog. He directs her into a stanchion, fastens it about her neck. To one he's finished milking, he says ee-ow, and she walks through the door to the lot. Outside, the farm has its own music: the lowing of cows, the clucking of chickens, the mesmerizing buzzing of flies and bees, the chirping of birds, the chattering of squirrels in the trees, the occasional tire-hum of a passing car. The rumble of afternoon thunder draws a worried whine from a dog.

I stand, breaking the spell of the past, and I walk through the barn to the brick milk house. The warped wooden door is stuck. I throw my shoulder into it and on the third try, the door pops open and I stumble into the room. I brush the whitewash from the shoulder of my jacket. The bulk tank still sits in the center, the once-gleaming stainless steel now chalked with dust, the temperature gauge clouded over. Against the far wall are the sink, hoses for cleaning the tank, and shelves for supplies. The air that always smelled of fresh milk is now pungent with the acrid smell of rodent urine. The windows are filmed over with a grit that gives the sun a honeyed cast, a beatific light falling on the stillness.

A feed store calendar hangs on the wall. Its year is 1988, five years after I sold the farm. The faded photo shows a herd of Jerseys grazing a sunny meadow, tall green corn growing beyond a white wood fence. The month is June, and a number is written in red pen on every other day: 2,432, 2,340, 2,419—the poundage of milk collected by the milk company truck. June 22 is the last day with a number. Later that morning, a livestock truck must have pulled up to take the herd to a new farm where they would be milked that afternoon in a different barn. That's what I want to believe. But maybe the girls were sold for slaughter.

When I leave the milk house, I look to the sky. Feeling disoriented, I realize that the silo is gone, the silo that had stood like a marker, the first thing you saw driving down the road. The corn crib is missing, too. It must have been dismantled and sold for scrap. The calf barn, where I gave Sam a face scratch that cold spring morning, has collapsed, its walls and roof folded atop one another like a fallen house of cards.

When I get back to the car, the woman reappears on the front porch, baby in her arms. She has thought of a couple of questions. What is the deep hole under her deck? What is that stone structure at the back corner of the yard? When was the house built? The hole would have been the cistern and the stone structure a smoke house where my grandfather cured hams. The brick house was built in 1943, and I tell her the story of the fire, from my grandmother cleaning in the attic to fleeing with the family Bible. When she shifts the baby back and forth between arms, I realize I've been running off at the mouth, so I smile and thank her again. She steps back inside. I pull out of the driveway. My last look at the farm is a glimpse of the decrepit milking barn in the rearview mirror.

The next day, I skip the football game for a solitary walk. Comradery and glad-handing are beyond me, and that night my seat at the fraternity dinner remains empty. When I return to California, I lie to my wife and tell her the homecoming events were fun. I do not know how to explain that I flew across the country to spend an hour wandering a dairy farm in ruins, the rest of the weekend lamenting the past.

Since the visit, I've been having vivid, deeply unsettling dreams about the farm. I have inherited the dairy, but I've forgotten about milking and the cows go dry. Or for unknown reasons the crops wither and die. Or my grandmother is still trapped in the nursing home, but I've somehow forgotten and have failed to visit her for years.

Retraction

Taylor Akiko Shoda

She'd given me that little pill and expected me to down it quick. "Just do it. One go. You think it's like jumping off a cliff and maybe it is a little, but not really, because there's water below. And it's not that far a jump. I promise. One good swallow and there! You'll be done and won't be up so high anymore and you won't have to be scared. You'll be in the water and you can float. That sound good?"

I'd nodded. It was easier that way.

"See. Then just one go. Go for it."

My mom is the kind of woman who looks like she's always ready to pull her hair out. She's tall. When she'd stood above me like that as I sat in the chair below her, I could see up her nose, the clean canals of tiny hairs, and I'd wanted to take the little pill and shove it up her nostrils.

I didn't, of course. But I didn't swallow it either. I wanted to tell her that I wasn't scared like that. I'd been okay at taking leaps. But Mom kept moving her hands and arms in this flailing way, like a kite cut loose, that made her hard to disagree with.

I'm twenty when I call her to come home for a few days. I'd only been moved out for six months. She believed that a girl needed to learn how to make it on her own, but I'd said something like "I can't deal with Dane right now. We won't stop fighting. I think it might be over," and she hates Dane so she told me to come. She was absolutely hysterical when I let her in on my little secret, even though I'd asked her, fruitlessly, to try not to react or anything. Her whole body reacts to things like she's boiling inside. Dane always tells me that I care too much about what she thinks, that we have a toxic relationship, that she is a very angry woman, that I come home angry after spending time with her, but he's wrong. I just don't want her to break her back for me.

I told her I couldn't take the pill, especially when she spoke to me like that. She'd asked, "Like what?" like she didn't know, and I'd rolled my eyes and made a face. "Just do it, Clare. Do it." I didn't do it, and she'd gotten pissed off the way she always did so fast, and walked out of the kitchen to the living room. I shouted at her that I was in pain, that I was crampy and the most tired I'd ever been in my entire life. I'd started to cry, not even forced, and she wouldn't come back. She yelled my name again and again after I said anything.

I waited a little bit and looked out to the yard at the dead garden Mom had tried to plant, and then I followed her to the living room and told her that I did it, and I was relieved, and she'd said she was too, thank God. Effusively, she told me that I'd really dodged a bullet coming to her. It was a good thing to leave the man out of it, sometimes. She'd given me a hug and said into my hair, "Life is full of tests." I gave the hug back, my palm grabbing at the fabric of her shirt, unaware that by returning the gesture I was saying, "I'm okay. We don't ever have to talk about it ever again. I don't need you to ask me about it or try to make me feel better." But that's what she heard, I'm guessing. I'm still having a baby in eight months.

I'd fallen asleep on the living room couch feeling as though I'd endured and then conquered some very great thing. I thought of the King Palm trees in the front yard receiving whip after whip of aggressive wind, persisting, through the rare California storm, sustaining.

I hang up on the lady a third time. It's not like I know the woman. Dealing with Mom yesterday engendered a rotten mood today. She left for the day and I plan to leave soon.

The lady calls back. She tells me to just hold on and let her talk, please.

She needs me to schedule the appointment and I try to comply from my bedroom floor. I made a pillow bed in the middle of the carpet. My insides suspend in an uneasy halt, running up to a cliff and stopping right before the fall. I always surprise myself at being such an easily unnerved person. She goes on talking, and I try to listen but I keep getting distracted by the movement inside me, like a fish running into the glass bowl that is my stomach, again and again.

The lady says that though the consultation will be in person, the doctor will give me the details and tell me what I should expect through a Telehealth phone call in a patient room. Yes, the phone call has to be at the office, in the patient room. Over the phone because the doctor is only in-office every few weeks.

It all feels very pointless then, like maybe this is one of those signs I've been asking for.

I want to cry, "Over the phone?" but I stay quiet and take a deep breath. Sometimes I forget I have to be an adult about things.

"It's just that, I know you've called before. And I'm not saying any of this to scare you, but you need to know that time isn't on your side. It's important to have all the information before you make any decisions. You know, look before you leap."

What is up with all of the leaping? I raise my brows and she goes on, "This isn't something that's going to go away on its own. It's not a cold. It isn't a sickness. You can't just ignore it." The receptionist chooses her words like Mom does—careful and tight, like each word is a fragile piece of china. I wonder what she sounds like talking to her kids.

I set the phone to speaker and put it in my lap. I flip off the screen to see what it feels like. I listen to her with this face on like a little kid. But I want the lady to say it, say the actual word instead of "treatment" and "procedure" and "this choice." I want to hit her like a piñata and watch the truth scurry out of her mouth in a mess on the floor.

I picture my mom in her magenta pajama shorts with the bow in the middle, too young, a big belly stretching a pink tank top to its last stitch.

I'd been getting these gatherings in my gut for the last few days. Some sort of rush. I couldn't tell if it was baby or me. The cramp turns a little bit and then the phone goes quiet. I think about telling the lady about the gatherings, but then she might say something about it being normal. I don't want to hear it. I don't want to be pooled into a category that confirms what's happening to me.

"Clare, are you still there?"

"Yeah. Sorry. I've been having trouble focusing." I get up to try and appease the ache and pull apart my curtains and open the window. Every time I stand up I picture tiny little teeth and fingernails spilling out of me. Last night I had a dream of its skull rolling around inside of me, and its sausagey intestines, the teeth, the fingernails, and strands of hair, crashing and conjoining together, then ricocheting off the walls of my stomach lining. The dream wailed and whimpered, assuaged by the rub of my belly, the coo of my lips. I ate breakfast this morning with an elevated purpose. I'd looked in the mirror at my eyes, the bearer of such early life. I want to tell the receptionist that.

"I'm wondering if maybe you can talk to someone about this. Are you in contact with the father? Maybe a friend or a family member you trust?"

"Yeah. I'm gonna come to the appointment. Thanks."

The receptionist sighs and I feel bad for a second. I flipped her off like four times. Then, "That's great. Okay. We'll see you then."

We hang up.

On my phone Dane sends me pictures on Instagram. They're stupid but they make me laugh a little. I wish he could distract me fully without me knowing that's what he was doing. He doesn't know what he's doing—he doesn't know anything—but he knows something's up. I know that because he texts, "are you coming back?" Later, "everything okay?" I text back that everything's fine, and so then he tries to FaceTime me. I don't think I can look at him without spitting everything out. Baby, baby, baby, baby running through my head, assembling in my throat. The decision hovers over everything. Hovers, clouds; I can't look at anything without seeing a big round belly plopped in the middle of my vision. I can't even have my morning coffee. Seeing Dane face to face is too perfect a catalyst for a confession.

Instead I message that I'm leaving my mom's in a minute. I also ask him what he thinks about going camping maybe. Storm in a teacup, Mom always says. I'm seeing what sticks. Dane can be unpredictable, even to me. A trip feels good, sounds good. I haven't been able to make any decisions lately and this one is immediately soothing. Right like a good pair of jeans. I'd had few of those lately.

Dane is a good boyfriend. He doesn't need to make the effort because he's naturally even-tempered. I told him that once, along with that it was relieving he always knew what he was doing. I told him that it put me at ease. He said he was glad I didn't worry. He said he had me. Sometimes he could get angry at things—the world, the TV, his game—but never me. But it was like watching your parents fight, or get too drunk. I wanted it to stop but had no right.

I wonder if I still feel all those things for him. I marvel and maybe even enjoy, for just a moment as I'm driving back to the apartment, at how quickly everything has changed. It's almost incredible.

When I get to the apartment Dane is on the sofa with his back hunched over his phone and a bowl of cereal on the coffee table.

I look at his profile and imagine our baby, somehow too white and too big to make sense, and see it in my arms, a little girl, dressed in light pink and white gingham. I can't see its face but it has that baby mouth where the lips are always pursed.

Looking at him now I'm confronted by a deep knowing. I know what Dane would say. He's good at calming me down, at saying things he feels are mobilizing and powerful, and he would get me, he really would. I'd do whatever he told me to do. He'd say money and young and money and career and money and hurry and please and Clare, Clare, Clare. He would never say baby. He'd probably be angry, but he'd say it's because he cares, and then probably hug me and then grab his hands onto my shoulders like he does sometimes when he thinks I'm not listening to him.

But I'm too hormonally warped to bring it up. I'd feel needy in a childish way, tugging at the fabric of his pants from the floor, help me, help me, tell me what to do, asking questions that feel so important, concerns, but no concept, hanging on every word. Yes, the sky is blue. No, I don't know why.

I couldn't feel like that now.

When I think about a baby, really, really think about it, I'm so sure it's all I've ever wanted that I can't believe I thought I wanted anything else. I can almost trace the instinct, or the infiltrator, inside my body probing at my heart and my brain, kicking every morsel of my body into some protective mode, a "keep me! keep me!" swarming every thought, nervously guarding my womb as if it's being held over the edge of a cliff.

I look at Dane and I'm thinking of nothing sometimes.

I don't know if the apathy in our relationship is Dane-caused or my own. Before we were in love he could be so hard to reach. He was always on his phone but never answered texts or picked up phone calls until the last second acceptable within romantic propriety. I never knew what he was thinking or if he wanted me in a serious way. Every time we found ourselves spending time with one another it was happenstance, which made the meetups simultaneously precious and almost burdensome on his part, like he'd just barely squeezed me in. Our relationship happened faintly, almost by accident, like slipping to the floor and then staying down. As if Dane couldn't, wouldn't, take responsibility for our coupling, but was merely complicit, then slowly grew to rely upon, maybe even enjoy in a satisfying way, my partnership, my admiration, my dependence, my body.

We talk about camping, that he can free up some time and go tomorrow. He asks no questions. He looks at his phone a lot when he talks but I think he makes a point of looking at me when I talk. I tell him about Cypress Lake, how it's only a couple of hours away, and that I've always wanted to go. He says something like, "You and your lakes," and it's cute. It's pleasant, like floating, to feel so known. I press into the feeling like packed snow.

He mentions something about his day, work, a coworker, then looks at me to maybe talk about my own. I don't, and he is amicable with my silence. Short-lipped. He knows I'm withholding, so he withholds back.

I get in the bath. He leaves me alone. The suds spread across my body like moss over a rock. I look at my belly. There's some little thing inside me, whatever it is. What a thought to have. What a thing to feel. I miss being bored, because now it's just baby, baby, baby. I Google how much childbirth costs at the hospital. Like 25k. I start feeling like I have to use the bathroom so I get out of the tub. I lotion myself all over, too fast, and my face turns blotchy and red. I press my palm into my stomach and try to send a signal or something. I don't know. I think about having a glass of wine while I get ready for bed, so out of my character, like with a towel wrapped around my hair and gliding lotion up my leg, like a movie, and everything's white and I'm skinny and there's no fleshy bits of me sticking out anywhere, and the wine perches in my fingers like it weighs nothing.

I'd stopped drinking after finding out. Dane will bring beer on the camping trip, and I'll have to say something. We are big drinkers, for occasions. He thinks we're fun together when we drink. He said, couldn't I tell that everyone gravitated toward us at parties? He said we're the fun couple. I could tell this meant a lot to him. He walks into parties with his arms and mouth all wide, without a care in the world, and ushers me in, presents me like I'm very special and important to his entrance, a mound of meat to the centerpiece of the table. Maybe they'd eat me.

I don't imagine these attributes—fun, unattached, carefree—would survive in fatherhood. I think about never seeing Dane smile again. I picture his head in his palms, his hands trying to hold up what he can't on his own.

I hear a rustling, and then Dane opens the bathroom door. I close my towel. I want to cry. My face aches like a sore muscle. He leans in the doorframe to watch and study me like a hippo might a butterfly. I stare at myself in the mirror then catch his eye in the reflection.

"Flâneur Dane is my least favorite."

"Flannel?"

"Flâneur. It means you're hovering."

He wonders at me. He tilts his head.

"What time do you wanna leave tomorrow?" He tells me that he dropped everything to go on our camping trip. It was convenient that he had the weekend off from work and I'd called in all of my sick pay at the restaurant this morning, two and a half weeks' worth. I'm doing my best to trap myself, puppy guard my mind into a corner so that I'm forced to do something, make some sort of choice, I guess, do anything.

"Whenever." I close my eyes and its water. I take a big breath.

"You okay?"

"Yeah? A little tired, but that's it."

"Y'sure? Have you drank enough water today?"

"Yeah. I need to pack." I feel him behind me as I walk to the bedroom. Ask again, in my head. Ask again.

I make quiet work. I wish he would leave and stay at the same time. I suppose that is to say that I want him around but I don't want him with me, and somehow those things amount to the same one feeling. Summer is still warm but I pack big, loose sweaters and shirts, piling them into my duffle bag, then force it to zip shut so it heaps in the center like a pillow stuffed underneath a little girl's shirt.

"Shouldn't you pack too?" Dane is a last minute person. This attribute makes him seem easy-going, but he's actually just lazy and then necessarily fleet-footed when he's ran out the clock. Our child would be late to everything. It would grow up with an impatient look on its face, like its mom's and its mom's mom, always a hand on its hip and its gaze darting, watching dad, go, go, go.

Dane sits on the bed. He looks at me. I turn away quickly and catch a tear as though I'm rubbing my eye. I feel like a whale. A container. A clump of organs choked on a table. I want him to try and reach for me so I can jerk his touch away. For some reason I thought he would be able to tell. I'm hot inside and out. I'm angry over the possibility of waiting for him. Bitter.

"Go pack, Dane. Seriously," I snap.

"Okay, okay."

He gets up slow.

We pass a huddled group of raccoons as we drive through the park, dusk's dim field making their eyes appear struck and vigilant. They scamper up a tree as I stare them down. My mom calls me twice and I ignore both of them. She sends me texts asking how much I'm bleeding and that if I'm bleeding too much then I should go to the clinic. I've finished three stacks of saltine crackers when Dane parks the car. Our site is under a large oak and beside a dirt hiking trail. We didn't talk for the two-hour drive except he'd asked me why I wanted saltines instead of actual dinner and I said my stomach hurt and felt some relief at that small truth. The silence, instead of restful or unintended, is preparatory, tiny foreshocks making tiny cracks in whatever peace remains between Dane and me. His quiet is a fortifying battle practice. Mine is the slow drying of bricks stacking higher and higher.

First Dane does the fire. I set up our tent and put a checkered tablecloth over the lunch table. It is so quiet I can hear my heartbeat. I can feel it in my gut. My stomach is hard. The site next to us is a still, orange glowing tent.

"Come sit with me." We put a blanket next to the fire and brought cushions from our balcony chairs to sit on. He's housing a beer and one of the turkey sandwiches I made before we left. I think about nothing as I sit down next to him.

"Does your stomach still hurt?"

I shrug.

He pulls me into him, steers my body until I'm sat between his legs with the top of my head pressed into his chin. Everything smells like fire. I wish that we had never left home. I wonder why I put myself through it. No place to escape, how tonight we'll have to sleep next to one another, close with our bodies glued to stay warm. I wonder what I'm doing. I mouth silently, I'm pregnant again and again and then just preh preh preh preh feeling my lips touch and depart over and over. I have the sudden urge to get in the car and lock the doors. I imagine the whole thing. I love locking doors. I love looking at locked doors.

"Penny for your thoughts?" His voice a ceiling falling lower, lower.

"What."

My body runs cold. My chest picks up.

"I feel like I can physically feel your mind racing."

I could cry. I could cry and then he wouldn't ask that many questions. He'd have to attribute the tears to a whole mess of other things, dispense one of my problems like a gumdrop from a coin machine. My mother, my stress, my insecurity, my lack of direction, my anger, my stubborn resolve.

"Talk to me, please. You've been distant. I tried to give you space, but you have to talk to me. I wanna help. I hate seeing you like this."

Where's the pull? Where's that trigger that's supposed to fire when the man I love lends me a hand, says, I'll carry that weight for you?

The word between my silent lips like prehg-nin, pregh-nin, taking impossibly long to say, taking such a toll with so much tongue work, a whole mouthy procedure of precise movement and perfect timing to say one word. Where's the pull? When will I give? How far could I go, how long?

"I'm pregnant." I don't know how it comes out. I don't feel it. I feel like a very large clot trying to squeeze through a tiny tube.

"What? Are you being serious?" My mind parses out the insult in this response. I feel my fuse shorten, cut off at the waist. I see the easy way out with that fight, that rehearsed conversation, so trivial now, a drop in the ocean.

"Mhm."

"What?"

"What?" I repeat back to him.

"No, not you 'what.' Me what. Are you serious?" He pushes me up from him and moves to look at me as I steady myself with my hands behind my back. I feel sticky. His face is alert, a siren. His face is the instant "Clare" becomes "Clare, pregnant," inseparably. He looks all over from my forehead to my cheeks to my chin, I think, to see if I'm cracking a smile, on the verge of a laugh. I get red and hot.

"Why the fuck would I joke about this?"

"You have before!"

I don't remember. It feels only like something I could do, not something I have done.

"Dane."

"Okay, sorry. Okay. Are you sure?"

I tell him about the two tests. I detail the humiliation of buying the tests. How I'd worn my mom's ivory cable cardigan and her dark cherry loafers, tied my hair into a bun, I don't know, tried to look old enough. I tell him about my mom's house. I tell him I lied to her.

I am a flood.

I tell him when, approximately, and he goes Ohhhh okay, casual. I tell him I'm so tired that I always want to cry. I tell him I feel like I'm not in my body. I tell him I don't feel like myself no matter how hard I try and I feel lost and I can't find my head and I don't get it. I tell him I'm sorry I couldn't say it earlier and I'm sorry I iced him out. I tell him I'm a cold person. I tell him I don't know what to do.

"What do you mean—like, do you mean like, what, like you don't know what to do how? Like you want to keep it?"

"No! I mean I don't know. Why don't you think I would've thought of every possibility? I don't wanna talk about this."

"Clare—what? We have to talk about this." He grabs my shoulder after I shrink down. "Look at me. You know this wouldn't work. We're like—we're practically still kids. You were a teenager like three months ago! How would this even work? I mean, it wouldn't. We can't."

I wish I never said anything. The remnants of the impulsive blurting smolder like heartburn, from my chest all the way down into my stomach. The wind changes direction and smoke courses between us. I hear the wild all around us, small sounds.

Dane stands up. For a long time he paces around the fire pit as if circling his prey. "Clare, you know we can't. Don't make this hard on yourself. Now we're like—I mean what the fuck are we doing out here? We're frickin—two hours from the nearest clinic. What are we doing?"

"Like I'd go and do it right now? Are you kidding?"

"I don't see why we'd wait. I don't get why you didn't just do it at your mom's house."

"I can't believe this." The tears tickle my neck like fingers tapping against my skin.

Dane squats down in front of me. I sense he's come into his thoughts rationally. His demeanor has shifted back to its usual ease, if only for a moment, as if I've barely disrupted his life, as a bird might fly from a falling tree.

We're quiet then. He does not move to touch me. He falls back from his squat into the dirt.

I imagine I could move to a small town and get an apartment and a good paying job. If I can't get an office job maybe I could waitress or bartend, when I turn 21. People make their livings off things like that. I have skills. I can cook all right and learn most things quickly. I really do. I almost have a degree. Or I could move to the coast. Or I could live in the country in the middle of nowhere. Maybe a farm. In the middle of nowhere I could probably afford a house, a modest one. The baby would grow up in nature. We'd know flora and fauna and the feeling of good silence. Mom would come around. She is hardened but she is moveable. She'd take one look at the baby and understand.

Dane takes off one of his shoes and chucks it into a tree. He yells like I haven't heard him. I startle. The glowing tent next to us stirs. I tell him to stop, please. I cry harder and he mumbles at me. I thought I knew every Dane. I'm somehow periphery to his thoughts in a way I thought was no longer possible. I don't know when it happened or if it has always been this way, but somehow, we've ended up a couple who survives their battles stood side by side, but not hand in hand.

"I'm not having a kid, Clare. You can't do this. There's too many things going on. We don't have enough money, for starters. My job now only just barely covers the rent. You—you're in community college, Clare. You're a waitress, Clare. I want to be perfect when I have a kid. I want us to be perfect. I want you to be—to be good." He says something else then, deeply in his chest, that I can't make out.

"You want me to be perfect?"

"Clare, no. Jesus. Seriously? You know what I mean."

"Yes, you do. You want me to be perfect. That's what you meant to say."

"What? No! I'm just saying that I want us to be good before we even think about having kids. If we even have kids. We're not ready. You're frickin' twenty years old!"

I'd have a baby shower and invite every person I know. I'd meet rich people, quickly. I'd tell them my story. I wouldn't spend a dime. I'd say, no, no father in the picture. I'd take what I could get. I'd collect welfare. Mom would help as much as she could. I could live at home. I don't have to move. I could stay with Mom and we could replant the garden with a little baby cheeky and giggling.

"When, then? When will you be ready?"

"I don't know? What does that have to do with anything? That's not the point. We wouldn't even be talking about this if—"

"But we are. You act like having the baby isn't a possibility."

"Because it's not. It shouldn't be."

"Because I'm not perfect yet. Right."

"Clare, I swear to god. Not that this like, matters. You know I want to be with you forever, and I love you, but. We've only been together for a year. I mean. I don't know."

Something inside me zips up, if at first I was flayed for whatever of Dane's pickings.

"I know I'm supposed to say that it's up to you. And like, I would—I mean—I don't know. I don't know. We can't do this, Clare. Please."

Would I look at my baby and always remember her dad begging her away?

His eyes unable to meet mine as he told me to vacuum out my insides?

Would she look like him?

"Say something." He sits down next to me. I look at him to see how it feels. I stare. I let that sit.

"You think I would be a bad mom."

"Clare, please."

"You do."

He opens another beer. I hadn't noticed the pile, five or six, growing behind us.

"I think my life would be over." His face is the moment a bee realizes its sting.

What a poisoned way to start a life.

I want to walk away, storm off dramatically, but I'm someone who cannot help getting lost. And I don't want Dane to have to help me. He had wanted to avoid labels when we first started dating, but when we moved in together, something changed, and he made me promise we wouldn't give up, that we'd always be kind. He'd said couples could get so ugly. He said when people are in love and it gets fucked up, they turn on each other that much harder. I feel what must be a misplaced sense of relief, or perhaps some form of hysteria, that all of this time he always could have, but never did until now, really hurt me.

I stare at the fire for a long time. Dane does too. He offers me a drink of his beer and I look at him. Probably out of pride he doesn't retract his offer or move the bottle back into his chest. Eventually he takes a sip. He attempts to reminisce on our last camping trip, when we saw a bear walking along the shore of the lake. All of the campers swarmed to the parking lot as children cried into their shirts, while the bear sniffed along the rocks and algae clomping one large paw with great effort in front of the next one, not looking up at us, not looking at anyone, not even once.

We somehow watch the fire give out, walk to the bathrooms and get ready for bed, lie in our sleeping bags on our phones, and finally turn out the lantern without speaking. Dane somehow falls asleep.

My stomach turns. The nausea waves over me. I can only lie on my side otherwise it feels like a stone is pressing me into the ground. I want to wake Dane up just to tell him how tired I am. I want him to say, I know, and turn back over, maybe rest his hand near me, so I can touch it if I want. Tomorrow I am eight weeks. This means, according to the lady on the phone, that I have one more week to take the pills. Otherwise they'll put the vacuum inside of me. I can't imagine an actual baby-looking thing sucked up in the vacuum-looking thing, suctioning down a tube, I think because I know somewhere inside that it might not really be a baby thing, not quite. But I feel that my anger, that Dane's anger, and the culmination of energy from this very violent moment, discussing the life or death of the unborn thing, I guess, has certainly infected the entire pregnancy, maybe even the thing itself, the confusion, stress, and complete lack of desire for its fruition, absorbed right into my belly. I wonder when love is enough, how much you need. I wonder how to explain, or how to make sense for myself, that it isn't one way or the other, want or not. But mostly I wonder how I know that I would make it all right, with or without Dane, with or without my mom, just me and kid. This, more than anything, prompts the decision to begin unwrapping itself in my head, spread over my brain coating every inkling of want, distrust, tenderness, hesitation, and love, somehow always love, driving deep deep, until there is only the duty to do the Right Thing.

And yet.

Good Form

Ben Carter Olcott

In the big white house, it was game night.

Helen slapped down an UNO card, ironically drawled, "Draw four," and winked at me, purred. My cheeks burned, hot with liquor. I smiled. I glanced at Andrew, who was raising an eyebrow at me, watching my every move with a strangled electric attention, urging action like a pubescent teenager outside a woman's window.

"How sultry, Helen," Maddie said. "How bad of you."

"Helen's hot," Andrew said, staring at me, "for beating you." He made a hand-job motion, gushed some spit around his mouth in time with his thrusts.

Maddie, sitting next to Andrew, slapped his groin.

"You're gross. You're bad."

Andrew's eyes dragged toward Maddie, his soon-to-be wife, the coiled sexual thing between them. I smiled my immaculate white teeth. I liked Maddie and Andrew, their repartee, their balance. They were still having sex, it was obvious. I imagined they yelled at each other when they fucked, profanities of all colors and stripes. Then sweating, naked, they'd admire photos of the gazebo in which they'd be wed.

I drew my four cards.

These were my friends, people like me—handsome and solvent, smart but loose—and I was pleased to sit with them on this white pleather couch in the white expanse of their white-walled living room.

Helen, her eyes melting, breathed through her mouth, cooed, "Your turn, Robert."

Later, in the kitchen, Andrew clapped me on the shoulder, gripped. He was built thick and muscley like a bull, all energy and kick. His fingers burrowed into my well-formed muscle. He lingered there for a moment, massaging me, his face close to mine.

"What do you think?" he said, his voice hoarse.

"Helen's great," I said.

His gaze gripped me, that same electric attention begging the silhouette: undress. Then he stepped away, leaned on the marble counter. His shirt was buttoned down to his waxed, well-formed sternum. It looked like he'd started game night the moment he got home from work, wasting no time. I liked that. It made him seem desperate, like a desperado.

"Helen's hot," he said.

"And a coworker."

"So was Martinique."

"That was different."

"Different how?"

It wasn't different—I knew that—but it was different to me. Helen's posture, her bearing—the way she breathed too hard, the way she looked at me—so eagerly, too eagerly. I wanted to work for it. I'd gotten to where I was in life by working hard. By making plans and testing them and leaving no stone unturned.

I said, "It's not good form. To date in the office."

Andrew actually bent over laughing. He spilled his drink. I became conscious of my crossed arms, my frown. I tried to laugh with him, loosen my hands.

"You're too good for us," Andrew said. "You're a goddamned saint."

I smiled. I splashed some water into my whiskey.

Then it was a blur, and Helen and I were outside waiting for Ubers. She hooked her finger into my belt loop. My nose was filled with Texas spring and Helen's lilac perfume and her rye whiskey breath. She pressed her cheek into my chest, rubbing herself into my abdomen. We were drunk.

"Just gonna lay here," she said.

Her fingers released the belt loop and began walking down my thigh.

"Don't tell anyone," she whispered.

I grabbed her hand, raised it to my mouth, and sucked on her pointer finger. She groaned, said my name, kept saying it, until the headlights caught us. Then I led her to her car and bid her goodnight.

I liked to spend Sunday mornings at the farmer's market in Alamo Heights. At this time in my life, I considered patience my greatest strength—I'd cultivated it for years and applied it to everything I did; it was a modus operandi, a way of seeing, of being better. I would spend hours at Quarry Market on Basse Street carefully selecting the best produce on offer, searching for ripe fruits in places most shoppers never looked—four layers deep in a pile of apples, underneath a blueberry carton on display—easily findable if you made the effort, if you cared. This was the secret to unimpeachable quality: effort, patience. I enjoyed figuring the stone fruits most, peaches and plums whose decay hid beneath the skin. I'd clasp one, shut my eyes, and read all along its pressure points with my fingers, detecting the contours of its pith, its suppleness, my sensitive instrument seeking the broken flesh. I would accept nothing less than perfection. This was the last ingredient to success: knowing what you want.

The day after game night, I was holding a candidate plum when my sister called.

"It's terrible," Lara said. There was a tinkling, rustling sound in the background of the call. "It's so awful."

I was used to this from Lara. I simply continued to test my plum and told her it would be fine.

The sounds over the phone crescendoed into a glassy crash. "You don't understand," she yelled, and I could hear something shatter. She swore. She was panting, then she screamed.

I made the final pass on the plum, double-checking around the style. I pressed in with my thumbs, found the rubbery give that meant that even at its weakest points the plum held its structure. It'd be a tangy one, a fruit you had to cut through, as I preferred. My method was once again affirmed. I felt a surge of pleasure. How pleasing it was to master every element. How worth it.

"Do something. Say something," Lara said.

I said I would come over soon. I had a presentation I needed to focus on that week, and Andrew's bachelor party was the weekend following—I'd need to make sure everything at the office was in order before I left.

Then I felt the depression at my thumb.

"Bobby, please."

I hung up. I looked down at the plum, astonished. I'd missed the rot, dead center in the suture, the cinch where the lobes meet. My thumb stroked the crease once again, confirming the disintegration with disgust. Then I put the plum back on the display. Every fruit, then, seemed defective, abject. Suddenly sure that everything I had built for myself with great attention to detail could at any time slip from my grasp, I told a manager about the situation. "Talk to your buyers," I commanded them. "This doesn't work for me." Then I left the market and headed for the gym, where I lifted until my muscles screamed and I no longer felt a need to punish myself for my carelessness.

We had a new development officer at work. Their name was Jaim—"they" was their preferred pronoun. There had been chatter about this—I ignored it. Helen had come to my office and said, "So. I wanted to talk to you about something."

"I've forgotten all about it," I said.

"Forgotten all about what?" she said meaningfully.

"Nothing," I said, furious with myself for slipping.

"What I wanted to talk to you about. This, I guess, person—this new person, I mean. Jaim?"

"What about them?"

"Just . . . you know."

"No, I don't know."

Helen blinked at me. She blinked and fluttered her eyes, trying to show me she was having trouble understanding what I was doing without saying anything—and this was precisely why I didn't want her. So I told her what was going on: Jaim had excellent credentials, that's why I hired them. End of story. Helen left smiling, pretending not to care.

Jaim was my subordinate, below me—I was the head of the San Antonio Mayor's Office of Philanthropic Initiatives. Jaim was well-dressed, clean, fit. Most days they wore their blonde hair up in a ponytail that accentuated and revealed their side buzz, wore dangling sapphire earrings and boxy glasses that seemed to perch on cheeks angular and stately like the cliffs of Dover. Jaim would pair this with anything at all: one day, a white collared shirt underneath a mustard cardigan, sensible slacks and shoes. But another day, they'd come in with their hair teased and crinkling, wearing a short sleeve button-down shirt, a tie, black jeans, a look almost punk-rock, almost New York.

Jaim and I had our first development meeting together that week. We sat in a conference room alone for the first time since their final interview. They were dressed "normally" that day, and I felt an overwhelming urge to comment on this—which I muted, understanding very well that I had gotten this far precisely because I never—never—made this mistake. There were rules to uphold, and they were there for a reason. I was kind, harmless. A gentle giant, I'd heard, among other comments and prognostications about my physical appearance. Martinique and I had disclosed our relationship to HR. Everything was above board with her, how I liked it. It just hadn't worked out between us, and she'd moved on to a different municipality.

"How are things going?" I said to Jaim.

"Good!" they said. "Really looking forward to this first meeting. I think this is a really strong opportunity, something the mayor can really get behind. I'm thinking about climate change, of course, I think we want to show that we're blue around here, you know? Or at the very least purple," they said, laughing. "And I can see the need to project a softer touch, in general. The mayor is concerned with nature. You know, and not just politics as usual."

While Jaim spoke, a lightness fuzzed into my brain, soothing and smoothing. I was listening to their voice, mellifluous, so smooth, but missing some of the words—but I couldn't stop the fuzzing. Usually I listened with tenacity, missing nothing: but not with Jaim. Their voice made me smile, made me resonate, as if it were vibrating not just in my head but throughout my body.

"I love that," I said.

Then the executive from the Arboreal Society entered, and we all shook hands. He was a Texan through and through: ruddy-faced and round, white with a rawhide cowboy hat and rawhide leather boots. He got to it. "The trees need savin'. They are the root of our great republic . . ."

I smiled my white teeth and nodded. I kept throwing to Jaim, kept wanting to hear their voice, vibrating in me so sweetly. And I liked the way Jaim's earrings dangled when they spoke, always impassionedly, about mission, belief, "our goals." As Jaim handled this rough Texan like a damaged dog, I began to imagine Jaim telling me what to do—I couldn't stop myself. They could tell me to do anything with a voice like that: I would do it. Jaim in charge, telling me how to dress, telling me how to be. Jaim finding the rot in me, telling me to stop fucking around you worthless piece of shit, shape up. Jaim telling me to dress like a woman: put on a dress. That's right. And lacy underwear that goes up your suture. That's right. And I realized I would if they asked, as the Texan crumbled like cake. "The mayor is doing things the right way, now," Jaim said. They were effective—highly effective.

When the executive left, pleased and promising to send a gift in the mail, Jaim and I were left alone again. My heart was pounding. I could feel my palms very keenly, their thin skin and their itch, as I pressed them into the table, subduing their revelations.

"You were great," I said. I kept the breath out of my voice or thought I did.

Jaim said, "Thanks," showing their white, well-ordered teeth. They gathered their things. "I thought it went really well."

They were standing. I was sitting. They were tall, my height, but I felt small and usable. I put my hands in my lap.

"I'm gonna make a call in here," I said.

Jaim smiled and left. I watched them as they went. I watched.

My hands pressed and pressed. I tried to think of trees: their beauty. But then I thought of trees being pulped to paper, stretched and beaten ceaselessly until they surrendered their shape.

"You could be mayor someday," Andrew said.

We were having lunch in the office cafeteria—I was eating a salad, a rainbow of vegetables with a lite dressing, Andrew a fried chicken sandwich from Chick-fil-A.

Andrew was in City Planning, and we often worked together. Our first project had been managing a gift by the Zurleins, a wealthy family, earmarked for a substance recovery center. It'd never been realized, the patrons died, and the children were dissolute, lazy, addicted—they squabbled, nothing ever got done. We'd wiped our hands of it and become friends as our departments commiserated over beers three years ago.

"I was thinking of it the other night," he said, "after game night. You're magnanimous as fuck, you know that?"

This was not the first time I'd heard something like this, but it was the first time I'd heard it from Andrew.

"That means a lot to me, Andrew."

"You got it, pal. Of course. I'd fucking vote for you."

We ate our meals in silence. The thought of running for real political office had of course crossed my mind—I'd spent my adolescent years seeking election. In third grade, I'd been told there was an activity called student council where you got to make decisions with sixth graders, whom I revered. As a third grader, I could run for treasurer—the lowest ranking officer in the cabinet. I did run and I did win. I became the favorite to win vice president the next year, and I won that hard-fought race. Every subsequent year through my senior year of college I was elected to a leadership position. At Baylor, I was the class VP. The president, Mary Beth, whom I'd desired desperately at the time, was now working in Washington, DC, as an operative for the NRA. I stayed in politics to outmatch her, at first—and I was still here.

Andrew said, "You ever imagine where you'd be if you were someone else?"

"Of course," I said. "I think everyone does that from time to time. It's healthy."

"You could be anywhere. On a private jet, about to do something massive. Something awesome. You could have a yacht with a bunch of girls around you, like that guy, just floating around some fucking beautiful fucking scenic fucking ocean."

"But you wouldn't have Maddie in that scenario. So, you know, there are reasons to be grateful for what you have."

Not hearing me, he squeezed out mayonnaise from a packet into a mound of ketchup. At work, Andrew was different than he was at game night: he always seemed half-present, as if he didn't realize or didn't care what it looked like to be so detached. I didn't like this about Andrew; in fact, it made me angry, at times. Because Andrew got promoted anyway. No one seemed to notice that he didn't care. He mixed the pinkish glop together with a fry, and said absentmindedly, "I'd be different, I think."

"No one's perfect," I said.

"Yeah," he said. "Maybe you are though." He faintly shook his head, as if clearing his head of these delicate ideas. "Anyway. You ready to get fucked up next weekend?"

"Sure," I said.

"Good," he said. "Yeah. I just need to let loose. Time to get messy. Right? It's good to make a fucking mess sometimes, right? Healthy."

"Sure," I said, not sure at all.

He glopped the fries again, making a mess of his meal, getting pinkish ketchup-mayonnaise slop all over his fingers, which he licked absentmindedly, his mind on the yacht in the Adriatic and the women he'd pay to look hot beside and to fuck him.

After work the next day, I drove out to Sabinal. It was hot, muggy; things went still that deep into the country. It was around six when I arrived at Lara's, a trailer just beside Sabinal Creek, which is what we called the rut in the road that once held water. Not that I'd ever seen it. The air smelled of dogwood and silt, humidity and dust and hot metal. A dust devil swept up a few feet away. There was some kind of grit in my teeth; I spat out sand.

The trailer door was open—a bad sign. I went inside.

Astrid, Lara's eight-year-old daughter, was sitting on the floor, playing with a bit of tin foil, shaping it into a hat with a pointed top like the kind eccentrics on TV make to protect themselves from alien communications. I'm sure Lara had been watching something like this, babbling fearfully to Astrid.

"Hi, Uncle Robert," she said. Her thin gingham dress was spread out on the false wood floor, her legs splayed at an odd angle. She was blonde, fragile, and gentle, like Lara had been as a child. Her curls were tucked back in a red clip.

"Where's your mom?"

She pointed toward the bedroom.

I had to step over the usual crap to get there—boxes filled with junk, scraps of broken things, mounds of materials, creaky stained half-destroyed furniture. Lara was, according to her, an antiques seller. But I paid for everything, she never sold a thing— what was there to sell?—and I felt a familiar frustration as I struggled to get around a rocking chair encrusted with some blue syrupy liquid that smelled like antifreeze. Plates of old food, flies hovering around them, littered the plastic counter—I was disgusted. I was ashamed. That was familiar, too.

The bedroom smelled of charred foil, a faintly chemical musk. But there was no sulfurous curling smoke this time, no arms flashing out, no frozen moment of desperation—I was grateful for that, at least. Lara was tucked into the creaky pull-out bed, groaning and muttering under the covers. I lay down next to her and stared at the ceiling, the tin shell of the trailer blackened from my mother's constant cigarette smoke. She was dead, and I'd given Lara the trailer, our childhood home, to live in. My mother, so much like Lara, had wisely entrusted me with such decisions. Lara had changed the curtains years ago, it was going to be the start of something new, and they matched the old covers and the goldenrod floral wallpaper so in the setting sunlight the room glowed yellow then gold then tawny. But that was the extent of Lara's efforts, and the room was now filthy.

I shook Lara awake. She resisted at first, brushed me away. Then I said my name. She turned to me.

Her eyes were glazed, half-open. She looked serene, blissed out, beyond reach—I couldn't help but think of Helen, drunk out of her mind, drawling at me, thoughts floating to the surface, fading away—of Andrew, brainless over the Chick-fil-A.

"It's you," she said.

I flicked Lara's forehead—she didn't react at all.

Two seconds later she rubbed the spot. "What . . ."

I could smell her hot, metallic breath—unclean.

"What do you need, Lara?"

"You're . . ."

I waited for more. The room was hot, and I could feel myself begin to sweat.

Lara turned away. She was quiet for a moment, then she smashed the mattress with her fist. She began to sob, to heave, and then abruptly stopped.

She was asleep again, just like that.

Suddenly full of energy, Astrid was running around a rusted jungle gym at the school nearby, an unvarnished, latticed dome stuck in patchy crabgrass. The sun had set, but it was still humid, still hot. The only other apparatus to play on was a swing set a few feet away. Standing there, watching Astrid exhaust herself, I remembered all these playground pieces having paintjobs, having color, when I'd lived here as a boy. But they didn't now. Someone had graffitied the word "TITS" on a swing.

"La-di-da-di-da-di-da," sang Astrid.

The sight of the swings made me think of sixth grade, when I was president of the Sabinal Elementary School Student Council. I would hang out here, on the swings, after after-school meetings, with Jordan, the vice president. Although he was a fifth grader, I respected him. He could piss his whole name into the dirt, in cursive, using a single stream.

"See?" he said the first time he showed me, his tiny dick still out.

I tried, but I couldn't do it. I could barely even piss in front of him, which was humiliating.

"You have to practice," Jordan said.

Even after months of practice, I never got the trick right. My letters always looked boxy and uncontrolled, jagged-edged— Jordan's name came out in perfect script. And I didn't feel the impulse like Jordan did—even when he wasn't trying to show off his talent, he'd do it. I saw. If he just needed to piss, he'd spell Jordan anyway, letters looping in the dust. I thought that was impressive. Although I was president, he had that skill on me, and I'd seen his dick and he'd never cared. I always cared, always hid myself, and peed in straight lines when we weren't competing—I feared my lack of talent would be exposed if someone ever saw me try, only myself to blame. Jordan died of an overdose at age nineteen. Heroin, I think.

Astrid was now sitting in the dust, looking at a rock.

"Hey. Wanna swing on the swings?" I asked.

Her face brightened, and she nodded vigorously.

Jordan could do backflips off the swings. He had taught me how.

Astrid sat in the seat and tried to propel herself up, but she couldn't do it. She started to get frustrated and kicked at the dust.

"Do you need a push?"

She nodded vigorously again.

After a few shoves, she got the hang of it, and I watched her pump up and down, arcing into the twilight as the swing set squeaked.

I thought of Jordan revealing himself, and then, weirdly, of Jaim. Those sapphires, dangling. How clean they were, so put together—how unafraid Jaim was of themselves, of showing themselves to the world, of letting people bend to them, while I, on the other hand, accommodated everything, everyone. I was always trying to get elected. But I could never speak like Jaim could, I could never make someone's brain fuzz and melt. But I wanted to. I wanted to be soft and wear dresses so Jaim might like me, my "softer touch, in general."

I felt blood pulse in my eyeballs as a whisper in me said no, then yes. No—then yes.

And then Astrid, at the top of an arc, leapt off the swing's saddle. On her landing she collapsed in a heap, as if the momentum of the fall had brought her, catastrophically, straight through her legs.

I bolted over, my panic complete. I turned her over, fearing the worst—but she was laughing, laughing hysterically, a feral addicted look in her eye.

"Again!" she squealed. "Again!"

I spent the rest of the week stealing glances at Jaim whenever I could, inventing stupid things to ask them about, taking trips to the bathroom to pass by their desk. Had we heard back from the Arboreal Society? Had we received the executive's gift in the mail? No, and no—but yes. That yes flared every time I passed them. And every time it flared, I felt a need to crush myself into softness or piss my name in script. I was absentminded. And that made me want to punish myself at the gym, so I did.

On Friday, I went over to Jaim's desk with every intention of asking them to Andrew's game night. I needed to see them outside of work, it had gotten to be too much. I wanted to touch their leg under a table and have them bat my prying profane hand away, teaching me to behave, to be good. I wanted them to make my brain fuzz and soften and then penetrate me, telling the bad part of myself that it was good, but not too good. But when I planted myself outside their cubicle, these words did not arrive. Jaim was wearing a version of their "punk" outfit that day, and I couldn't make eye contact, let alone look in their direction.

"Still nothing?" I asked. My loose words sounded pitiful to my ears.

"Still nothing," they said, sighing a bit.

"Keep me highly updated," I said seriously.

They said, "I'm so glad you're so interested in this. My last boss wasn't really like that. But this is so great."

I said, "Well, you know, trees. They're the lungs of the earth."

They smiled strangely, as if acknowledging the outward awkwardness of the conversation—or was it thoughtfulness, Jaim truly considering the idea?

"Yeah," they said. "I guess they are."

Afterwards, I closed my office blinds and did as many pushups as I could without breaking a sweat. I wanted my muscles to scream at me, Jaim to scream at me, like I was screaming at me for my stupid fucking comment.

After the pushups I told everyone they could go home after our weekly wrap-up meeting in a couple of hours. I wanted to feel magnanimous, and I wanted to treat people—to treat Jaim. I'd be off next Friday, too, so there was a practical reason for it: next week was bound to be busy. I had to keep the ship steered straight. The mayor depended on that.

At the meeting, everyone was in good spirits, I observed out loud, especially Jaim, who was really fitting in nicely, really settling in.

"It's great to see," I said, smiling pathetically.

Some nodded their heads in earnest affirmation—some subtly rolled their eyes at one another. Helen scoffed, masked it as a cough. Fuck you, I thought. Yesterday, Jaim had worn blue jeans and work boots and a plaid shirt, no makeup. They astonished me, I had to stop myself from saying. I wanted to say, "you astonish me," and let the words sit there, sparking something in Jaim's face, watching the others' faces redden and burn in shame and embarrassment. Fuck them.

I instead talked about the Arboreal Society. Gave them an update on the latest. They'd asked for funding for a seed bank, we energetically had agreed and asked for a photo-op and their public support on a few upcoming propositions affecting property taxes. I looked knowingly at Jaim, who looked at me inscrutably.

"All this thanks to Jaim," I said.

There came applause, a smattering. Jaim blushed.

"Thank you," they said. "That's very kind of you, Robert."

I winked and smiled with my teeth. I fiddled with my hands and breathed with my mouth closed. I thought of crushing stone fruits with my bare hands in the middle of Quarry Market. I thought of Jaim at game night, their body glowing in the white of Andrew's living room, making me draw four over and over and over again until I had no more breath and no more brain and no more cards.

Andrew passed me a shot of the premier tequila he'd brought straight from work.

He shot his back, I threw back mine. "Doesn't even burn." He smacked his lips.

It didn't burn.

Andrew poured us both another shot.

"You know," he began, then halted. Andrew was in an aggressive mood, his shirt was undone all the way, as if to signal something had been unleashed, ready to strike—the bull alerted, having seen red. "I didn't think it'd feel this way."

I listened. I watched. His eyes were darting, darting at me, looking me up and down, devouring everything they saw.

"I thought I would feel like I deserved it. I'd have Maddie, I'd have this fucking house. I'd feel good. But I feel like . . ."

Then he settled on me. Magnetizing me—inflamed.

"Look at you. Look at you."

"You should feel good about what you have. Maddie is wonderful."

He smiled cruelly. "I don't have what you have."

"What do I have, Andrew?"

He gripped my shoulder, bruising me.

"I don't have a story. I don't have a past. I don't have Sabinal motherfucking Texas."

Andrew never spoke to me like this. I felt I had to defend myself. "I consider those things impediments."

He laughed at me then—just laughed with that full-chested guffaw that seemed to uncoordinate his limbs for a moment.

"You lucky bastard."

Andrew picked up his shot. I did too.

"To your marriage," I said.

"To fitness," he said, and threw back his tequila.

Then he tried to sack tap me: to strike me in the nuts. I barely avoided him, but I felt his hand brush my penis.

He just laughed and went back into the room.

A few shots later, Andrew and I were sitting together on the couch, legs touching. He wrapped his arm around my shoulder. He slapped a draw four down and grabbed me by the neck and whispered in my ear, "Draw four, bitch." His tongue licked my ear.

"Whoa-ho! Andrew!" Maddie cried, clapping and rocking back, pumping her arm in the air.

"He's a touchy guy," Diane said. Diane was Maddie's old friend from college, in town for the weekend. Andrew wanted me to get to know her. "He's hot-blooded."

I laughed. I showed my white teeth.

Andrew said, "If I'm touchy then this guy's feely, am I right?"

He elbowed me in the stomach. It hurt, but I grinned anyway.

"Hard as a rock!" Andrew roared. He grabbed my bicep.

Maddie said, "Robert's a hard body. Or so I imagine." She purred at me, like Helen had.

"Okay, wife," Andrew said.

It was as if the music had stopped, the record scratched. Something passed between them I'd never seen before. They just looked at each other.

"What, we're not married yet," Maddie said.

I suddenly felt dizzy. I excused myself and went to the bathroom.

I splashed water on my face and breathed for a minute. I was thinking of my mom. I was thinking of the dialysis machine whirring, the cigarette smoke pooling on the ceiling, the rollers in her hair. She was screaming something, her jaw was open wide, her black rotting teeth leaning out, leaning unnaturally from her gums as if over a cliff, about to dive out of their mouth to a rancid, violent death.

I went straight to the kitchen. I took a shot quickly, secretly, and then Andrew walked in. He passed me and slapped my ass as he passed.

"Hard body, eh?" he said.

"Guess so."

He poured another shot for both of us.

"To strength," he said.

I woke up askew on my bed, a vague taste of puke or weed in my mouth. My head was pounding. I opened my phone and saw I had ten missed calls from Lara. When I called her back, she didn't pick up. The world spun.

Two hours later I was in Sabinal again, the day hot and punishing—my reward, I thought, for last night's excesses. I stewed in my shame, turning over and over the black gap in my memory, revealing nothing. My hands shook. You'd think after years and years, Lara's descent and my mother's death, I would have learned some things. But I was pathetic. I was just like them. I wanted to crush something in my hands. I wanted to crush my head in my hands.

I opened the door to the trailer. Astrid was sitting there, playing with foil. I sat down on the floor with her. My teeth and gums felt coated in acid or sugar. My vision wobbled randomly, my stomach lurched after it a moment later.

"Hi, Uncle Robert."

"Where's your mother?"

"I dunno."

It felt as if my brain were being pried open by tongs.

I picked up the roll of tin foil Astrid was playing with, ripped off a long sheet and laid it over my face like a shroud. I shut my eyes.

Lara never came home. She never picked up her phone.

I stayed on the floor with Astrid for a while, and when the throbbing pain subsided, I cleaned up and made dinner on the stovetop, where I had made so many desperate dinners before. I couldn't believe the kitchen still functioned—in fact half the burners didn't, the microwave bulbs were burned out. It seemed the refrigerator couldn't stay cold enough to prevent food from rotting: most of the produce had devolved into formless fetid juice. I slapped together cheese quesadillas, which Astrid loved.

She was a good kid—she stuck to herself mostly, even as I tried to ask about Lara, her mothering, the truth. She didn't tell me much, and I recognized that old pact I'd had with my mom: I never told on her, though I had every reason to. There was devotion, despite everything, and I respected it because I knew it by heart. We had become entangled in our depravity, and to have told on her was to have told on myself: was to have told the world that I was as unworthy as she was.

Later, Astrid asked if I could help with her homework. She was talented at math, it was obvious, and as she talked through her problems in a sweet singsong I realized she'd be an arresting, enigmatic person all her life—she already was. Men and women, friends and lovers, would break their hearts on her, as they had with Lara. But Lara broke hers on them, too. She was addicted to that, to breaking herself. And then it registered, somehow deeply for the first time, that Astrid was growing up without a father, like Lara and I had, and I had to step outside for a moment to grieve. Then I did a minute of high knees, which did not help.

Astrid slept with me on the couch—she tucked in just as my eyes were shutting—and slept soundly even through the commotion that woke me at six in the morning.

It was Lara, sitting in the dust, her dress spread out around her, her legs splayed. She looked petite and vulnerable, just like Astrid, except she no longer had an excuse, no longer had innocence to protect her. She sat there staring into the blue expanse as if her mind were broken and what she saw had no weight, as if she were somewhere far, far away, a world where no one needed to sacrifice anything good for anyone.

"He doesn't want me back," she said. "He doesn't want Astrid."

I watched the grasses sway in the dry wind. I thought of our mom. I felt an immeasurable burden, anger that Lara had refused to take it up. I felt grief spreading outward for miles and miles into the Texas flats. I felt resentment spewing from me like an oil leak.

I looked down at Lara like she was a scarab scuttling in the sand. I did not help her up.

Andrew called later. He apologized for how weird Friday got. I said it was okay, even though I didn't remember everything that had happened. He hoped I was still excited for the bachelor party. I said I was. I wished him well and hung up.

I didn't get to the market that day, or the gym. I ordered pizza, watched reruns of Friends, and, for reasons I couldn't then explain, looked at photos of women's clothing online until three in the morning. When I woke, I had several carts full of sun dresses.

A new mandate came down from the mayor, as well as a congratulatory email. He greatly approved of the Arboreal Society deal, it was a terrific message and showed canny alignment with the mayor's thinking. One of the mayor's aides, a prominent person we all knew, came down to my office and shook my hand.

"We're keeping an eye on you," the prominent person said.

When he left, I stepped out onto the office floor. I felt inquiring eyes directed toward me, even a sense of pride. Helen smirked. I saw Jaim look up from their desk. They wore the dangling sapphire earrings that day and their "normal" clothes. I felt good in that gaze, accomplished, like I'd done something right. I gave Jaim a small silent clap.

I called Jaim into my office every day that week. I wanted to put them on the new mandate—partnerships with local agricultural interests—but also wanted to get to know them better. Needed to. They were from the area, it turned out. They'd lived on the East Coast for a while but wanted to come home and make a difference. They had aspirations, ambitions. I said that I did too, and they said, "I know," with a smile.

Late on Thursday, Jaim and I sat next to each other during a meeting. All I could think about was their proximity, their heat, their smell—Jaim smelled like dust and dogwood and lilac, like Sabinal, like home. They wore a burgundy cashmere sweater, a bit big and retro-seeming. Their hair was up in a top knot, revealing their buzzed hairline like a secret. It felt so intimate to see their scalp up close, as I would if I were lying in bed with them, and my heart skipped and caught at once, a delicious warning.

A small nudge against my knee interrupted my thoughts of Jaim at game night, Jaim meeting Lara, Jaim meeting Astrid, Jaim with me at Quarry Market, Jaim burying my face into a pillow, suffocating me, my penis erect. It was almost bizarre to recognize it was real-life Jaim who'd touched me. They laid their pencil down casually on a legal pad, as if accidentally pointing toward the words: "Most boring meeting ever?"

Playing it calm, I nudged Jaim back and coughed. Jaim chuckled under their breath ever so coolly, almost undetectably.

By the end of the business day, I could not take it any longer. Jaim was bursting from my skin, tearing through my skin.

I called Jaim into the office. I asked them to sit.

"I'm just going to cut to the chase. You inspire me, Jaim. You're beautiful, you're talented, you're like no one I've ever met. I want to get to know you even better than I have. I want you to meet my friends. I think you're what's been missing in my life. I want you."

I knew instantly. Jaim didn't need to sigh, shake their head, try to find a smile.

"I'm sorry, Robert," they said.

They didn't need to say a word.

"I think you're a good guy? But it's not really like that for me. Let's just . . . put it at that. And maybe this is not so appropriate for work?" And they smiled gratefully, honestly, and said, "but I think I can forget it, because we're doing such good work together, and I'm really excited about that. And I really do think you're a good guy, but maybe just . . . confused?"

"You're right. You're one hundred percent right. It was incredibly wrong of me."

"It's okay."

"I'm bad."

"That's—not what I said."

"I'm disgusted by myself. And I understand that you're disgusted too. I'll tell HR personally that I crossed the line."

"No, Robert. Jesus. It's fine."

I tried to stay calm. I remembered everything I had built for myself with patience and great attention to detail.

"Thank you for your understanding. I am sorry, Jaim."

"Again—it's okay."

They stood. They smiled their well-ordered teeth. I felt so small and usable.

"Have a great weekend, okay? Maybe . . . do something relaxing."

"Okay," I said. "I will."

They walked out.

Alone, I wanted to explode. I wanted to explode out of my skin with Jaim. But I did not. I gathered my things and left. I went to the gym, because that is what I do. That is what I am.

We gathered at Andrew's house for the bachelor party—a couple of guys from the office, a few college friends, some whom I'd met before. Andrew's attentions were on the group, the night, the party, and he barely paid me any mind. Friends lavished Andrew with praise, put him in chokeholds, made him do shots. I took a few too, had civil conversations with the men, who were all interesting. I was healthily buzzed when the limo arrived.

We piled in. Andrew took out a bag of coke, we all did bumps.

We ordered cocktails at dinner, several bottles of wine. I had a full branzino. We talked about women, money, sex, and sports. I told the men about my workout routine, all my supplements. I explained in great detail what it is I do for work.

At the next bar, Andrew sat down next to me. I was drunk and high already, and I didn't give a shit anymore. He put his arm around my shoulder, drew me close, and licked my earlobe, said "bitch" into my ear. I told him to fuck off, and he laughed—everyone laughed.

Andrew was drunk, dancing on the dance floor. I came up to him and told him I didn't like how he touched me. He told me to just fucking dance.

I did. I drank. I hit on a woman, and we danced. The woman kissed me, grabbed my bicep, then disappeared into the crowd. The men bought me a shot for that.

"To the next motherucking mayor of San Antonio!" Andrew roared.

Then we were at a strip club. Things were spinning fast, really fast. I wanted to talk and talk, and I was talking about talking about I don't know what. Then Andrew was talking about me. "You're the trailer park mayor," he screamed. I was trash, I was a saint. "You're the fucking soul of America, you bastard."

He slapped my ass again. This time, I grabbed him by the throat. The boys had to rush to pull us apart—I wished they hadn't. I wanted someone to fucking punch me. I begged someone to punch me. No one did. They gripped my shoulders, massaged me. They complimented me on my appearance.

I did more coke. I watched a stripper dance. She was skinny, lithe, had small breasts. Her hair was shaved at the sides. I was in agony, dreaming of Jaim.

"How much for a private dance?"

She reached down and said a number. I agreed to pay it. There was a roar, men cheering, calling my name.

"He's the king," they said. "He's the goddamned king."

In a room, she began to dance. I stopped her immediately and asked whether she had any duct tape. She called me kinky and fetched it. When she returned, I ripped off a long piece and wrapped it around her breasts, taped them back so she looked flat.

I told her her name was Jaim. She used the pronoun they.

They said, "You can call me whatever you want, king."

But it wasn't what I wanted, not at all. I threw down the money and stepped outside.

I was calling Lara. I was telling Lara to pick me up.

I was sitting on a curb. I was crying into my filthy hands.

Then Lara showed up, I don't know when, don't know where. I remember seeing Astrid, asleep in the front seat, looking so quiet. But she was frowning, even in her sleep. The careless, fatherless world was already imprinted on her face.

I wanted to be hit. I needed to be punished for what I'd done.

I slammed my head into the roof of the car and howled at the top of my lungs—to the entire city, to anyone who would listen.

"What the fuck is wrong with me?" I howled.

The blood dripped into my eyes, stinging me, and my head throbbed. It was a relief.

I smashed my head again.

And then it was not a relief.

Go On Ahead

Suzanna C. de Baca

When you were dying in the hospital / resting uncomfortably in an adjustable bed / the kind with the hard metal sides that go up or down / you told me to go on ahead to China. / Don't cancel your trip on my account. / But I stayed. /

You told me about when Grandpa had a breakdown / and you'd driven to St. Louis so he could get shock treatments / but of course you couldn't tell anyone / because that was in the 1950s / and shameful. / You said how terrifying it was to be married to one person one day / and then to another person the next. / No one could know about the violent outbursts / the erratic behavior. / It would have ruined him / if anyone knew he was not in his right mind. /

You told me that even when he was better / you kept separate accounts for the farm. / He did his bookkeeping too like always / but you had a backup for the real numbers. / At first I thought you were just protecting his ego / as women do, / but years later / I realized it was because you loved him, / even when you had to care for him like a child. /

Who cared for you? / Maybe you went to your sister / or the priest. / But you probably worked it out alone / in the garden. / After all / you were the kind of person who was always thinking of others, / saying / go on ahead to China. / You told me you'd probably hang on another few weeks / and I should enjoy myself / but that was unthinkable. / I sat with you / running my hands back and forth / over the cold rails of the hospital bed / while you told me your real stories. /

For You

Victor Oliva

September 21, 2013

No one prepared me for how much of a social gauntlet college is.

For the school's part, they're doing everything they can to ease our anxiety since for most of us, this is the first time we've lived away from home. Welcome picnics and pep rallies. Free merch that makes us all into walking advertisements. And this cute little bonfire in the woods outside of the school. Throw enough distractions at us, and maybe we'll buy into the mentality that we belong here.

I'm trying to figure out where my roommates went when I see you across the bonfire. I remember we met at orientation, but it was only a quick conversation.

Firelight like this can make people's features harsher. Something to do when the light comes from below. Instead, I get this impression of a warm, orange glow around you.

You approach me and say, "What's up!"

"Hey!"

"I saw you over here and thought I just have to say hi."

"Aw, thanks. I'm glad to see a familiar face."

"I feel you." You gesture to the cup in my hand. "So, did you sneak in alcohol like everyone else here did?"

"I don't even know if you could consider this sneaking in alcohol. Seems like an unofficial tradition where the school puts on this event and lets us do whatever. But no, I didn't bring any with me. Someone else handed me this cup of what I think is beer?"

"Sounds just a little suspicious. Want some of mine instead?"

"I shouldn't trust this beer from a stranger, but I should trust yours because we've met once before?"

You laugh and say, "Okay, fair. Fair. I saw a cooler over there with some cans. We can get you another from there." You put a hand on my shoulder to direct me where we're going. "So, you getting along with your roommates?"

"Still getting to know each other. It's been only a few days, but I like them . . . and most of the people on my floor at least. Honestly, I was worried about making friends here, but I think I'm going to be okay."

"Yeah, it takes a bit to get to know people. I think I'm one floor above you. So, you have them, and I guess you also have me now."

We spend the rest of the night sitting by the fire. The flames give off a faint heat, but I feel part of the warmth on my face is also from this intense eye contact you keep giving me. Eventually, your friends call you back over to them so they can head out, but you turn back to me and say, "Can I get your number?"

"Yeah. . . sure!" I call my number from your phone so I can save it later.

"Okay, I'm gonna text you so you for sure have my number."

"You're very thorough, you know?"

"Well, I would beat myself up if I messed up getting your number."

September 24, 2013

Maybe I'm just a little bit excited when I run into you at the dining hall. You make room for me at the table you're sitting at with your friends. After introducing us, you turn to me and give me your full attention.

You say, "I found this sick mural when I was exploring campus yesterday. I remembered you said you wanted to see the different art pieces around here. Want me to show you?"

I pause for a little and say, "Oh, yeah, sure! Thanks for remembering." I quickly look to the side because I'm unsure on what to do with how direct you are.

As if picking up on my mood, you say, "Unless you don't want to?"

"No, no. That's really nice of you to show me. I just don't want you to feel like you have to since I told you I was worried about making friends."

"Oh! No, I want to hang out with you. You're chill, and I don't know, I get a good vibe from you."

"Yeah, I feel a good vibe from you too."

The beginnings of something deeper start building in me. I try to brush it off. I've had crushes before, and I'm really not trying to make it weird between one of the first genuine people I've met here.

September 27, 2013

"Please don't let me fall." I hold my hands out and steady myself on your shoulders. Why did I say I wanted to try this?

"Don't worry. I got you. Longboarding is easy once you get the hang of it. I'm right here."

Oh, right. That's why.

October 13, 2013

"You know Passion Pit?" you ask me.

I turn to you and say, "Uhm, yes of course."

"Check out this video I made when I was a dumb teenager."

"Aren't we still dumb teenagers?"

"Hey, we're a little smarter now, right? We're on our way to getting college degrees."

"Yeah, like four years from now! I can't even imagine what life will be like then."

"Details," you say with a dismissive gesture. "And for the record, I think we'll be just as cool as we are now even when we're old people about to graduate."

"I really do admire your optimism."

You pull up your Instagram and scroll down a bit. In the video, you're lip syncing to the vocal effects that start off "I'll Be Alright." Contrary to what you say, I think the video is cute, not dumb.

I say, "Okay, that's funny. I'm embarrassed of what I was putting on my Instagram when I first made it."

"Oh, now you have to show me."

I sigh and scroll down to the heavily filtered photos of my junior year in high school, trying to find something really cringe-worthy for you. You stop me when I get to a selfie from that time. "You look hot in this photo. I can see your cute eyes very clearly in this one."

I sorted our hang outs into the friend category to avoid getting my hopes up. But this has to be flirting, right?

October 25, 2013

A group of us are playing truth or dare in someone's room—fighting our way through gulps of cheap Kirkland vodka. There's a certain cruelty that kids on the cusp of adulthood give in to. Playing games like this is just an example of it when the questions start getting personal and malicious. Like asking who's the ugliest or who we would kick out of our floor if we could.

In what seems like a question designed to personally torment me, someone asks you who you have a crush on. I don't know what I was expecting, but hearing you say a girl's name cuts me in a way I've never felt before.

I manage to survive the night without causing a scene, but I break down in my room. I never thought I was capable of crying this much until this moment. Sobbing in the dark at 3 a.m., I learn a simple truth: we build up our expectations in life and nothing hurts more than when they come crashing down.

November 2, 2013

"When are you coming back?" reads the text on your Snapchat. It's the first weekend I'm away from campus.

The picture I send back to you has the rave I'm at in the background. "Sooooon!" it says.

A reply less than a minute later: "Have fun, party boy. I miss you."

Putting some distance between us feels like a good idea after you made it very clear I'm not your crush. I try to lose myself in the sounds of where I'm at. It feels like one of those moments where I'm supposed to be present. This is my first rave after all! But I'm still thinking about you constantly, even here.

How am I supposed to deal with existing between joy and longing? I don't even really register all the shirtless, sweaty guys around me. I just want to see you in your faded, plaid shirt.

November 17, 2013

"This calc class is kicking my ass," I complain loudly. I sigh and put my head on the desk.

"I got just the thing. Study fuel." You hand me some sour candy.

"I feel slightly better. Only slightly. I used to be so good at this in high school. And now it's like I can barely get a B on assignments. Not to mention the B– I got on my midterm."

"I'm going to share some very special advice I got about college: C's get degrees."

"A C?! How am I going to get into med school with C's?"

"I think you'll figure it out. But I think you need a break."

"You have to drag me out of here. I have big plans for the future."

Surprisingly, though, you turn my chair around, put your hands under my shoulders, and lift me up. There's a brief moment where we're hugging each other close, but I quickly pull away.

I stamp down how I'm feeling inside and instead say, "Okay, fine. You win. Let's go for a walk, but if we happen to somehow make our way to that burrito place, you're paying for me."

"I live to serve."

December 18, 2013

There's nothing sweeter than when you turn in your last final and run to the closest pregame. You step away to get us drinks and come back with a cup full of liquid that's too blue to mean anything good for me. I shrug and say, "Fuck it." The first gulp goes down harshly, but I've been getting more used to downing suspicious liquids.

You smile at me and say, "There's my party boy."

"Yeah, I'm officially free and ready to burn all my notes. I know I've been a little stressed lately. Thanks for being chill about everything even when I wasn't."

"I mean, I get it. Also, I thought I was going to be the stressed one, but you've been really good energy to be around."

"Oh, why's that? Okay, I get why I'm good energy. I'm wonderful and perfect. But why did you think you were gonna be stressed?"

You let out a chuckle, but it dies as your face takes on a more serious look. "Ah, I'm not trying to be a downer, but I think it feels right to tell you. My dad's been sick for the past year. It seemed to get better, but lately he's been doing worse. My mom says it's not too alarming at the moment, but I'll be glad to be home this winter break to spend time with him."

"Oh, wow, I'm so sorry. I didn't realize. That must be really tough."

"No, it's fine. I mean, it's not. But there's really not much I can do. He wants me to be here, and I think he would be happy to know that I'm meeting such great people like you."

A ridiculous grin blooms on my face. Even when I'm trying to comfort you, you manage to make me feel better too.

December 28, 2013
"So clutch that we got to meet up on our break," you say.

"Yeah, very convenient that our hometowns are like twenty minutes from each other. Perks of being at a state school I guess. A lot of us come from the same places."

The whole of the city spreads out before us as we sit on this rooftop in the hillside city you're from. We just watched a movie together, and you said you wanted to show me something beautiful after. At no point did we say this is a date, but what else do you call the two of us sitting next to each other, with this constellation of city lights as a view? What else do you call feeling like this moment, this place, was made for us?

January 18, 2014
I'm definitely paying the price for how much I drank last night—my first time blacking out.

You find me hungover laying in the quad. I don't mention how even though everything's a blur from last night, I can still distinctly remember the sound of your voice in my ear as you got me to drink water. You don't mention the way you held me close to you. Or how I said things felt right with you nearby.

We talk about the class I missed.

February 2, 2014
The noise of the party keeps the words between us private. A little island of isolation in a crowded room.

"I'm glad you were able to come out tonight," I say.

"Yeah, of course. I gotta keep up with your party boy life," you say in a teasing tone.

I lay my head on your shoulder, feeling a little more comfortable being close to you. "Very funny, dude. I'll have you know I lead a very balanced life. And this semester is all about learning how to be less stressed about school. I'm evolving."

"Of course. But really, I always have fun with you. You help me take my mind off things at home."

"Any update on your dad?"

"Not really. Not doing better, but not doing worse at least."

I move my leg to drape over yours since I'm not sure what else I can do to let you know I'm here for you. You start rubbing it in slow circles. Anyone that looks at us would think we're a couple. What a nice piece of fiction.

February 19, 2014
Your text reads, "Where are you?"

I send back, "Chilling in the lounge. Why, what's up?"

"We're drinking right now. I want to see you!"

I'm not sure how we end up in the dorm hallway—just the two of us. Our shoulders brush. Our fingers dance around each other, not quite touching and not quite hand holding, but getting just to that point.

I begin to notice these moments of physical intimacy can only fully happen through the excuse of alcohol. I chase down that feeling with another shot.

February 27, 2014

Your voice comes through the closed door, making me feel more alert like some fucked up Pavlovian response. I'm sitting in a study room and hear you ask my friends in the lounge outside if I'm around. After hearing you knock on the door, I tell you to come in.

"There you are!" you say.

"Hi! Looking for me?"

"Yeah, kinda. I mean . . . okay I was walking by and saw your friends. And then I got excited that you were nearby. I guess I just wanted to see you."

I smile and say, "Well, here I am. I'm working through this study guide for a midterm. But you can squeeze in here and join me if you have work to do."

"I don't really have anything to do right now, but hold on. I'll be back."

Soon after, you return with a book and the sour candy you know I like—well, I only like it because you keep giving it to me. You settle in next to me, and I can't help but feel how natural it is for us to be together.

March 5, 2014

You flash a bright smile at me and say, "Hey! Thanks for saving me a seat."

"Of course! Did you eat yet? I want to get food after class."

"Yeah, I did. But I'll come with. Make sure you're taken care of." You wink at me.

When you say things like this, I really don't get if there's meaning behind it. But I'll take any affection you throw my way. The class drones on, and I steadily get more sleepy. I find myself nodding off, and my head falls on your shoulder. Your body tenses, and I quickly sit up.

"Sorry," I say. "I guess I'm more tired than I thought I was."

You don't immediately respond but you say, "Nah, it's fine."

You're the first person that's made me feel this way. But no one told me what to do when I like a guy. It's like we're playing a game, and I don't know the rules.

March 28, 2014

Watching sunsets together has kind of become a thing for us, but this particular golden one feels different. It's usually only after some time has passed when we get to appreciate how significant a moment is. Somehow though, I get a sense of how big of a shift this is for me.

Is your heart beating fast too? Do I ever take your breath away the way you do mine? Seeing you glow in this fiery light, do I have any other option but to fall in lo—

April 10, 2014

I feel this strong need to just tell you right now. But I'm so scared that if I say something, I'll scare you away. Holding this in hurts, but losing you would hurt more.

"You're my favorite person, you know?"

I think to myself, "Oh, shit, this is it."

But you continue and say, "I like how we are. There are no complications."

"No complications?"

"We can just be us. You know how hard things are for me with my dad being so sick. I like how easy things are when we hang out."

"Right, things are easy. I feel the same too."

Why can't I say more? Why can't I confess right now? Why can't you?

April 27, 2014

Homesickness hits me hard so I leave for the weekend. My friends run into you at a party, and I get texts saying you're asking for me. That you miss me. I don't know what to do with that.

In a way, I'm becoming a bit desensitized to your affections—our intimacy. It feels hollow. Does it really mean anything if we're perpetually stuck in this limbo?

I go to parties and see people making out. My friends tell me about their hookups. There's even a guy on our floor who's in the middle of his third relationship just this past year. When it comes to us though, I have no words to describe what this is.

May 3, 2014

Someone does eventually ask me what's going on between us. I can't bring myself to say how much you mean to me. Yes, it scares me to come out so openly, but I'm even more afraid of outing you. I end up telling them we're just good friends.

Spending time with you is one of the most beautiful experiences I've ever had. But it's also one of the loneliest. I can't tell you how I feel, and I can't tell anyone else. Where are these feelings supposed to go if I keep pushing them down?

May 17, 2014

"He totally stole the girl I wanted to dance with," you say to me.

"Are you looking for girls to dance with?"

"It would be nice I think."

"Okay, well I won't hold you back then."

"It's fine. I think we can have fun by playing beer pong."

The lights of the party start swirling around me. I try to follow you to the table, but everything starts feeling too hot. People become dark figures around me, and I lose you among them. At some point, I end up outside—the cold air is only helping a little.

I convince myself I just drank too much.

May 28, 2014

After a series of unanswered texts, I can't help but spiral. I think I did something wrong. I think you finally found a girl to take your mind off me. It finally hit you how I want us to be more, and you decided to cut me off. The fear I had of losing you is finally coming true. I should have learned to just be happy with what we have.

Later, I find out from someone else that your dad has passed away. In my self-centeredness, I just want you to tell me that yourself. I try to rationalize your actions, but it still hurts that you shut me out, and won't tell me how you're doing.

June 13, 2014

A month passes without having seen or talked to you, and it takes me right to the end of the school year. As I pack up my dorm room, I decide at this moment that I won't let you dominate my thoughts anymore. I throw away the things you gave me and delete as many pictures of us as I can.

My feelings though, are a little harder to deal with. I settle on pushing them away. Not thrown away—but like locking something in a box and placing it on a closet shelf.

July 9, 2014

Of course I run into you at this local carnival. Nearby hometowns, remember?

"I'm so happy to see you. Oh my God," you say. You go in for a hug, but I pull away.

I say, "Hey. How have you been?"

"I've been good. Excited to start school back up."

"Yeah . . . hey listen, my friends are waiting for me. So I'm gonna go back to them. Great seeing you."

"Okay . . . yeah. Good to see you too."

Forgiveness isn't something that comes easy to me. I wish I could tell you just how much seeing you again excites me. But the way you abandoned me still feels so raw.

Were you ready to let me back in then? I wish I could have admitted I was.

September 28, 2014

I purposefully seek out guys that only want something casual from me. It's harder to get hurt if there are no feelings involved.

October 18, 2014

"I was wondering when I'd run into you again," I say.

"Me too. I'm living on campus this year. You?"

"Yup, right over there."

"Ah, I'm in that building right next to you. Neighbors still, I guess."

"I guess we are. We should hang out again."

"Definitely. You have my number."

"And you have mine."

In my head, you have to be the one to make amends. I can only see things in black and white—that there are people who wrong others and people who are wronged.

I learned to put my ego aside too late for us.

April 5, 2015

My friends finally ask me about you. They tell me there was definitely something between us. It helps to get some external validation, but it feels empty. I just want you to own up to everything.

June 19, 2015

As time goes on, I'm becoming more and more sure of who I am. I officially come out to my friend group from high school, and they ask me if I'm dating anyone. I say no, but I can't tell them it's because I end up comparing everyone to you.

I think I keep my heartbreak open for you just in case you come back. I convince myself I can pick up these broken pieces and patch together our "almost." Our "close enough, but not quite" relationship.

Fixing this hole in myself means I have to face the fact that the strongest I ever felt for someone was based on something tangible, but not concrete. I want to keep the smoke and mirrors. They're all I have left of you.

February 10, 2016

I've gotten more involved in campus life and joined an org. I'm helping run a booth at a school event when you walk up.

"Hey!" you say with the same smile I'm still fond of.

"Hey! Interested in buying a raffle ticket?"

"Okay, sure, I'll buy one."

"You save if you buy five, by the way."

"Ah, spoken like a true salesperson. Okay. I'll take five."

"Yay! Thanks so much. Alright, here's five. You can place them in these different bowls for different prizes. There's a raffle for a really cool longboard I think you'll like."

"Oh sweet! You know me so well."

"It hasn't been that long."

"No, I guess it hasn't."

I look and see people waiting to buy their tickets. "Ah, shit. There's a line and the person helping me run the booth went to the bathroom."

"It's chill. I have to go anyway, but it was good seeing you."

"You too."

July 28, 2016

Turning twenty-one feels both anticlimactic and exhilarating. My friends and I end up at a house party. It's something we've done dozens of times before, but now it's legal. The party is a nice pregame they say. We can put my ID to use at the club after.

Catching sight of you feels like a relief. The rational response this whole time, of course, was to just reach out to you. But you can't convince an early twenty-something to take the logical approach. It's too simple.

"This feels familiar," you say.

"Yeah, we used to go to so many parties together."

"We did. But after freshman year, I stopped seeing you at the ones we used to go to."

"My friends got a little tired of them, and we started to go to some different ones. But I don't know, we got nostalgic I guess and wanted to come back to one of these. Even if the usual crowd skews towards dumb guys, at least there's always a lot of alcohol."

"Yeahh, that's fair. How have you been though?"

"I've been good. Actually, today's my birthday! I'm officially allowed to legally drink."

"Happy birthday! No wonder you look extra good tonight."

"Oh, I look good, huh?" The alcohol, just like it always did, makes me feel bolder with you. I feel the old sense of comfort I used to have with you.

"I mean, yes, of course. That's also why sometimes I felt you were too cool for me."

I playfully push you and say, "Shut upp. I loved being around you. Remember when you made me play that super complicated board game? I don't think I ever saw you that ruthless. I would want to play just so I could see you throw away your nice boy personality and just get absolutely savage."

"The rules of courtesy don't apply in that game. I'm not responsible for who I become when I want to win."

My friends find me and make me take two shots back to back so we can head out. They cast a knowing glance at you. They probably feel like they have to save me, but I would take any moment with you, though.

"Speaking of personalities, it looks like you're still my party boy," you joke. Do you catch the "my" in there? How easily we slip back into our routine.

"Hey, you're also here taking shots. And I remember you dragging me to parties too." My friends call my name again. "Damn, I guess our Uber's here. Please hit me up. It's been too long."

"Yeah, okay. I will."

August 7, 2016

You text me, and we try to solidify plans to meet up. But life has gotten busier for me, and it seems like it has for you too. I keep trying to play it cool with you. I want to just be honest and say, "Look, I really, really miss you. Things got weird between us, but let's start again." But it feels too real, and it's not like you're really giving me a lot over text anyway.

So, I let things slip between us again. I can't really explain this fear I have about going for what I want when it comes to you. These old habits really do die hard.

October 1, 2016

"I feel like I can only catch you at parties," I say.

"We're really bad at keeping in touch. But really good at finding each other eventually."

"I guess so." What you don't know is that I convinced my friends to start going to these parties again just so I could run into you again.

You say, "So . . . that guy you were with earlier . . . what's the story there?"

"Why do you think there's a story?"

"I mean, you two were pretty close to each other."

"I don't think I need to explain myself, but he had weed and I wanted some."

"So, you were just flirting for weed?"

"What the fuck is this judgmental attitude?"

"I'm not being judgmental! I'm just curious if you're dating him."

"I don't think you've ever been concerned if I was dating someone before."

"Okay, what? Why are you mad?"

We've never fought like this before, but at least this is starting to feel like real honesty. Even when you cut me off, I didn't feel this furious. I think I understand now what it means to be so angry that you see red. Where do you get off thinking you can just interrogate me about guys I talk to? After all this time? It's probably because of the alcohol, but I just want to push this more and more.

I say, "Alright, you know what? I don't owe you an answer to this. And it's not like you're really in my life to keep tabs on who I date."

"It was just a fucking question. Your socials don't leave the impression that you're dating someone right now. I just wanted to see what's new with you."

"I don't know if you know this, but people don't really post everything online, especially who they're dating."

"So, you are dating someone?"

"And if I was?"

"Then, good for you."

"Good for me then."

You walk away, and I feel dumb for expecting a better outcome.

June 17, 2017

Graduation is an evening ceremony and the sun's beginning to set slowly—the shadows lengthening. This time, I'm expecting to see you.

Our old RAs want to get a photo of everyone from our dorm just before the ceremony. A pair of pseudo parents bringing their former charges together for one last memory before we go into the real world.

We're drawn to each other as usual, and like so many other times with you, it feels like there's no one else around us. We hug first, and I take a moment to just look at you in your cap and gown. Looking into your eyes, a sense of finality settles around us. There's no denying that we're at the end of the line.

You say, "I was hoping you'd come to this reunion. Look, things got weird last time I saw you. Are we cool?"

"Yeah, we don't have to get into it. We're good."

"Okay, I'm glad we got to see each other before we're officially done with college. Feels so weird now to be at the end of it."

"I feel the same. Sometimes, I still feel like that scared freshman just arriving on campus."

"Yeah, back at that bonfire when we first got to really talk to each other, you said you were scared no one was going to be your friend. But I never quite got how you didn't see how wonderful you are. It didn't take long for you to become someone special to me."

"That means a lot to hear you say that. Sounds like you've been reminiscing a lot about that year?"

"I've just been thinking—nothing like starting the next chapter of your life to really get you thinking. But I think about our freshman year, and how much time we spent together. Things weren't the best for me then, but you were always there for me. I don't know, it just feels . . . significant."

"Yeah . . . significant. Let's call it that. And so we're here now. Anything else you wanna say about that time?"

You take a moment to just look at me. I'm holding my breath. Waiting for you to make the first move, like always. "Just that I'm going to miss you."

"Okay." I sigh, once again letting go of any hope I have for us. "I am too. So, what's next for you?"

"I'm not sure yet. I think I need a break for a bit. No job at this point, but I'm gonna travel for a little. Figure things out. Maybe I'll see you back home whenever I come back? Unless you're going to move for med school?"

"Oh, wow, no. We really did lose touch, huh? I dropped pre-med like sophomore year. I'm staying here because I start an internship in a week. I barely get a break before I start my first adult job. And going home is weird for me right now. I don't know when I'll be back."

"Why is it weird?"

"I'd rather not get into it at the moment, but it's family stuff. I'm better off staying here for a while."

"Okay, well, I'm sure I'll be back here at some point. We can catch up then."

"We can see what happens." I'm done keeping myself in suspense for you.

"This feels like such a goodbye. I guess this is it then?"

"I think it has to be."

We can't rely on chance to put us in the same place anymore. Do you hear my voice breaking as I realize that fate has gotten tired of throwing us together?

We hug each other one last time—tightly. Even though we're years older, we still have the same trouble with letting each other go.

April 5, 2018

I have a dream that I'm in your arms, but I wake up in the dark with nothing but our memories to hold on to.

I feel pathetic realizing that you never fully left my thoughts. Did I leave that big of an impression on you?

October 12, 2019

I move across the country and start to seriously date for once. My circle of friends changes, and it's no longer a given that people in my life know who you are. You feel like a footnote in my story as time moves on. I decide that it's easier to say you're "just a serious crush I had in college."

September 19, 2023

"Look, I have a lot to say about how we were back then. So just hear me out because I really need to get this off my chest. Time has helped me understand why it was so hard for us. At least, why it was so hard for me.

"I was so scared of pushing you away that I held it all in. I choked on my words to let you breathe and blurred my edges and lost my definition. I convinced myself that I still had you, not in the way I wanted, but it was still something. And I loved you in a way that only makes sense to an eighteen-year-old.

"But I realize now, that type of love burns brightly—and it burns away everything you are. You were my first love, and maybe it was a little superficial because of how young I was, but that made it feel all the more real.

"I had to start again after you stopped talking to me. I know your dad died, and I'm not blaming you for the space you needed. I get it. But I didn't get it back then. Even if we weren't anything official, we were still friends at the very least, right? We still told each other things.

"I had to make you into a villain to move past it. I was so cold to you when I saw you again, and then after that, we just fell into a new routine. One where neither of us reached out. My life became full of other things, and it made less and less sense to hold on to someone that I never was actually with.

"I would run into you now and then, and I would regress back to who I was when we first met. Someone who only had eyes for you . . . and who was still scared of going for what he wanted. Before I knew it, we were at graduation, and it all felt like a lost cause. What was the point? The only thing that felt worth mentioning was our goodbye.

"I never saw you again, and I really did feel like that was our closure. But every now and then, I'd dream about you or I'd see a photo from that time. All that love I felt? And all that hurt? It felt as real as it did back then.

"Please don't get me wrong. I don't think that I need to be with you. I don't know who you are now, and you don't know me. I just feel so grateful to you for showing my younger self what love could feel like.

"It's also clear to me now that hurt wasn't your fault. Or mine. We met in a fucked-up world that teaches boys to feel shame when we love each other. What chance did we stand against years of people telling us what felt so right was wrong?

"Maybe that's why I can't find peace with this. Why you're still someone I think about even when time has washed away the details of our moments. Because accepting what happened means I'm okay with the world denying us love. Maybe I just have to keep our story alive in the hopes that one day, it will be given a chance to fully unfold in another lifetime."

There are so many iterations of this conversation. The final one between us. Where I get to unload everything I've kept from you. But we always get to this point where I get to say my piece and just as you're about to respond—the whispers of closure slither away from me. I'm snatched back to reality as the early morning light wakes me up. Or I shift back into focus after daydreaming in the park. Or, I reach the end of this story.

This time, though, did I finally reach you?

For Nex Benedict

Ren Wilding

I hope that when we think of him, it's the
tucked away dimple that we remember first.
I hope it's his eyes and his cheeks, those hands
shoved into his pockets and how sharp he
looked in his vest.

—Carmen Phillips

Let your dimples
        be a memorial
   to the ways
   you should have been
loved, softly
      as the vulnerable fur
   of a cat's belly.

I want to read
    the tracery of lines
       that would have mapped
  your life   across your face.

At sixteen,
    girls bruised you
        into the bathroom wall—
            no one held
    accountable
        for your absence.

            At thirty-eight,
            I can see the beginning
                of furrows curving
                    down from the corners

                of my mouth—
            seams
        in place of the dimples
                I will never have.

Inspiration Point

by Michael Bronson

The ordeal happened right after I turned seventeen. I was at college. A freshman in football camp. Classes hadn't started yet. I'd been there a week. Centre College. Danville, Kentucky.

Everyone else on the football roster was older. I skipped the third grade. I wasn't gifted. I was big. Dad said my school photos looked like cover art for *Gulliver's Travels*. Made him laugh every time. So my parents pushed me on ahead. They didn't want the size difference to stand out so much.

I was in the dorm when the call came in. It was late. 10:47 at night. My roommate wasn't there. He was breaking curfew. Partying with teammates.

"Toffy," my little brother Brody said.

"Something wrong?" I said.

"Daddy's dead," Brody said.

I didn't say anything at all for a long time. "How?" I said then.

"Fell off Inspiration Point," Brody said.

Christmas that year was hard. For me it was. Couldn't think of much else. We were sitting around after supper when Jack knocked at the door. Jack was Dad's friend from over at the hospital. Jack was a nurse. Dad was an assistant administrator of some sort. Never was sure exactly what he did.

"Merry Christmas, y'all," Jack said. Our old German shepherd Blanda wagged his tail. Jack gave Mama a pie and a handle of Maker's Mark. He patted Blanda's neck. "Been a while. Y'all hangin' in there?"

"Toffy's feelin' better now that you brung a pie," Brody said. "He'll get to it soon as he finishes them cookies."

Brody sat beside his boyfriend Garrett. Brody's hand covered Garrett's. Jack looked at them.

"How was your season, Toffy?" Jack said.

Season hadn't crossed my mind in two months. Nothing to remember, really. Blanda walked back and lay down by my feet.

"The boy's name is Cade," Mama said. "Those college kids are calling you Cade, ain't they?"

"I don't care what people call me, Mama," I said. I ate a cookie.

"Where does Toffy come from, anyhow?" Garrett said.

"Started out as Tons of Fun," Brody said.

"That's mean," Garrett said. He squeezed Brody's knee.

"And it ain't even true," Brody said. "He ain't especially fun."

Mama set the bourbon on the counter. "Why you always talkin' dumb shit?" she said. "Be nice to your brother."

"Maybe you oughtta play football, Brody," Jack said. "Looks like you been hittin' the iron."

Brody flexed his arm. He used to be heavy. Heavier than I ever was. Then on a dime he only ate chicken and broccoli. Spent his free time in the weight room. Wasn't another high school kid in town who could take him.

"Football ain't my cuppa tea," Brody said. "Skintight pants. Bulges. All the huggin' and gropin'. Too gay for my taste."

Garrett laughed just then. Jack looked at the floor.

"Your daddy didn't like you talkin' such nonsense," Mama said.

"Yeah, well, Daddy didn't like a lotta things," Brody said.

"Now's not the time, babe," Garrett said.

Jack slumped his head. Stuffed his fingers in his back pockets. "Everyone at the hospital, we miss him a bunch," he said. "Y'all made it up to . . . It happened at Inspiration Point?"

Mama stripped wax off the Maker's Mark knob. Poured some in her coffee mug and drank. "Ain't the time for that, neither," she said.

I ate a cookie.

"He right loved Grand Teton," Jack said. "Mused about y'all retirin' out that way." Jack swung his foot like he was kicking a pebble. "I hiked Inspiration with him once, too," he said. "'Member? His fortieth. Same trip we fly fished the Snake. Place is heaven on earth. S'pose it's fittin' he should pass there."

"Cade don't need to hear this," Mama said.

Jack kept his eyes on Mama. "Heard it was nearabout sunrise?" he said. "Awful early. Y'all musta been the only souls on the mountain."

"His idea to get crackin' and beat the crowd," Mama said. She gulped the bourbon. "You know how he was. Set his mind on somethin', wasn't no talkin' him out of it."

"Sure," Jack said. Made a sound like a sigh. Kicked the pebble. "That's true alright."

"Appreciate you droppin' in and all, Jack," Brody said. He stood up. Rounded his shoulders. "You done your good deed. Prob'ly time to get on back to your house, ain't it?"

Blanda barked just then.

"How was he managin'?" Jack said. "Just curious, on account of . . ." Jack's eyes went over to the bourbon bottle. "On account of the cliff's awful sheer up there, ain't it? Trail boundary ain't real firm, as I recall."

Brody stepped toward Jack. Blanda growled. "Daddy wanted to see Inspiration Point," Brody said. "So that's what we did."

"Sit down, Brody," Mama said. She smiled. "Send our best to your family, Jack. Merry Christmas to y'all."

"I'll do that," Jack said. He didn't smile back. "I'll be checkin' your schedule online, Toffy. Like to make it to a game this year."

"Can't promise I'll be on the field," I said. "College ball moves fast."

"Might move slower if you put down the goddamn cookies," Brody said.

"Your daddy was awful proud of your football," Jack said. He scratched Banda's ear. Then he turned and left.

"When you gonna learn bein' a hothead don't help nothin'?" Mama said.

Brody flipped a bird at the closed door. "No one invited his ass here," he said.

Blanda showed his teeth at Brody. Snarled. Barked twice.

"You got a problem with Jack?" I said.

"Worry 'bout yourself, Toffy," Brody said. "Three hundred pounds, soft as Charmin. That's why you don't play. And you," he said. He grabbed Blanda's scruff. "I ain't afraid to put you out of your misery."

Later on, I was in my bed. Mama came in the room. She crossed her arms. "Don't mind your brother," she said. "He's just bein' childish."

"He doesn't bother me," I said.

"You sure 'bout that?" she said. "You gotta be able to talk 'bout these things, Cade."

"Brody didn't call me till nighttime," I said. "Dad really die at sunrise?"

Mama sat on the bed. Rubbed my forearm. "It took mosta the day to get folks up there to help us," she said. "We needed a stretcher and so forth. Had to move him so as the coroner's van could get to him. Even where he fell, we was high. Couple miles from the trailhead, anyhow. Then we followed them to the mortuary. Day passed turtle's pace and bat of an eye, all at once. A daze. You know. But that ain't an excuse. Shoulda called you sooner."

"You didn't call at all though," I said.

Mama closed her eyes. "I didn't have it in me, Cade," she said. "I couldn't tell you. You got that big old heart, just like your daddy. I couldn't hear the hurt. Not from you."

"Gather Dad was drinking a lot," I said.

"What makes you say that?"

"The slurring, for one," I said. "Before I went to Centre. Just about every night I saw him over the summer. Left me a voicemail before you all headed out to Teton. So slurred I couldn't even understand."

"No doubtin' he liked his bourbon," Mama said. "So do I. But he wasn't no alcoholic, if that's what you mean."

"Can't see how you're so sure," I said.

"Well, how can you be so sure, Cade?" Mama said. "You was a ghost last summer. Right up to the time you went away. Never 'round. Workin' at the movie theater day and night, s'posedly."

"That why you didn't take me along?" I said. "Wait till I'm gone and have a family camping trip? Then Dad . . ."

I had to stop talking just then. Mama scooted herself closer. Put her fingers on my cheek. "Big old heart," she said. She pulled her hand away. Shook her head. "Didn't reckon you'd wanna be there with us."

"It was weird here," I said. "That's why I kept scarce. Brody and Dad always arguing. Dad was flustered I didn't get D1 scholarship offers. And nothing was the same after the affair, near as I could tell."

Mama stood straight up. "That was three years ago, Cade," she said.

"You ever forgive him, though?" I said.

"You don't know what you're talkin' 'bout, boy," Mama said. "I took him back unconditional. We all make mistakes, every one of us."

Mama glared for a long time just then. "You got somethin' more you wanna say to me, Cade?"

I dug in my pocket for a piece of paper. Unfolded it and showed her. "Life insurance policy," I said. "Less than a year before he died. Half a million dollars. Found it in your drawer."

"We're done here," Mama said. She started to leave.

"Thought we needed to be able to talk about these things," I said.

Denison beat us by a field goal in our home opener. I played a series in the second half. Starter had a cramp.

After the game, fans gathered on the track between the field and the locker room. Mostly teammates' families. I held my helmet by the facemask. Kept my head down as I passed. Someone grabbed me by the shoulder pad.

"Toffy!" Jack said. "Awful nice work out there, fella. One more possession, y'all woulda had 'em."

"You didn't need to come all this way," I said.

Jack looked right at me. "I did, actually," he said. "Somewhere we could talk? Won't take but a minute."

I followed Jack to an empty spot by the bleachers.

"Been aimin' to circle up with you for months now," Jack said. He was near whispering. "Got the sense at Christmas you might not know everything you oughtta know."

"Got the same sense myself," I said.

"First off, it was sporadic," Jack said. "You understand what that means?"

"Haven't a clue," I said. "What was sporadic?"

"Your daddy's ALS," Jack said. "Mosta the time it's sporadic. And that's a good thing. Means it ain't genetic. So you and Brody, your kids—you ain't likelier to get it."

"ALS?" I said. "You talking Lou Gehrig's disease?"

"Jesus and Mary," Jack said. Shook his head. "You musta seen the symptoms? He was gettin' dysarthria. In his voice. The slurrin' when he was tired? Already becomin' less sure of foot. That's the reason I thought your family, they coulda picked a less precarious place. Now he did treasure Inspiration Point, so I 'preciate the sentiment. But he didn't belong up there. Unnecessary risk, in my estimation."

"Why didn't they tell me?" I said.

"'Bout the specific disease?" Jack said.

"What else?" I said.

Jack's eyes got big just then. Toed at the invisible pebble. "Can't answer that one," he said. "On account of you were a minor, it was up to your parents what to share. I'm certain they didn't want you to be havin' extra worries, top of football and college. It's your own medical history too, though. So. Important you should know."

"Assume you were helping with his treatment?" I said.

"Sure, son," Jack said. "You can bet I was there for him. Woulda done anything for that man. But it was gonna be an awful tough road. All the way to the end."

"You saying Dad was fixing to die? No matter what?"

"Ah, shit, Toffy," Jack said. He put his fingertips to his nose. Collected himself. "Yeah, son. That's what I'm sayin'. He mighta had some time left otherwise. A few months or a few years. Woulda ate away at him, bit by bit. Debilitatin', eventually, to the point he couldn't swallow. And then, yeah. He woulda died horrible."

I skipped showering and jumped straight in my truck. Still wearing football pants. Undershirt cut off around the arms.

Near four-hour drive but it went by fast. Didn't stop once. Truck was running on fumes as I got close.

The garage was shut. Brody's moped was outside. I parked so as nobody could get around me.

Barged through the front. Flung open the screen door till it slammed against the house.

"Watchu doin' here, Toff—?" Brody said. He didn't finish because my hand was on his throat. Lifted him up off the ground. Pinned him against the wall.

"You killed Dad," I said. "You and Mama both. You shoved him over the cliff."

"The fuck off me, Toffy," Brody said. He tried to shove me away. "You ain't in no position to lecture."

Blanda ran up excited. I let go of Brody's collar and punched the wall above him. Plaster came down. Fell in his hair. "Son of a bitch," I said. "Planned it all, didn't you? For life insurance money. Neither of you intended on looking after him when he got sick."

Brody's face changed just then. Looked me in the eye. "He was sick already!" Brody said. He bawled, real hard and loud. "We was losin' him already. There was days Daddy couldn't tie his own shoes. Droppin' things. Draggin' his leg. You wasn't here to see it!"

Brody's head fell on my chest. His tears got my shirt wet. Blanda sat and watched.

"It wasn't your right," I said. "That's God's business to decide."

"Daddy decided, Cade," Brody said. Sobbed again. "He decided when and he decided where. Inspiration Point. That was his place."

"He didn't wanna tell you nothin', baby," Mama said. She walked down the stairs. "And I ain't gonna lie—I supported that. Bad timin', we figured. You had too much goin' for ya."

"So you just . . ." I said. Gulped. Had to stop talking for a second. "You threw him off?"

"He wasn't with us no more by then," Mama said. "We got out middle of the night. Long hike. Brody half-carried him mosta the way."

Brody leaned back on the wall. Shut his eyes.

"I gave him the meds soon as we made it to the peak," Mama said. "Timed it up so he saw that first hint of sunrise. All pink on the horizon. Just like he said it would be."

"Didn't take but twenty minutes after the jab," Brody said. Sniffled. "He went to sleep. Stopped breathin' not long after."

"So it really was about the life insurance," I said. "Couldn't collect on a suicide."

"His idea," Mama said. "I swear it to you, Cade. He wanted you to stay in college. He wanted us to have a good life. Figured if he went over, fell all that way, wouldn't be no questions about cause of death. No autopsy or nothin'."

"Jack knows he had ALS, Mama," I said. "He knows Dad shouldn't have been up on that mountain. Not in his condition."

Brody laughed just then. Mama came and gave me a hug. I let her.

"Oh, sweet Cade," she said. "Jack was a good friend to your daddy."

Blanda licked Mama's leg.

"Jack was just bein' jittery at Christmastime," Brody said. "Neurologist that diagnosed Daddy, handful of others down at the hospital who knew—they was askin' after it with Jack. Why we took on such a demandin' hike and like that. Found it peculiar, sure. But they wasn't ever gonna accuse us of nothin'. Community's too small. And they don't think we're smart enough for no schemin'."

"Jack does," I said. "He was suspicious."

"That's what I'm tellin' ya," Brody said. "Only thing concerned Jack was gettin' caught."

"He gave me the cocktail, Cade," Mama said. "The meds. Explained how to use 'em. How to make your daddy comfortable as possible."

Mama started shaking. Brody put his arms around us both. Squeezed.

We all cried then. I rested my cheek on the top of Brody's head. Kissed Mama's temple. Blanda lay down at Brody's feet.

"He wanted us to have a good life," Mama said. "He wanted us to be happy."

Melancholy Is the Nurse of Frenzy

R.C. Goodwin

One afternoon, three months after my twelfth birthday, I came home from school and found my mother in the garage, her car engine on. She'd put towels under the bottom of the garage door and the door leading to our downstairs family room.

I'd had a good day at school. In English class we studied a book I really liked, *Shakespeare for Young Readers*, and discussion in the class was livelier than usual. My introduction to Shakespeare, and even then his work drew me into it like nothing else I'd read. I especially liked *The Tempest*. I envied Miranda, living with her wise and loving father on an island far from everywhere.

When I came home that day, I looked through the house for my mother the way I always did. She might be anywhere. Watching TV, or reading on the back patio. Or lying in the bathtub with her wrists cut, amid swirls of bloody water. Or kicking the carpet and spouting gibberish as she stomped around the living room. Or waiting for me in the kitchen, a glass of milk already poured and a plate of Oreos on the table, but that didn't happen often. The Oreos signaled a good mood, by her standards. My favorite cookies, as she knew.

When I didn't find her in the house, I checked the garage. Not that I expected to find her. She'd leave randomly throughout the day and night, for unknown reasons and destinations, and I wanted to see if her car was there. It was. So was she, sitting in the driver's seat, slumped over the steering wheel. She'd opened all the windows. Her favorite CD was playing, Diana Ross's *Blue*.

I could tell from small movements of her chest that she was still breathing.

My cue to become the heroine. The script was supposed to go like this—I'd turn off the engine, open the garage door, call 911. Pull her out and start CPR. I doubt most children of twelve know how to do it, but I did, of necessity. Today would mark her sixth suicide attempt, or maybe her eighth or tenth. Hard to keep track of them. Her method of choice, an overdose from her cornucopia of meds. Pain pills for her fibromyalgia, Xanax and Valium for her nerves, lithium and antidepressants for her mood swings. Half a dozen different kinds of sleeping pills. I used to wonder why the nitwit doctors gave her so many, but I knew she could be shrewd about obtaining them. She doctor-shopped and used different pharmacies, and the pharmacies' computers didn't yet keep track of every pill.

Among her other suicide attempts: twice she tried to slash her wrists but she went about it wrong, cutting across instead of up and down. Swimming to the middle of a lake near us. The lake stays shallow for quite a distance, though. Exhausted before the water got deep enough for her to drown, she headed back to shore. Her closest call involved a car, but it didn't involve carbon monoxide. She took off in her Audi and aimed for a tree at high speed. That might have done it, or at least put her in a wheelchair for the rest of her life. But she tried to brake as she neared the tree and began to swerve around it at a crucial point. Even so, she fractured four ribs and a shoulder. Plus, she had to have part of her face reconstructed. Another close call involved my grandfather's insulin. My father was at work and I was at chorus practice after school. He often worked into the early evening, and I often stopped at a friend's house after practice. If both of us had come home a half an hour late, she would have died of hypoglycemia. But we both came home when she expected us.

Back to that particular day—I was supposed to be the heroine again, but I didn't. I didn't turn the engine off, or open the garage door, or call 911. Instead, I took a walk around the block. I didn't feel heroic, I wasn't in the mood.

Dr. Hollander, the best of my shrinks against scant and sometimes toxic competition, believes I went into a dissociative state. A fugue, she called it. Perhaps she was right, but I doubt it. My mind remained too clear for me to be dissociating. I remember wondering what I'd say when I got home and called 911, and would I call my father or let the cops do it, and how would he react. Would he start to cry or throw a fit? Unlikely; not his style. In fact, he might not show much of a reaction of any kind. Or he might have shut down and collapsed into a stupor.

I wondered if he'd blame me for my walk around the block. That struck me as unlikely too. It was a perfect afternoon in late April, a cloudless sky, light breezes rippling through budding trees. I liked to take walks after school, and this had been an ideal day for one.

I could give you the key facts about my mother. Where she grew up, what my grandparents were like, where she went to school and such. The smaller ones are more telling, though. She smoked very little but when she did, she liked Gauloises, a French brand that smelled like burning decomposing leaves. Her drink of choice had been a liqueur called Blue Curaçao, which looks like what you'd clean a toilet with. She always had to be different, always. Forget the violin or piano, she learned to play the English horn. In medical school she planned to go into forensic pathology, among the least popular specialties (young though she was, death called to her). Despite good grades she never did become a doctor, though. The summer before her final year she dropped out, no reason given. She cherished her unpredictability. In her twenties, unattached and financially secure—a wealthy uncle died, leaving her a bundle—she could have done what she wanted and gone where she pleased. Boston or New York or San Francisco. Or even London or Paris. Instead she moved to Nebraska, knowing no one there, her job prospects so-so although she didn't really need one. "I wanted to live on the prairies," she told me, without elaborating.

What else? Snakes fascinated her. She would have had a python if my grandparents or my father had allowed it, but butterflies terrified her. She had the greenest eyes you've ever seen, in which she took great pride. Her favorite holiday, if you can call it that, was Halloween. Every year she dressed up in a different outfit, each more elaborate than the previous one. I remember her as Marie Antoinette, complete with a tiara on top of a foot-high wig. She might stay awake for three days or she might sleep for fifteen hours straight. She married my father because he got her pregnant with me. Otherwise she never would have married him, as she repeatedly told us. The women she most admired included two with successful suicides, Sylvia Plath and Virginia Woolf.

And something else, she smiled once every three or six months, if that.

After the funeral service, we had a catered reception at the house, kind of fancy. They served a buffet featuring crab canapés, baked stuffed mushrooms, and a hot artichoke dip. Finger sandwiches, beef and smoked salmon. Deviled eggs, the yolks sprinkled with caviar, which struck me as too festive.

Not many relatives attended. My parents had only one sibling apiece, and three of my grandparents had already died. A number of friends and neighbors showed up, though. Mrs. Westbrook came, my fourth grade teacher, a sweet huggy woman, fiftyish, sort of retro with her clunky shoes and spit curls. Mr. Izzo, who lived across the street and owned a hardware store, sad-eyed ever since his wife left him for another man three years earlier. Harry and Ava Gelb, our accountant and his wife. My mother deemed Ava her closest friend although she might not contact her for weeks or months. Half the time she ignored Ava's texts and phone calls. A better friend than Mother deserved, in my opinion.

Only six or seven of my classmates came, but Kelly was one of them, thank God. Kelly Kiernan, my only confidante, whom I loved like the sister I never had. A pretty, round-faced girl with a slightly upturned nose and an abundance of reddish-blonde hair. Kelly knew about the suicide attempts, and how I came home from school each day unsure if she'd be waiting for me with milk and cookies or lying unconscious in the bathtub. She knew about my gut-deep yearning for a normal family life, whatever that might be. She knew about the lava-hot rage that never left me, my generally unruffled manner notwithstanding.

Kelly had the sense not to give me advice, which I didn't want and would have ignored in any case. The closest she came to it was this: "Justine, you have to stay open to the possibility that things might improve." What Kelly did—and she did it better than anyone else I've known, even Dr. Hollander—was to listen. She listened when I called her in the middle of the night, barely coherent. She listened when I told her how I prayed for my mother, how I offered to do whatever God asked of me if only He'd make her happy. If He wanted me to go Africa and take care of dying Ebola patients, or if He wanted me to become a Catholic and join an order of silent nuns, I would have done it. Kelly listened when I called her vile and wicked names that stunned us both, using words I didn't know I knew. When I cursed her as a useless pathetic self-pitying failure, a travesty of a mother and a woman, incapable of an unselfish thought, no more an adult than our canary.

I began to sabotage myself. It started about four years after her suicide.

I turned in papers late for no reason and left tests unfinished when I knew the answers. I skipped so many choral practices that Ms. Sorenson finally kicked me out, although she said I had an outstanding voice. Increasingly I skipped school altogether.

I also began to wreck relationships. I never had a host of girlfriends, but I lashed out at the ones I did have. Even at Kelly, who hung in there anyway. Greg was my first serious boyfriend, lanky and handsome despite his acne. The sort who'd send me flowers for no reason. An idealistic youth who hoped to become an urban planner or social worker. Driven by testosterone, of course, but gentler than you'd expect a boy of seventeen to be. My final text to him, I can't see you anymore. No, we can't be just friends. Have a nice life, J.

After Greg came Zack, a soccer star with a raunchy offbeat sense of humor, sort of narcissistic but surprisingly tolerant of my snits and topsy-turvy moods. One night, when we were drinking high octane rum, we got into a stupid argument over who was worse, Hitler or Stalin. I don't remember how, but it turned nasty. I told him to get lost and stay lost. Prudently, he didn't badger me to take him back.

Greg and Zack were the only ones I cared about, but a pack of others followed. Boys and men I found everywhere, in bars where they didn't check IDs too carefully, and in the lobby of the ten-screen Cineplex, and at the Six Flags down the road. In the bus station and at the airport. I preferred the bus station, it was grungier. Some were my own age, maybe younger. Some were fifty, maybe older, balding men who wore clothes two sizes too small that emphasized their spreading bellies. Many of them sweated mightily and marinated their faces in generic aftershave.

Cautiously, I used the internet. I didn't want to get hooked up with the sort of man who's a candidate for Death Row. Self-abasement was one thing, but getting dismembered by a psychopathic madman was something else.

Throughout this time, I wasn't altogether slothful. My father had all of Shakespeare's work in one impressive volume, over 1,700 pages. I'd pick a play randomly and read it. Not having a teacher made it harder—they did teach his plays in Honors English classes, but my poor grades kept me out of them. My father's book had lots of footnotes, though, which helped. I mainly read the tragedies. My favorite was *Macbeth*. I found Lady Macbeth more interesting than anyone else I'd ever read about.

At first she was so strong, much stronger than he was, and then guilt brought her to her knees. I suppose guilt can do that to a person. I wondered if it would do that to me someday, because I could have saved Mother but I didn't.

I began to cut myself. I preferred X-Acto knives but in a pinch I'd use razor blades, or the scalpel from my dissecting kit for high school biology. I went about it cleverly, picking sites that no one would notice. My site of choice, the inner part of my upper thigh. Not wanting to risk infection, I sterilized the blades with matches and candles. The heat intensified the pain, an added benefit.

One evening my father came into my bedroom to say goodnight. I forgot to lock the bedroom door (Dr. Hollander thought I forgot on purpose). He caught me slicing up my leg. "Oh, God, Justine. Oh, God." That's all he said. He took me in his arms, holding me tighter than he ever did before.

He made me see a psychiatrist, the first of five or seven, whatever. Some were smart and some were dolts, some were fake-jocular and some were as somber as hanging judges. Some tried to draw me out and some didn't care if I sat stolidly in silence throughout the whole session. I hated all of them.

Mostly they coalesced into a blur, but I do recall a few. Among the more memorable ones were the Bird Doctors. Dr. Hummingbird, Dr. Buzzard, and Dr. Parrot.

Dr. Hummingbird, a short nervous twerp, was the youngest, about thirty. Restless, prematurely bald, given to twitching and tapping. A man who looked as if he'd gone on an espresso binge. Every so often he'd stand up and walk around for no reason. Like a real hummingbird, he ate constantly. Throughout our sessions he munched on jellybeans and protein bars, on Hershey's kisses and pretzel bits, but you'd never know it from his weight. A thin man, probably had an overactive thyroid. Or else he tapped and twitched away the calories. I remember nothing he said to me.

Dr. Buzzard was also thin but at least ten inches taller than Hummingbird, with a hooked nose and wing-like arms that he didn't quite know what to do with. He wore dark suits and jackets, white shirts and solid-colored black or navy ties, as if in perpetual mourning. I imagined him perched on a scraggly tree in the desert, or flapping his arms as he flew around in search of carrion. Nice enough despite his doleful manner. He had a sad half-smile that made me want to ask him what was the matter. Unlike Hummingbird, he asked reasonable questions. How much responsibility did I assume for my mother's unhappiness? How did I feel about my father's inability to protect me from her, or protect her from herself? What did I think might have happened if she'd lived? I wish I'd seen him later, when I was older and less sullen. He might have helped me.

Dr. Parrot, a heavyset woman in her fifties, had short-cut salt and pepper hair and tiny eyes behind thick glasses. The most Freudian of my shrinks, with an office that gave away nothing of her. No family pictures on her desk, no knickknacks or framed diplomas. A few watercolors of winter days on the wall, and that was all. She could always wait me out. When I finally said something, snottily reluctant, she'd parrot it back. "This is a goddamn waste of time," I muttered once. "You think this is a goddamn waste of time," she echoed dutifully. "I killed my mother," I told her on a different occasion. "You killed your mother," she repeated, with maddening calmness. "YES, I KILLED MY MOTHER," I yelled. "What part of I KILLED MY MOTHER do you not understand?" But she did make a comment for which I'm grateful. I'd been talking about my mother's oft-repeated statement that she wouldn't have married or had children if my father hadn't knocked her up. The clear subtext, we'd ruined what would have been her otherwise idyllic life. And I, especially, bore responsibility for the angst and failures that came to pass because I had the gall to be conceived. "There are things for which we're absolutely not responsible," said Dr. Parrot with a jot of affect for a change. "They include the circumstances of our conception."

That might seem obvious to you, but the obvious can be remarkably elusive.

My father tried.

He tried to talk to me, to plead with me. You're smart, Justine, your grades could be spectacular if you applied yourself. He tried to jolly me out of the worst of my moods (serious himself, he did this poorly). A busy man, who ran data processing at a utility company and did consulting work on the side, he still managed to find time for me. We went to the beach in the summer, we cross-country skied in the winter. He took me to the Chinese and Italian restaurants I most enjoyed. He took me to movies and once in a while to plays. Knowing how much I liked Shakespeare, he took me to *Romeo and Juliet* and *A Midsummer Night's Dream*.

He must have lacked for female company but never dated. I guess he felt he always had to be available to me, and he worried that girlfriends might cut into his availability. Of course, it's possible the last thing he wanted was another woman in his life, after all the sound and fury with my mother.

We almost never talked about her. Next Wednesday will be her birthday, one of us might say. Or, Halloween is coming up. I wonder what she'd have worn this year. Or, one evening at Rudolfo's, her favorite restaurant, she would have liked that eggplant parmesan. But these were passing comments, and neither of us took them any further.

He must have known, I often thought. Had to know I still cut myself despite the fortune he spent on shrinks. Had to know I slept around, had to know about the alcohol and marijuana. Maybe he feared it would make things worse if he confronted me, that I'd have more sex and drink more out of spite. Or, maybe he simply disliked confrontation. Or, maybe he thought I was only kicking up my heels. Getting it out of my system. What the hell, the kid's been through a lot. Or, maybe he really didn't see what I was doing, didn't want to see. Who wants to see his daughter as an apprentice slut and an early-onset alcoholic?

We rarely talked about her, but my mother was never far from us. Never far from me, in any case. Memories of her ambushed me when I least expected them. When I brushed my teeth, or shopped for a sweater, or watched *60 Minutes* with my father. Memories of her hysterics over nothing, of her sobbing marathons and suicide attempts. But there was a scattering of pleasant memories as well. How we had a tea party for my dolls and stuffed animals. How she helped me put together a puzzle of the United States, each state a separate piece. How she taught me to make French toast. We'd have it ready, the maple syrup warmed and the bacon crisp, when my father came home with a Sunday paper. You could almost mistake us for an ordinary family.

I remember with particular clarity something that occurred while we sat on the back patio, a couple of weeks before she killed herself. When she suddenly began to talk, I couldn't read her face or interpret her tone of voice the way I usually could. Her monolog, a mix of anger and despair, of self-doubt and fatalistic self-acceptance, of threats, with a scintilla of love and affection thrown in for good measure. But mainly she spoke in a soft voice and a low steady monotone, and she might have been talking about the weather. A gifted actress would have been hard-pressed to capture all of it.

This is what she said—You are my daughter, my creature, the flesh of my flesh. You are my redemption and my scourge, my greatest hope and my heaviest burden. You are my pride and my shame. You think you can escape me but you can't, not if you move ten thousand miles from here, not if I die tomorrow and you live to be a hundred. My life and yours are intermingled. There are no boundaries between us.

I graduated from high school with barely passing grades. My only extracurricular activity consisted of writing the morbid, mordant poems I sent to the school literary magazine. They made me an assistant editor.

Instead of college I held down a series of mediocre jobs. Barista at a Starbuck's wannabe, assistant manager at an overpriced precious bakery called Cupcakes 2Die4. Receptionist at Harry Gelb's accounting firm, gate agent for a no-frills airline. I usually quit after five or six months. Despite the brevity of time I spent with any of them, despite their paying little more than minimal wage, I managed to save money. Living at home with my father made it easy.

Looking back, I suppose the jobs proved useful to me. They prompted me to go back to school, since I knew I'd face a lifetime of those jobs if I didn't.

I lurched and stumbled into life as an adult, or a replica of one. No longer did I sleep around. In fact, I lived a celibate existence, not unpleasant to me. I gave up weed and drank no more than a glass of wine when my father and I went out for dinner. Finally leaving home at twenty-two, I moved into a small but pleasant flat I decorated with reproductions from the local art museum. My favorite prints were of Edward Hopper's paintings. I liked the way he captured isolation.

I took courses, first at a community college and then at a branch of the state university. At the age of twenty-seven, six years later than most of my high school classmates, I graduated with a BA in English. I took enough education courses to become certified as a teacher.

At twenty-eight I met George, eight years older than I am, divorced, with twin boys who lived with their mother a time zone away. Nicely featured, neatly trimmed brown mustache, with a high and rather noble forehead. Well-dressed but not a fashion plate, fit but not muscle-bound, serious but not ponderous. He didn't want more children, a big plus. Didn't ask many questions about my past, another plus.

His biggest draw was his family. His parents, soft-spoken and good-natured, came across as two people satisfied with their lives and with each other. Satisfied, a word from a foreign language I barely spoke. When one of them came into a room, the other smiled. An unforced smile, near-impossible to feign. They listened to each other without interrupting, rolling their eyes, or looking pained. George's sisters, good-natured too, struck me as close friends as well as siblings.

The first time I met them was at Thanksgiving dinner. They made me feel at home in minutes. I found myself caught up in interesting conversations interspersed with banter and laughter. An excellent wine accompanied an excellent meal, consumed freely, but no one got drunk. His parents hugged me when I left. They said they hoped I'd come back soon.

George and I began to live together about six months after meeting. His job, as regional manager for a major car rental company, called for quite a bit of traveling. One week he planned to be out of state from early Monday morning until late Wednesday night. His mother, who worried that I didn't eat enough when her son went out of town, came over Tuesday evening with lamb stew and a wedge of homemade cherry pie. She found me in the garage, in my Mitsubishi, slumped over the steering wheel with the engine on, towels stuffed beneath the garage door.

They kept me a week and a half on Three West, the psychiatric unit of a local hospital. I know that doesn't sound too long, but in fact it's a fairly lengthy stay these days. Some patients, including pretty sick ones, are in and out in forty-eight hours.

A jumble of memories of Three West: a paper gown, lest I try to hang myself with a cloth one; fifteen-minute checks around the clock for the first two days. Pills that made me nauseous and gave me the worst headaches I've ever had. Group therapy sessions with a mute guy, a manic woman, and a man not quite over the DTs. Nurses going through piles of paperwork, too busy to talk with anyone for more than ten minutes, usually closer to five. The food—cold oatmeal and warm ice cream—a fried egg that kept its shape when someone thumb-tacked it to a bulletin board. George's visits, and the pain that marred his placid, handsome face. My father's visits, and our unaccustomed awkwardness with each other. Playing Ping-Pong with Melanie, a transgender teenager who looked neither male nor female. The small pleasure of getting back my belt and shoelaces when they judged me safe to have them. The unrelenting thoughts about my mother.

One unequivocally good thing did come from my being there, my meeting Dr. Hollander.

Lana Gaye Hollander might have worked her way through medical school as a model, although she didn't have the borderline-anorexic thinness of so many of them. Just under six feet tall, with long dark hair and deep brown eyes, she moved around Three West with a yoga teacher's fluid grace. When you asked her about herself, she provided just the right amount of information. She didn't inundate you with it, but neither did she give you the old Freudian copout—Why are you asking, hmm?

Among the things I learned about her, in the course of our nearly three years together: her father and older sister are both doctors. As an undergrad at Princeton she majored in anthropology. She did fieldwork in Brazil, learned Portuguese there. Although she liked surgery, she thought psychiatry would hold her interest more than any other specialty. She's married, has a boy and girl. To unwind, she does Zumba and reads British and Scottish crime fiction.

There's also this—part of her interest in psychiatry comes from the suicide of her great-uncle, a Vietnam vet with posttraumatic stress disorder.

I began to meet with her, as a private patient, immediately after my discharge. She changed my meds and found a combination that helped me without making me want to throw up half the time, or making me feel as if a wad of gauze lay between my brain and skull. If I start to get evasive or tangential in our sessions she brought me back, gently but firmly. I've always been skeptical about the Freudian stuff (do people still believe that folderol about primal scenes and castration anxiety?) but I believe in transference. She became the trustworthy mother and bighearted older sister I never had.

She's also preparing me for the day when I no longer need her. I've known shrinks who foster dependence. Maybe they get off on becoming indispensable to their clientele. Or, maybe it's due to money. If you keep a patient indefinitely, it's like having an annuity. Dr. Hollander doesn't work like that. "I want you to be your own person, Justine," she told me once, "and it won't happen if you're too dependent on me." Then she added, softly, without an iota of rejection, "You can't be my patient forever." I used to see her twice a week, and now I see her once a month.

Except for my father and Kelly Kiernan, I love her more than anyone else I've ever known.

My father and I enjoy each other's company as we used to, and we no longer walk on eggshells around each other. I've grown fond of a woman he's crazy about, a professor of art history widowed young, whom he met online. I wish they'd met years earlier.

I still see George, although we no longer live together. We talk often, we go out occasionally, and once in a while we take trips together. I think he has forgiven me for the suicide attempt, but I doubt that he'll ever fully trust me. It's as if I cheated on him. But a lot of couples make it work when one of them has cheated, so maybe we can too. I like him very much, and maybe I love him, but I'll be okay regardless of what happens with us.

I'm still teaching in a high school, but not for long. Next year I'll start working towards a PhD in English. My dissertation will be on Shakespeare, who still touches me the way no other writer can. I plan to do a dissertation on *The Taming of the Shrew*, which always bothered me. I've read it three times, and I've seen the movie with Taylor and Burton twice, and I still don't get it. Here's Shakespeare, the greatest writer in the English language, and he writes a play about a woman completely surrendering to a man. A man who's a manipulative schemer, kind of frivolous when you look closely at him, a man who's simply not worth the trouble. How could Shakespeare have written a play like that? What was he thinking? Besides, he never touches the real mystery, he barely hints at what made Katharina such a shrew in the first place. But he's Shakespeare, so he must have had his reasons.

Maybe, with yet more rereadings, I'll come to understand the play. And maybe—I know this is a long shot—maybe it will help me understand my mother. She wasn't a shrew, not really, but she could be quite Katharina-like when it suited her. There's a line in the play that always makes me think of her: *"too much sadness hath congealed your blood, / And melancholy is the nurse of frenzy."*

There's another line in the play I especially like, a line that applies to both of us. *"My tongue will tell the anger of my heart, or else my heart concealing it will break."*

A Slow Spiral

Jordyn Lillibridge

Fluorescent lighting wasn't the least inviting part, or the night-gown that didn't close in the back. Not even the poking and prodding with needles, or a stranger's hand shoved up to my cervix, or the mesh panty with a giant puppy pad shoved in them. No, the worst part was knowing in this moment, while I was cared for, I was a vessel to the life inside me. Anything and everything would be done to get them out, whether I consented to it or not. Who wouldn't consent to whatever measure it took to get their baby out safely? Some mothers don't hesitate to be ripped open at a moment's notice or cut to make more room for a too large head. Maybe I was weird, or selfish, but I would hesitate, because it was my body too, that I carry through life, which would be affected by these snap decisions. My very devotion as a mother was questioned before I even had the chance to be a mother.

Being wheeled back I was terrified, praying silently for a safe experience. Keeping my tears to myself so as not to alarm anyone close to the fear I felt. Joking with the staff about finally getting this 'thing' out of me, while wishing I could get out of this god damned wheelchair and go home to my safe, comfortable bed. Try this whole birthing thing another day. It doesn't work like that though, does it? Birth doesn't care how unprepared you are, how terrified you are, how you feel like you are at death's door itself during the last stretch. It comes when it wants, not stopping for anyone.

Hobbling from the wheelchair, in my too revealing nightgown, I sat in the firm, and unyielding bed. A young, blonde, spritely nurse came up next to me. A large needle in her hand, before we even exchanged pleasantries she stuck a vein, with the largest fucking needle possible.

"You're a hemorrhage risk," she said while, taping the iv line in place. Before I could even register what had happened, I was being instructed to move to the end of the bed and put my feet in stirrups. My wrist throbbing from the rushed stabbing. Attempting to finish the command, while still moving, a hand reached up as far as it could to attempt to stick a finger into my cervix. One quick motion and a flood of water poured out of me. I didn't even know they were going to do that. My wrist throbbing, my cervix cramping, drenched in my own fluid; I lay there, staring at the ceiling, knowing this was just the beginning.

"I just need to place these monitors on you, so we can hear and monitor baby," another young but brunette nurse said as she was actively reaching around my giant belly. No one had asked, no one asked about a single thing. There was no explanation, and I never asked for one or told them to stop either. My desire to be a good patient, to take up as little space as possible, took more precedence than my own well-being, than my own birth experience.

A cold liquid pulsed through the vein the IV was lodged in. Cold until it burned like fire throughout that entire arm. I gritted my teeth against the pain, not wanting to make a scene, hoping it would just pass soon. It didn't. The pain got worse until I had to say something.

"This really hurts," was all I said, while I said it calmly it was a desperate plea for relief. The nurses apologized, diluting the solution enough to make it bearable. I looked at the very full bag, then at the clock, and then back to the ceiling. Allowing myself to get lost in the stark white paint and blinding florescent lights.

All settled for a while, the liquid fire ceased to drip, no one stuck their hand up my vagina, or stabbed me with needles that you can see through. Cramps started, as the medication to encourage them dripped steadily through my line. They were tolerable. I watched TV to settle my mind from the happenings of earlier, and the happenings that were to come later. An hour passed when the doctor came in to check how things were progressing. Shoving another hand in a private space, she informed me they were not. She walked to the box on my IV pole that controlled my medicine and began pressing buttons.

"What are you doing?" I had asked, completely in the dark, about what was now going to be entering my body.

"Oh, turning up the Pitocin. You aren't progressing, so we need to encourage stronger contractions." She turned and left the room after that. I felt the liquid increase in my veins, wondering when it would hit, when the medicine would "encourage" more contractions. I didn't have to wonder very long because a few moments later I had a large and painful contraction. There was no work-up to this pain level. No gradual increase of meds to stimulate labor. Zero to seventy in a matter of five minutes.

I instructed my husband to turn the TV off, turn those damn lights off, and bring me the medicine ball. I swayed my hips in circles, trying to breathe through each wave, my husband massaging my back. The contractions came faster and faster, my ability to cope diminishing with each one. Nurses only coming in to aggressively readjust the monitor because my attempts to position myself into a bearable pose shifted them. Pain began to blind my thoughts, I could no longer cope, I was tapping out.

"I need the epidural," I begged, holding in a sob. Trying to hide how much I hurt, how afraid I was to continue this journey, to not alarm anyone, even the person I trusted the most. My husband flew out of the room to get a nurse, desperate to make this all stop.

"The anesthesiologist will be in shortly, he's just finishing up with another patient," the blonde nurse said as she looked over my IVs. She turned on the lights to see her chart better, not considering I turned them off intentionally and that the hallway had plenty of light to offer her. I don't know how much time passed before the guy with the needle came in, but I do know it was agonizing. My cervix was being hammered by what was sure to be the cutest head I'd ever see in my life. My spine felt as though it was ripping in half, a consequence of the baby being turned the wrong way. My grip on it all diminished greatly.

"I'm going to need you on the edge of the bed. Round your back and tuck your chin in for me," the man with the needle said. "I'm just going to disinfect the area; I won't poke you without warning you." The only time that courtesy had been extended during the whole ordeal. "Okay, round your back again and breathe out."

"I'm having a contraction." I could barely get the words out through the searing pain. The words came too late, he stuck me, the shock making me jump. In turn making the brunette nurse gasp. I was paralyzed, I was sure my reaction had paralyzed me.

"You're okay, it's okay," the man with the needle said trying to calm my panic. I schooled my face back into that mask of calm I had worn this entire stay. Relief never came. Before the man could push the drugs into my back that would offer any refuge from this pain, the doctor appeared out of nowhere, casually sticking her hand back up to my cervix.

"Oh, that's a head, hold off on that, get her on her back, this baby is coming," she said as she prepped herself to receive the baby careening itself out of me. For the first time during my stay, I cried. I sobbed, I didn't care if I was a bad patient, or if anyone saw my fear. I was beyond that. I sobbed and screamed as I was sure that with his exit, my baby was breaking my spine. I was sure there would be permanent damage done.

"He's stuck," was all I heard the doctor say before her hands were inside of me, ripping my baby from my womb. I screamed at the pain, which reached levels I didn't know existed. Staring at the ceiling again, the same stark white paint, the same blinding lights, I felt myself bleeding out, I felt the energy drain from my body. The blood pouring out from in between my legs taking parts of me with it.

"She's hemorrhaging," the doctor said, before a nurse, I'm not even sure which one, began kneading on my stomach, sending blinding pain through my already obliterated abdomen. More bags went on my IV line, more fluids through my vein, more kneading. I didn't know what my baby looked like. I didn't hear him cry. I saw my husband standing over the bassinet, looking between our baby and me. I was too tired to really register the gravity of the situation.

A loud cry finally broke the sound of the nurses rushing into the room, getting this and that in an attempt to stop my bleeding. I let out a breath I wasn't even aware I was holding, as a new nurse brought my baby to me and placed him on my chest. He was perfect, nowhere in the world had there been a more perfect baby, I was sure of it. I loved him, instantly, but not in the overwhelming way I had heard about. Not in the way I had been promised. Not in the way I expected. I held him as he began his search for food. Helping him latch, we stayed there together for a while as the nursing staff continued their efforts to get my bleeding under control, to get tests done on him, to prick his small tender foot for a blood sample.

My bleeding did stop. The staff left us for an hour. An hour of peace with our new baby. Placing our son in my husband's arms I tried to sit up, but the pain was too uncomfortable still. In between my legs was swollen and bruised, my spine still ached, and my abdomen was still cramping. My lack of ability to move was noted by the nurse who came to take us all to the postpartum area. The room had to be changed for the next poor woman. She placed her feet under mine and hauled me up, shifting me carefully to the wheelchair. There was no graceful way to do this, so I plopped myself on my sore bits, without so much as a grimace. I was back to being a good patient, now that my feral lapse had passed. I was wheeled through the halls, my husband maneuvering the bassinet that held our bundle. The song indicating a baby was born played on our behalf as nurses congratulated us.

The room was fine, quaint, and sterile. The bed offered no relief for my broken body. I was carefully helped into the bed by my new postpartum nurse, a lovely woman with tan skin and black bob. At least I thought she was wonderful until she also began kneading on my tender stomach, causing it to contract aggressively, and dispel blood clots from my body.

I wasn't holding my baby; I made no reach for him either. Allowing my husband to hold and swoon over him. I love him, I repeatedly told myself. I knew it was true, but it wasn't right. I didn't love him the right way. I loved him, but I was okay not holding him. Preferring to watch my husband bond. When my husband wasn't in the room I held him, though my attention was elsewhere. I admired the baby toes, the soft newborn grunts, but if I had been able to stand, I would have placed him back in his bassinet.

Two days passed. Two days of being woken up around the clock for meds, stomach kneading, and help to the bathroom. After that time had passed, we were handed pages of paperwork to fill out, large documents detailing how much we owed and why. Fifteen hundred dollars for an epidural I didn't even get to use, our responsibility now. Invoices, latch help, purple crying, how to spot depression, pamphlet after pamphlet shoved in our faces. All while my newborn was trying to maintain his latch to my breast.

Newborn in my arms, crap stuffed haphazardly into bags, I was wheeled to the same entrance I had come in from. Back in the real world, away from the round-the-clock care, that while I was grateful for, I was ready to be home. The car ride home was uncomfortable, still swollen and raw, every bump in the road was noticed. The baby began to cry in the backseat, prompting us to pull over.

"I think he's hungry," I said trying to get out of the car, my abdominals useless to assist me. He was too. Even after feeding him ten minutes prior, he was ravenous. I just want to be home. I wasn't enjoying this feeding, just like I hadn't enjoyed the other ones. Sitting up to nurse hurt, the latch hurt. Once he was filled with nourishment, I strapped his little body back into the giant car seat, and we were on our way again. This time we made it to the destination. I didn't take in our surroundings; I didn't notice them. I was just focused on getting home and getting in bed.

I only remember waking up to my husband telling me the baby was hungry, sitting up in a daze I was reminded of my wounds promptly. Latching my boy, and gazing down at him, I wondered when that earth-shattering bond would kick in. Finally opening my phone, I saw the mass amounts of missed calls and text messages. Everyone asked about the baby, wanting pictures of the baby, wanting to bring meals, to come hold him. A few close friends asked how I was. Fine I replied, not sure how to tell them about the whole ordeal, but relaying I was indeed okay.

Visitors stopped by, bringing food like a ticket for admission. All excited to hold the baby, swoon over the baby. I wasn't up for any of it. I leaked from my breasts, my nether regions ached still, the cramping hadn't gone away, and I was wearing diapers to catch the flow of excess that still poured from my body. These are not details guests want to hear. They want to hear about how you love the baby, how you're so happy to have the baby. I wasn't though. I loved him, but he cried so much it threatened my very sanity. I loved him, but his latch had caused my nipples to crack and bleed. I loved him, but when I looked in the mirror, I had no idea who was staring back at me. This new foreign body stretched and sagged, barely able to get around. Breasts so full they hurt. Grease lining the strands of my hair, dark circles taking permanent residence under my eyes. I loved him, but I didn't love him enough. I put him down every chance I got. Opting to watch an old familiar show instead of snuggling with him. Picking him up and comforting him when he cried, which seemed to be around the clock. Wondering what happened? This wasn't how it was supposed to be. This is not what I was told. Why were there so many people over all the time when I was having an extended existential crisis, did no one see that?

No. How could they? I welcomed them. I put on the polite smile, I shoved my fat ass into jeans that hurt and didn't fit, covered by a large engulfing sweater that was difficult to nurse in. I chatted for hours pleasantly while inside of me screamed for answers to these uncharted and murky, spit-up-filled waters. Why wouldn't I let them in my home and chat about baby toes? They paid for that right with their mystery casserole admission.

I was always fine with people holding him, I never asked for him back. This was my second indication that I was not a good mother. I could go the whole day without holding him and be okay. What was wrong with me?

"Nothing," my lovely sister-in-law had said when I confided in her one night. "I didn't bond with my baby right away either; give it a week. Don't worry. You're doing great," Her words comforted me in ways I didn't know I needed comforting. I needed to hear that because I didn't feel like I was doing well. I felt like I was failing miserably. Despite the Broadway act I put on for our barrage of visitors. When the show was over, I was left empty, walking circles with my bundle of joy while he gave me tinnitus. Sleep wasn't even a reprieve for me, not that it mattered, it was a rarity.

Gradually the guests stopped coming, the phone stopped ringing, and I was left alone. This is worse, this is better and worse. Being alone with the baby all to myself was a stark reality that this was everyday life now. Even with my husband home to help. A luxury I'm well aware of. Each day blended into the next seamlessly, and endlessly. Tasks were left undone, clothes piled up, smelling of rotten milk.

The crying finally slowed in frequency about two weeks in. So why didn't I feel better? I was getting rest; I was sure when I got rest, I would feel myself. When I got rest, I would feel that unbounding love for my son who slept soundly in my arms. I got the rest, but the bond didn't come. This is too long I remember thinking. How could any sane mother not bond with her baby after two weeks, and while finally resting? It didn't make sense.

How could I still look in the mirror and then quickly look away from the stranger on the other side? Why was I watching the same goddamned show over and over again instead of turning it off to be present with my quickly changing baby? Why did I not enjoy this? I only asked myself those questions, and since I was the one asking, I knew I didn't have the answers. There's no casual way to bring up the fact that motherhood isn't wonderful for you. I tried once, I was told I needed to be thankful for my healthy boy, other women don't have that same outcome. I never talked about it again.

Days turned to weeks. Sleep, cry, eat, repeat. Laundry, dishes, dinner, dishes. I was going through the motions. Doing what needed to be done, what was expected to be done. Ignoring calls and texts from well-meaning loved ones. This wasn't working. In an attempt to feel something, anything, I set my baby down, walked to the bathroom, and looked at the woman in mirror. I faced her finally, stared her down. I didn't know who she was, but she sobbed with me. She had a complete mental breakdown with me, silently of course, we didn't want to disturb or alarm our husband. I hated her, this stranger sobbing with me. This stranger who resembled me in physical appearance and nothing else. I looked away, continuing my emotions on the bed, into a pillow, until a new small cry brought me back to my cycle of mothering. Sleep, cry, eat, repeat.

The bond did come, it was able to shine even through my own clouds. I did have that miraculous love for my baby. I rested as much as I could, I wanted to hold my baby all the time. Admire his little toes, his sweet smile. The clouds never lifted though. I felt wrong. I had this love for my baby finally, we were healthy, but only one of us was thriving. While he thrived each day, I withered gradually. Starting with the never-ending flow of silent tears, my daily stare downs with the woman in the mirror, turning into the voices that plagued my head. Encouraging me to do the right thing. There was no way I could mother like this. I didn't appreciate my baby enough to pull myself out of this slump, how then could I walk a whole lifetime with him through real trials?

Just take the knife, my own mind would say to me daily. *One little cut.* Holding the knife in my hand while the playful chatter of my family came from the dinner table behind me, enjoying a meal I had just prepared. Just do it! The voice would scream at me. I put the knife down and joined my family.

Swerve into the tree. Driving home from a grocery pickup, the urge to drive my own car off the road, despite my baby being in the back began to take over me. It would be so quick. Turning the music up as a feeble attempt to drown out the noise, the demands. I wouldn't do it. That unbounding love for my baby; the only tether to this world. Day after day I resisted the screaming in my head to hurt myself, to cease to exist.

My days began and ended with my meetings with the stranger in the mirror. She looked like shit. I knew she felt like shit too, but I couldn't worry about her right now, because the baby had begun to cry again. *Go get the knife*, the voice would say as I prepared a bottle in the middle of the night. *You aren't good at this; you didn't even breastfeed long enough. Now he's getting toxins, and you've created another financial burden. Selfish.* That stung; that made me stare at the knives a bit too long, wondering if it would be that easy. I grabbed one, and right there on the kitchen counter I sliced the skin on my forearm. *Just do it!* The voice hissed at me. My open wound slowly dripping fresh blood, I had what I wanted, relief. The expression of physical pain was a way to release the emotional pain building inside of my body. This was a slippery slope though. I placed the knife in the dishwasher, walked to my bathroom to stare at the woman again. She was thinner. There was no light in her eyes, there was no judgement either. Just a blank, lifeless expression on a tired face devoid of any emotion. In her eyes though I thought I glimpsed all she had been, it may have been there, somewhere, just trying to get out. Incased in this prison that wouldn't allow for such lovely things.

"Here's your paperwork, please fill out the Depression screening," a pleasant older nurse said as she handed me a clipboard. Do you cry for no reason? No. Do you want to harm yourself or your baby? No. Lies. I couldn't have the doctor knowing I had unyielding thoughts instructing me to end everything in such gloriously quick ways. They would lock me somewhere and take my baby away. No, we couldn't have that. So, we lied. The voices and I. Stuck in a never-ending dance together, that had no distinct beginning and no sign of an end. The endless questions about my baby, my body, and my coping came from the energetic doctor, who was rushing through this visit. She had a whole waiting room to see, I wasn't going to take up her time. I gave the generic answers, which were met with a nod of approval.

"You sound great, love on that sweet baby for me," she said as she walked out the door to go interrogate the next woman. I sat in the room for a moment, under the harsh fluorescents, devoid of anything. I had done well; they didn't suspect us at all. I grabbed my belongings and hurried home to relieve my husband of fatherhood demands. He had an actual job to do. *He hates you.* I knew he didn't, I knew him better than the voices. *He resents you for being like this.* That one hit. The sobs made their way from the depths I shoved them in, flooding out of me with such velocity. I couldn't breathe. *He works, has the baby, and now you to deal with.* I couldn't see, the tears obstructed my vision. *You, who can't even get herself together, spoiled girl.* My chest hurt from trying desperately to get a breath in, but the sobs kept coming in droves I had never seen before. *Crash your car and make it go away, make us go away.* The image of a small, sweet, familiar smile crept into my head. I pulled over, turned my hazard lights on and stayed there until the last bit of emotion left my shaking body.

Weeks turned into months. My morning and nightly run-ins with the woman the same. The voices still ever present, ever persistent. My beautiful boy was flourishing. Myself an empty vessel carrying nothing, trying to play this role expected of me. I did a good job too. The house was clean, the baby well cared for in every sense, food prepared, and laundry done. I couldn't be sad if I was accomplishing things. That was the rule. You aren't valuable. Anyone can fold a towel. The voices followed me during my daily tasks that I loathed. Loathed because they had no value to me, they had no weight, they were just stuff everyone had to do. Stuff that kept me from following out the voices repeated orders of violence against myself, but that kept me returning for bits of physical release during the long endless days.

Drop your baby down the stairs. I stopped above the first step. I looked down the stairs, counted each one, twenty-six. Twenty-six stairs to tumble down, a death sentence. I looked at the sleeping boy in my arms. That was it for me. That was the last straw with the voices.

"How are you doing this week?" my therapist asked me.

"I'm doing well," I lied. How was I supposed to say I could barely function, voices wanted me dead, and lady was staying in my mirror? I guess just like that. That's not what I said though. We went through the motions together.

"I'm just a little sad sometimes, for no reason," I said, shoving those violent sobs back where I kept them. The only slight indication that something was wrong. The voices all screamed at me. *Traitor! They'll take you away if you don't shut up.* Maybe that's what I needed though, maybe I deserved to be thrown somewhere to rot.

"Well, that's very normal during this transition, but what would you define as sad?" she pondered. The sobs inched a little closer to the surface.

"I just don't always find fulfillment in my mundane tasks." I didn't lie, though I didn't tell the truth either.

"Tell me more about that," she probed, waiting to see if I'd give up my lies to her. I didn't.

"I just don't enjoy the basic tasks, I feel a little useless," I said with a cheery tone to hide the impact of those words. The sobs inched closer again. I wasn't going to lose my grip though. Only thirty minutes left in this fucking session, then we could get on with my withering for another day.

"You know you aren't useless though, right?" she carefully asked. I didn't. The image of me standing on the stairs with my baby flooded back to my mind. That's why I was here, answering these questions.

"No," I whispered as the sobs crept closer.

"That seems to have brought up an emotion in you, do you want to tell me about it?" she said so gently. The sobs broke free, and I betrayed it all. The voices, the stranger in my mirror, my obsession with the knives. Never though, never the act of hurting myself, never the betrayal of the voices asking me to hurt my baby. I would never give those up. No one would ever forgive me for that.

We talked for the next thirty minutes about a plan to help with these feelings of hopelessness. Starting with a pill. I hated the idea of medication. I worried they wouldn't work and would tip me over the edge I was practically dangling from. I took them though, to be a good patient. I didn't notice any changes. A few weeks passed, I lied and said I felt better. I didn't want to jump from drug to drug. I knew there was nothing wrong with that, but the voices and I agreed it wouldn't be good for me. The only indication of a change came at night with my daily encounter with the woman. While I stared at her, I decided once to offer her a small, brief smile.

Months turned to more months, but I was feeling better. Not fixed, but better. I didn't have to hold my sobs down with such force anymore because they rarely chose to come out. My dear beloved voices had died down too, rarely instructing me anymore. *Hold the knife.* I did as they said, but they never instructed me further after that initial command. The woman in the mirror looked better. Her face was rounder, her eyes less sunken with fatigue. We hadn't cried together in a while, choosing now to watch each other apply our makeup in silence and understanding. Even smiling at each other sometimes.

"Can you just love me as I am?" she said to me one day, as we held our babies, and I thought maybe I could do that for her, for us.

Don't Tell Your Mom

Mark Cole

My favorite food is a highball. Dad has a highball when he comes home from work. He makes one for me. I like the cherry juice and cherry Dad puts in my highball . . .

Mom and Dad laughed when I recounted what I wrote. His laugh was pure melody. If it was scored it would be by Richard Rodgers during his Lorenz Hart years. Mom's laugh was high and piping. Sounded as if she was singing Hilda Hilda Hilda over and over again.

What, you may ask made a second grader write about a highball. Mom and Dad asked the same question.

The second grader watched his dad mix a highball. He selected the correct glass, a short one, wide, with silver trim. Sound effects included a squeak and crunch when the dad pulled the lever on the aluminum ice tray; and the clink of cubes dropped in the glass. The dad reached for a bottle of Four Roses, housed next to the Joy dish detergent and Bab-O cleanser in the cabinet under the sink. The bottle was filled with whisky. So much the second grader knew. What exactly whisky was, he didn't know. Only this: the elixir in the bottle was a pick-me-up for the dad every afternoon before dinner. The dad took a small silver cup from the cupboard. Filled it to the brim with the tea-colored liquid. How he then splashed the contents over the ice. Such technique. The casual toss of the cup, with a slight rotation of the wrist spoke to years of practice. Ginger ale, from a green bottle, effervesced the concoction. A quick dribble of cherry juice was followed by the best part. The dad plopped a Maraschino cherry (with a stem) into the mix. Maraschino. Mysterious word. Who wouldn't want a friend named Maraschino? Two more drinks were prepared. Parents and second grader repaired to the living room. While the mom and dad talked about school (the new superintendent wants to shift the paradigm), neighbors (their carport is the ugliest thing on the planet), or, since the dad was also an organist and choir director, the pastor at church (I told him he could take the organ keys and shove them where the sun doesn't shine), the second grader sipped his fizzy, sweet beverage. He imitated the parents and lifted the cherry by the stem. Dallied with it, tapped it against the inside rim of the glass. Finally, with the cherry poised between his lips, he'd extract the stem, and suck in the red-puckered fruit. If he was really lucky; if the dad was feeling generous, the highball came equipped with two Maraschino cherries. After liquid and cherry were consumed, it was time to masticate the ice. Had to be done on the sly though, since the dad's musically trained ears were sensitive and too much crunching would provoke a rebuke.

I was not able to articulate any of this at the time. So in answer to the question, "Why did you write about a highball?" I could only reply, with a giggle, "Because I like them."

Mom, if she were here, would want me to make one thing clear. My highball and Dad's highball were vastly different as to alcohol content. Zero for mine. At the time my idea of alcohol was limited to the isopropyl variety, used to sterilize a needle when extracting a splinter from my finger. Dad must have made me think I was getting the same drink as his. He was the magician who fools the eye with the cups and balls. The name of the tap-dancing curly headed moppet, Shirly Temple, was never brought up. The word mocktail (which strikes me as subpar Lewis Carroll) was not in our vocabulary. It would have been an ignominy to refer to my drink as anything but a highball.

Mom ceased laughing when I said, "I wrote we all drink them."

"You said I drink one too?"

"Yes. You do."

She said something like, "Not very often and not as strong as your father's."

What had strength to do with it? Extra cherry juice? As I've mentioned, I did not have a conception of proof regarding the liquid in the Four Roses bottle. I was about to.

Mom said, "We need to set this straight. I'll talk to Sister."

I feared the worst. Sister was to be dragged into it. No one was laughing anymore. I asked, "Why?"

"Because highballs are for adults."

"Why do you let me have one then?"

"Because you asked," said Dad. "And yours isn't the same as ours."

Mom said, "I don't want Sister to think we're corrupting our children."

Dad said, "Sister won't think—oh for God's sake."

"Can I taste yours?"

Mom said no. Dad said yes and offered me his glass. I sipped before Mom could intervene. I was repulsed. Yuck.

"There," said Dad. "Now you can say you've tried whisky. See," he said to Mom. "He doesn't like it. Isn't that good? I'd rather have him exposed to it at home."

I gulped from my own glass. Would all the ice, ginger ale, and cherry juice in the world wash away the taste of Dad's whisky? And he liked it. What a conundrum.

Mom taught Latin and English and concluded a second grader waxing eloquent about a highball was not grammatical. It was fine for other children to have parents who exposed them to all manner of worldly indulgences. Not for us. For example, going to movies that were Morally Objectionable in Part for All according to the Catholic Legion of Decency. My two older brothers and I only saw the Morally Unobjectionable for All movies. We went as a family to see *Ben Hur*, which was considered an acceptably Catholic movie. Even so, in the leper colony scene, Mom put her hands over my eyes to spare me the sight of what she deemed the morally objectionable part in an otherwise morally unobjectionable movie. She didn't shield me from the glistening naked male torsos in some other scenes, which interested me most, though at the time I did not know why.

Was whisky, i.e., a highball, Morally Objectionable in Part for All? Besides its vile taste, was it a corrupting influence? It seemed so according to Mom. Not so for Dad. Why then did we have such a good time drinking highballs?

Communication from on high was convoluted in the late 1950s. A nun revealed a message to Mom, and Mom, playing the prophet of old, delivered the news to us. I was afraid to raise my hand in first grade when I had to go to the lavatory, which resulted in the inevitable puddle around my feet. Sister had a talk with Mom, who had a talk with me. I learned to excuse myself. In regard to Mom's hypervigilance regarding Sister misinterpreting my disquisition about the glories of the highball, it is possible she relaxed her position on the issue after Dad's "Oh for God's sake." It is also possible she made the visit, had her say, and, taking a lesson from the Virgin Mary, held Sister's response close to her heart.

My encomium never came back to me. Besides the few sentences already quoted, I remember little more of my ode to the highball. Did I even ask Sister to return it? If the paper was returned, and in Mom and Dad's possession, it would have been inserted into the pages of the family Bible, the repository for all precious mementoes—holy cards and juvenile poetry—most likely in the book of Ecclesiastes. I have flicked through the pages and did not find it. No. I'm sure my paper was never returned. If Mom had visited Sister, one would think she'd have come home with paper in hand.

To make up for the loss of the paper, we invented a fiction, a sort of mythos explaining its absence. Mom came up with the idea (which makes me think she knew more than she ever let on). She no longer showed anxiety or embarrassment over anyone misunderstanding a child calling his nonalcoholic drink a highball. At least not discernably. The fiction was repeated and embellished at family get-togethers; and told to strangers as an example of how witty, clever, and perspicacious I was as a second grader. Eventually, without question, the fiction became fact. Here is how the story went:

Sister never returned the paper. It was passed on for the amusement and edification of all Sisters of St. Joseph near and far as a balm after reading the tedious, run-of-the-mill writing from tedious, run-of-the-mill students. Somewhere, in a convent, it is still trotted out, like a relic of some forgotten saint with an unpronounceable name, and venerated annually.

One day, also in second grade, the day after Dad conducted a concert, I asked Mom if I could wear the white carnation he'd worn. The stem was wrapped in green florist's tape, pierced with a pearl head straight pin. The flower was elegant, and wasted, stored in the fridge, between the milk and eggs. It was waiting for me.

Mom was skeptical. "To school? You want to wear it to school?"

I insisted, "Of course." I had become bolder. I raised my hand to be excused when the bladder was full, wrote about highballs, and now was ready to wear a carnation to school.

Mom looked at me with a look that looked beyond me. A look I recalled years later when I heard Ophelia say, Lord, we know what we are, but we know not what we will become.

After a Solomon silence Mom offered her imprimatur. "I don't see why not. The concert's over. Your father doesn't need it."

Mom's sense for composition and definition kicked in. "You should wear your suit jacket. A boutonniere needs a lapel."

Said lapel was attached to a charcoal grey wool jacket, nubby with flecks of white (no doubt a hand-me-down from one of my brothers). It came out of the closet and was accessorized with the flower. My boutonniere. French. A song in one word.

I marched into the classroom.

Normally the school uniform (grey slacks, yellow oxford button down shirt, and a purple clip-on tie) was worn jacketless.

Sister Marciana asked, "What's the occasion?"

I answered, "Beauty is its own excuse for being," which was something Mom often said. Sister gave me a noncommittal "Oh." She was not the first person, nor would be the last, including myself, who didn't know what to make of me. Whether or not my classmates knew what to make of me is lost to my recollection. Did it even matter? This was something I did for myself and the carnation. Was I conscious of a desire to be different? To show off? Possibly. More probable was a desire to emulate Dad. If I could have worn his white tuxedo jacket, pleated shirt with the onyx studs and cufflinks, bow tie, and black slacks with the satin stripes on the sides, I would have, most assuredly.

Once, though, when I was in fourth grade, my sartorial tastes made an impression, which has stayed with me. For Halloween, I wore an eighteenth-century suit our next-door neighbor gave me. She'd made it years before for a Girl Scout pageant. Just my size too. The character was George Washington. Satin jacket with deep cuffs amply trimmed with lace. Gold vest and breeches. A lace jabot. Even a powdered wig, made from the batting used for quilts. I thought this was my element and proudly joined the neighborhood troupe of ghouls, ghosts, vampires, and cowboys.

Mr. O'Neill, who was a history teacher, opened his door. I said, "Trick or Treat." He asked, "Who are you supposed to be?" I said, "George Washington," thinking, he of all people should know, and maybe he'd offer some tidbit of information about the great man.

He said, "You look more like Martha." Stung by the comment—somehow, being identified as a girl was Morally Objectionable in Part for All—I accepted my candy, returned home immediately, and changed. Mom noticed my bag wasn't as full of sweets as it usually was. I just said I had enough. A year later the outfit still fit me. I wore it for a Halloween party in the school gymnasium. I jettisoned the powdered wig, wore a hat with an enormous ostrich plume I'd gotten at the state fair, made a cardboard cutlass, covered it in aluminum foil, and called myself a pirate. Adaptability (some might say avoidance, others might say survival technique) was fundamental to my character. I won the prize for most original costume.

The sequence of happenings thus far related leads to a space where the real and the unreal meet. When I reached the age of eleven, in fifth grade, I arrived at the destination (by no means the journey's end; more like a motel with a swimming pool on a very long trip). For certain a multitude of occurrences crowded my life between grades two and five. In addition to the George-Martha-Pirate metamorphosis, only one thing stands out.

In fourth grade, under the rule of Sister Wilmette, who was more of a favorite aunt than a nun, I was one of a select group drafted to become altar boys. I learned the Latin responses, wore a costume, the cassock and surplice, and participated in what was, to me, the greatest show on earth. The mysterious and beautiful mass. I genuflected, lit candles, filled the cruets with water and wine, offered the linen towel to the priest during the Lavabo, rang the bells, carried the gilt-edged book on its gold filigreed stand from one side of the altar to the other; all duties I performed with reverence and precision, the way Dad made a highball. I played my part.

I realize now, these experiences in my strange, eventful history—drinking highballs, finding beauty in the crinkling bloom of a flower, and in the charioteer's pectorals, relishing the feel of lace at wrists and neck, offering myself to the otherworldly order of the Mass—primed me for the experience of experiences.

Dad took me to the opera. Gounod's *Faust*. Fortunately, the Legion of Decency had nothing to say about stage productions. This was in a metropolis of wide streets and towering buildings, about an hour's drive from our hometown. A biblical center of civilization. Nineveh or Tyre. The theater was decorated in a combination of *The Arabian Nights* and *The Tomb of Ligeia*.

I recommend *Faust* as a first opera for all fifth graders. It has magic, horror, a Walpurgis Nacht ballet, great tunes, and a sword fight. Angst, pain, suffering, and glory. Plus it has a devil. Mephistopheles. The name goes on forever. It conjures the darkness of an eternal night.

The devil appeared in a puff of smoke. Naturally he was a hero and the most interesting person on stage to a kid who was crazy for Vincent Price, Edgar Allan Poe, Roger Corman movies, *Famous Monsters* magazine, Boris Karloff, and mad magicians. The devil sported a red cape. A three-foot feather sprouted from his hat. A vestige of the wings he wore in another guise. When he sang, he owned the secret of all sound.

In the last scene of the opera, Marguerite, the woman whom Faust had tempted into his den of iniquity (as my young mind conceived of fornication at the time) is in prison and condemned to death for killing her child. Faust and Mephistopheles swear they can save her and guarantee her freedom. She stands up to them and says, "So long boys." Mephistopheles gets Faust. Faust loses Marguerite, and Marguerite gets a second chance. It was good preparation for understanding the dynamics of high school dances.

Much later I appreciated Gounod's technical skills, how he achieved emotional effects through melody, harmony, and modulation. At the performance, I responded to the physical thrill of the music. I was cracked open. Turned inside out. Shaken. Smoothed. Plunged into sounds I'd never experienced. This was the new greatest show on earth.

Angels sang. An organ sounded the chords of redemption. The music pulsed and pounded. Marguerite climbed a stairway to eternity. A living version of the full color picture of the Assumption in our Bible.

Something else happened at this moment of complete absorption. I could see the stagehands under the stairway (we were in the front balcony on the extreme right). The men pumped away at machines that delivered the Heavenly clouds. The sounds of Whoosh Clink blended with the music as they worked. Young as I was, this happenstance, of seeing the effect and the mechanics behind it burned itself into my sensibility. For the first time I was aware of the balance point between the real and the unreal, between an illusion and its inventor. Beauty may be its own excuse for being. Beauty also needed a lot of help to get there.

Where does a young sophisticate celebrate after experiencing his first opera? At Lorenzos, the premiere restaurant in this city of marvels.

A poster in the lobby advertised an exotic dancer. Pussy Willow. Live Onstage. The hostess, whose blue eye shadow and green and yellow blouse reminded me of our parakeet, referred to Pussy Willow as a stripper. I had heard of strip poker, and had been told by Mom to "Only, ever take your clothes off in front of your mom or your doctor." The hostess advised Dad to reconsider. He laughed off her suggestion and said we'd be fine.

"You will, won't you, son?" he asked me on our way to a table. I assured him I would be. I was sophisticated. I only wished I had one of his boutonnieres to lend my suit jacket a touch of class.

Lorenzos was all arbors of white lattice twined with artificial grape vines. The ceiling mimicked an evening sky; dark blue with stars in an arrangement no astronomer ever mapped. The table settings featured cloth napkins, the kind we only used for Christmas, Easter, and Thanksgiving meals. A bow-tied waiter handed me a padded menu, big enough to do a somersault on. I ordered a highball and a hot dog for starters.

Dad was on his second drink. I was eating a slice of cherry pie à la mode. An announcer's voice introduced Pussy Willow. She appeared on a platform, illuminated by pink lights. A far cry from the opera's environs. Instead of an orchestra she had a piano and drums nearby. Miss Willow wore a skin-tight black outfit fastened with a multitude of zippers and a marabou feather boa for a tail.

Two velvet cat's ears nestled in her black hair. Her skin was pearly and pink. The feather boa took on a life of its own. I coveted her boa.

Pussy Willow pawed and slinked across the stage. The pianist pawed and slinked across the keyboard. The percussionist rat a tap tapped on snare and tom-tom and thumped on the bass with an occasional sizzle on the cymbals. Unlike the opera, there was no attempt to hide the inner workings from view, as with the stagehands under Marguerite's stairway to Heaven. I saw the act and the puppeteer behind the act at the same time. The stagehands were Miss Willow's hands. Zip by zipper she unzipped and revealed first an arm and then an ankle, then a shoulder, then a thigh. She was in charge. Dad gripped his glass and tapped in time with the music. He turned it round and round in his fingers, as if he was screwing it into the table. I chewed my cherry pie and forgot to swallow, so taken up was I with Pussy Willow's act.

Having shed about 90 percent of her skin, Miss Willow was down to a kind of two-piece bathing suit. I was aroused. Not in the way you might think. I was yet to discover the booklet *Modern Youth and Chastity* (placed by Mom, the following year, in my dresser drawer amid socks and underwear). Still in the future was the talk from the priest, Father Fuchs, about what to expect when strange things happened to the adolescent body. Even with all this information under my belt, when the transformation came, I learned that "physical sexual impulses are easily aroused and hard to manage" (to quote Gerald Kelly, S.J., the author of the aforementioned treatise on chastity). At the moment, I was a chubby short fellow, with a pomaded haircut, and unblemished skin with no idea of what the next few years held. To me Miss Willow was a silken gown come to life. She was something Barbara Steele wore in a Vincent Price movie. Or the vestment I draped over the priest's shoulders at Benediction. Beautiful and dazzling.

The music jazzed and swelled.

Dad put money down for the bill, emptied his glass in one gulp, grasped my hand, and said, "We're leaving."

I resisted. "I want to stay. She's not finished."

He pulled me through the room. In his stern conductor's voice he said, "Yes, she is. You're just a boy."

At some tables people shook their heads at us. A few smiled. I never found out what good taste and the law deemed as Morally Unobjectionable for All at Lorenzos. Dad plunged me into the pleasures of grand opera. He wasn't prepared to let me wade into the waters of Miss Willow's repertoire. I was just a boy.

The hostess retrieved our coats. She dispensed with the performance and chirped: "Oh it's like watching your brother undress."

What kind of brother did she have?

When we got into the blue dodge dart, Dad directed me: "Don't tell your mom."

I voiced an "Okay," since it was a command and demanded only one response. Assent.

On the drive home I did not speak. My senses were overloaded. The lights of the oncoming traffic were a cosmos of winking stars. We might have been flying. We might have been Faust and Mephistopheles. I was in the place where the real and the unreal meet. I was elated at what I'd seen at the opera and Lorenzos. I was also angry and confused about Dad's reaction to Pussy Willow and our abrupt exit. Was he embarrassed? Ashamed? The instruction "Don't tell your mom" veiled it all in something conspiratorial. Why was trying whisky in front of Mom okay, but Pussy Willow was forbidden knowledge? I was also giddy with the sense of secrecy. A pact between me and Dad. At the time, I was not capable of holding the conflicting aspects of my personality in balance. The spiritual, the worldly. The desires, the moral codes. Salvation, perdition. All these things I kept close to my heart.

In the driveway, Dad said, "What's the matter? Cat got your tongue?"

"No," I said. "Just thinking about the opera."

At the front door he reminded me, "Remember what I said."

Mom was half asleep on the sofa. Whenever anyone was out late, she always waited up, and prayed. Before she had time to stand, I bounced in next to her. We hugged and kissed. The rosary she held whipped around my neck. I extricated myself and described the *Faust* performance in what I'm sure was exhaustive detail. I had a penchant for recounting the plots of movies and books. Mom always listened dutifully.

"And after, we went to Lorenzos," I added.

She laughed her Hilda laugh.

"Did you? Quite the night out."

"I had a highball and a hotdog. And cherry pie."

Dad chuckled his approval and sat on the other side of Mom.

He said, "I think your son likes the theater."

She questioned me with her hazel eyes.

No question, I liked theater. I nodded and agreed.

I'm sure it was not the answer she was looking for, though she accepted it and smiled. I believe she was searching for something infinitely more complex. On one level, I was a sentence with one independent clause and a few dependent clauses for her to diagram. And possibly recast. On another, I was a paragraph. She was concerned about unity, coherence, and emphasis. I doubt I ever achieved these elements to her satisfaction. I do know I never told her about Pussy Willow. I kept my word to Dad. Mom and Dad have been dead for many years. Whether Dad ever told her, I do not know.

At the time, however, I had a hazy sense of being on the threshold of something, something operating around me and within me, beyond my control. What this was I'd discover much later. At the moment, I felt closer to Dad than I had ever been. Closer, it turned out than I ever would be again. And more distant from Mom than I had ever been. A distance that even when we were closest, increased with the years.

A Day for Dying

Morgan Smith

Well before dawn that July morning in 1988 a friend named David and I began the ascent of Colorado's Pyramid Peak, 14,025 feet in altitude. David and I had been classmates in law school at the University of Colorado and he had been the best man at my wedding in 1965. We had climbed together many times. But now he was struggling—marital problems, his floundering law practice, drinking. I wanted to reach out to him; I thought that reaching the summit of Pyramid would help, would give him a sense of accomplishment. I didn't know how to talk to friends who were struggling; my only solution was to organize some form of athletic activity like climbing a mountain or winning a hockey game.

This didn't always work. Two years earlier, I went to my thirtieth high school reunion and joined Dick, my best friend in high school, for an early morning hockey game where we alums played the varsity. He too was struggling. Alcohol. A job change that wasn't working out. His wife Faye hadn't fully recovered from a fall in their kitchen. I thought that helping him score goals and beat these kids would give him a lift, so I was able to set him up for five goals and we won easily. Even though that was more goals than he had ever scored in our high school days together, he committed suicide less than a year later.

Nonetheless, I knew no other way to reach out to David; taking him on this climb of Pyramid was all I could offer.

We zigzagged up a steep trail in the predawn darkness. David looked strong, maintaining a steady pace. We climbed in silence. I hoped that this shared struggle would open up something between us and that we could talk when we reached the summit or maybe on the descent.

The sun rose; it was a cloudless day with no hints of the usual afternoon thunderstorms. Soon we were in the shadowed maze of steep gullies that led to the summit. This was where climbers often got confused and disoriented but I had climbed Pyramid six times previously and knew the route. I had a 9-millimeter climbing rope in my pack and took it out when we reached a short, vertical rock wall. I could climb up the wall and then set up a belay for David. If he slipped, I could hold him with the rope. He waved me off, however, and scrambled up easily.

Then we heard a noise ahead. A shifting of the loose talus rock. Someone was above us. A man came into sight, wearing a heavy green parka despite the warming day. He was hunched over, panting and moving unusually slowly. To attempt this climb alone and at such a slow pace seemed very dangerous. When we reached him, I said something like, "You look like you're struggling. You might want to turn back because the hardest parts are ahead."

He muttered. I couldn't really understand him. It sounded like he said, "Fuck you." His head was bowed and his face was thick with whiskers. He looked like a bear, shuffling upward, grunting with exertion.

David and I continued past him, reached the summit at 11:45 a.m., drank Gatorade, and ate the sandwiches I had brought. There were other climbers there, including a man from Aurora, Colorado, who had left home at 1:45 a.m., driven some four hours to the base of the peak, and planned to drive back to Aurora after descending.

In fact, I had never seen so many on the summit. We talked about past climbs, ate our sandwiches and candy bars, took pictures, and watched parties of climbers on the North and South Maroon Bells to the west. What a pleasant time on a mountain that, after six ascents, seemed like nothing more than a long hike with little exposure.

We didn't see the bear man; I assumed that he had either turned back or was still ascending via different gullies. I believed that I had done all I could to warn him and felt no further obligation.

Then we began the descent. The first gully seemed steeper, more full of loose sand than it had on the ascent. At the wall above the second gully, I struggled for handholds. Everything seemed covered with little round stones, like ball bearings. As we neared the bottom of the gully, climbers above kicked loose a volley of stones.

I realized that the rock wall we had climbed up so easily actually curved around to the east until part of it was above a sheer face. We couldn't see this face on the ascent but now as I descended, it opened up to my right; I felt my body freezing up as I looked into this abyss. All my life I've tried to get over a fear of heights—becoming a paratrooper in the Army, for example— but it had never worked and now I felt a moment of paralysis.

Then I turned to see David lunging downward, paying no attention to my warnings, his face tight as if he had forgotten our moments of happiness on the summit and was now refocused on his internal issues. It was as if he wanted to fling himself down the mountain. I scrambled to the base of the rock wall, reached up, grabbed him and pulled him to me.

Finally, we were safely out of the gullies, below the main bulk of the mountain, and on the trail we zigzagged up in the early morning darkness. Maybe now we could talk. Then a young man came running down towards us, his arms flailing.

"A man has fallen," he shouted hysterically. Fallen so far, he said, that he couldn't even spot the body. That was how we learned of the death of Dr. Heinz Pagels. We began running down the mountain to find help.

A day later we were back in Denver and learned that this man, Heinz Pagels had taken such a tremendous fall that his body had been torn to pieces. We learned that he was a renown physicist, that he and his family had been coming to Aspen for a number of years, that he had climbed Pyramid seven times, once more than me. Was Pagels the bear-man? Should I have done more to turn him back?

Then years later Dr. Elaine Pagels, his widow and a professor of religion at Princeton University wrote a book entitled *Why Religion?* I bought it not for religious reasons but because she wrote of her husband's death that day. It was a day I've never forgotten, a day when I tried unsuccessfully to persuade this bear-man to turn back because he was moving too slowly and was in danger. For all these years—more than thirty—I wondered if the bear-man was Pagels and if I should have done more to persuade him to turn back.

From the book, I learned that Pagels gave his wife little information about what she referred to as his "hikes." I did the same with my wife for many years, not telling her that the "hike" I had told her about was really a climb that involved risk, that I needed that risk just as I believe Pagels did.

Seeing the photograph of a young, handsome, vigorous looking Pagels in *Why Religion?* I then knew for the first time that the man I spoke to—the bear-man—wasn't Pagels. It is an enormous relief. I also learned that Pagels fell on the east face of Pyramid, a different route from the one David, the bear man and I took.

Reading *Why Religion?* opened other doors, however. Dr. Pagels quotes from her husband's book, *The Cosmic Code*, where he wrote that he had often dreamt of falling. "Lately I dreamed I was clutching the face of a rock but it would not hold. Gravel gave way. I grasped for a shrub, but it pulled loose and in cold terror I fell into the abyss." Continuing, he added that "what I embody, the principle of life, cannot be destroyed. It is written into the cosmic code, the order of the universe. As I continued to fall into the dark void, embraced by the vault of the heavens, I sang to the beauty of the stars and made my peace with the darkness."

I admire his words, and I did fall once on the Bugaboo Spire in western Canada, but my only feeling was sheer terror.

As shaken as I was by his death that day, I wrote an article about it for a local newspaper and cited some basic lessons about climbing safety. One of which was "Don't solo." Yet a year later, I found myself soloing Pyramid.

I also wrote, "Watch your companions for signs of fatigue, sloppiness, illness."

Four years later, I was asked to take John, the son of a friend up South Maroon Peak, the mountain we had observed from the summit of Pyramid on July 23, 1988. It was to be his last ascent of Colorado's fifty-plus fourteen-thousand-foot peaks.

John was overweight and I should have made him turn back. By the time we reached the summit, he was so exhausted that he said he didn't have the strength to descend via the much longer but completely safe route down a ridge. Instead, he insisted on going back down the gully we had ascended, which was now highly dangerous because the morning sun had loosened the rocks that had been trapped in the snow and ice. I shouldn't have agreed. We soon got caught in rockfall. A boulder clipped my left ear, an inch away from decapitating me. I can still see it—round, speckled, the size of a basketball, seemingly suspended in space beyond me, then crashing down the gully. I thought of Pagels, more experienced on Pyramid than me, but he died whereas I had been spared one more time.

Pagels wrote of "pitting my body and my skills against nature" as if his climbs were a competition with nature. I disagree. To me, mountains like Pyramid and South Maroon are alive. When you climb them, you're not competing against them or nature; you're there as a guest, tolerated but only if you obey the rules. I failed to obey the rules by taking David up Pyramid, by leading John down that gully on South Maroon. The speckled boulder that clipped my ear has always seemed like a messenger telling me that this time I would be spared but warning me that I wouldn't have more chances.

Mountains are full of objective dangers—rock fall, lightning, storms. The real danger, however, is mental. It's that loss of focus. I lost it on both Pyramid and South Maroon. But if that speckled boulder on South Maroon had killed me, there would have been no time to "make my peace with the darkness," to quote Heinz Pagels. There would have been nothing but the kind of grief that Dr. Elaine Pagels felt and that my family would have felt.

From looking at his photograph in Elaine Pagels' book, I wish I had met Heinz Pagels. He was just two weeks younger than me, both of us six months short of fifty at the time of his death. The photo of him showed a vigor, enthusiasm, love of life. I wish I could have done a climb with him.

As for David, my wife and I visited him in Wyoming last spring, the first time I had seen him in years. We drove out to his small ranch, looked at his scattering of Hereford cattle, and talked, but he didn't remember Pyramid Peak. That distant climb hadn't tamed his drinking, and he was slipping into dementia. When I hugged him to say goodbye, I knew I would never see him again, but he did recognize me, did understand that I was still his friend, that I cared for him.

In retrospect, it's easy to say that July 23, 1988, was a day of unnecessary risk, but for some of us, risk is part of our lives. On Pyramid that day, all of us were at risk—David and me, Pagels, the bear-man. All of us made mistakes. It now seems like a day when someone was destined to die. Pagels was just the unlucky one.

A Marriage

Donald Wildman

By mistake we fell into the same bed,
and night after night we repeated
the mistake till nights were ordinary
and she turned her face aside.

How wrong is a man and a woman's embrace.
How ill the damp warmth in the night.
The smell of two bodies pressed together
is full of doubt.

What foolishness trying to make one life from two.
You might as easily make
one rock from two by bashing them
together again and again.

How much better to have stayed in my mountains,
where shadows slowly fill the afternoon,
where the cool moon rises over the darkening ridge
and a single light is on.

Sleep with two hips leaned surely together
is a passing thought in a changing mind.
You will find yourself one day alone
with flat land all around.

Towel Collector

Mario René Padilla

Nothing made young Carlos happier than finding a white towel abandoned in his gym's lost and found or discarded on the street near the many homeless camps that had recently sprung up in his neighborhood. He was a humanist, and he refused to believe a lost or deserted towel, except for the ones severely torn and despoiled, could not be cleaned, refreshed, revived and put back into service to fulfill the manufacturer's designed purpose for its existence.

He felt no guilt or shame for rescuing what didn't belong to him.

"After all," Carlos rationalized, "a careless owner left it, or worse, maybe purposely disowned the damned thing. Such a waste."

When he got the towel home, he felt the thrill—and the challenge—reviving the product.

Lining up the bottles on the sink, he said to himself, "The entire operation requires the step-by-step application of special soaps, bleach, fabric softener, and rinse." And throughout the process, he'd confirm to himself while applying the liquids, with great pride, his expert know-how. He'd remind himself, "It's what I was made for—that and the study of philosophy." The latter was a compulsion begun ten years before in high school with a presentation of Schopenhauer for his tenth-grade English class at St. Bernard.

Now, it so happens that, one Saturday late-afternoon, on his regular walk to the beach to watch the sun set into the ocean,

Carlos spotted a white towel hanging over the fence at the Public Self-Storage building on the corner of Rose and 3rd Street. The entire sidewalk had become a homeless camp, with pitched tents and loads of discarded trash. Every day, increasing numbers were moving in "like bees swarming about a bed of flowers," he'd muse. "Until police arrived like lawn mowers."

But this Saturday, the police had already arrived, moving the inhabitants rapidly from the pavement.

From a distance, he saw it—a white towel that seemed a prime candidate for redemption.

Now, Carlos didn't keep all of the white towels he found. If on closer inspection he found serious flaws at first unnoticeable—if it was hopelessly unredeemable—he'd leave the towel where it lay.

But if the towel "passed mustard" (one of his mother's favorite phrases), he would slip it into his satchel, which he always carried for just this purpose, and take it home where he could apply all his skills to bring the white fabric back, as near as possible, to its original condition.

After completing the cleansing operation, he'd step back and look upon his work, like a surgeon who'd just replaced a hip. Pleased, he'd fold the towel in perfect thirds—precisely—and add it to all the others stacked inside his mother's large French antique chestnut armoire. He liked to think of all the towels in his collection as family members of a sort, each one absorbing his mother's Chanel No. 5 still emanating from the wood, though he'd long removed Ethel's clothes and donated them to Goodwill.

Once shelved, the towel's name and identifying details were meticulously logged into a leather journal Carlos had bought just for this purpose because it had embossed angels. In fine calligraphy he'd write,

Golden Touch 100% Cotton Made in USA

Welspun 100% Cotton Made in India

Martha Stewart Collection 100% Cotton Made in India

Hilton Worldwide 100% Cotton Made in Turkey

and so on. His favorite towel even had a birthdate. Ironically, it was the one towel that had no brand name:

Anonymous 100% Cotton Made in Bangladesh 4/15/99

This was the special towel he used on his lavender epsom-salt-bath night before watching his weekly shipment of Netflix movies—a well-earned break from his studies of Schopenhauer and Kant. He liked to ponder where the towel had been throughout its sixteen years of life, the bodies it had touched as it now touched his—reminding him of the intimate contact and exchange possible between humans.

But this Saturday evening, as he lifted the towel from the fence, he heard, "Whatcha doin' with my towel, mister?" It was a female voice coming up from the sidewalk and around the corner—half-hidden by dense foliage.

"Oh," Carlos stammered. He looked down to see a girl leaning against the fence. The stench she sat in was overwhelming. "I'm sorry. I didn't think the towel belonged to anybody."

"I put it over there to dry. It's mine."

"I'm sorry," Carlos repeated, replacing the towel on the fence, more nicely folded than how he'd found it. "As I said, I thought the towel was abandoned."

"Yeah. You think because it's on the sidewalk, it must be garbage, right?" The girl seemed a teenager. Hard to tell, Carlos thought, considering her boldness, as well as the wear and tear on her dirty sunburned face. Her arms covered in tattoos. Her wrinkled lips chapped by the elements.

"No, I don't think that," he said. "I simply thought the towel didn't belong to anyone."

"Well, it does."

"I see that now. And again, I'm sorry."

"I mean, Jesus, what are you, the official street cleaner-upper of towels or something?"

Carlos turned away to continue his walk to the beach, thankful to get away from the stench.

"Say, mister," she called out, stopping him, "you got a couple of dollars you could spare? I haven't eaten today."

Now, Carlos was stumped. He gave a short moment's consideration. "Sorry, I don't," he said firmly and continued walking. In his head, he heard his father's voice reciting his favorite creed: "We immigrants come to U.S. to work—we never beg. We work hard all our lives. Don't forget that, mijo."

The girl shouted at Carlos as he sped up to flee the scene, "Yeah, go on, mister. You're just full a sorrys aren't ya. Yeah, just keep on walking. If you don't see it—it doesn't exist, right?"

Continuing his walk to the beach, the girl's last comment weighed heavy on Carlos. Her philosophical cleverness. Her critical and accurate observation of human habit didn't match his notion of the homeless as ignorant and uneducated. In truth, he felt much sympathy for the less fortunate, but whenever he thought to intervene, his father's voice inexorably weighed in. To make things worse, his favorite philosopher, Schopenhauer, would step in, dressed in his best high white collar and black coat and tails, and, keeping pace, deliver his philosophical case against charity.

"My boy, what are you thinking? It's not the business of one man to alter another man's chosen destiny." He'd stare at Carlos with his blue-green beady eyes, his shock of white unkempt hair flying out from the sides of his bald pate. That was enough for Carlos, reaffirming the wisdom in his refusal. He stepped up his pace not to be late for sunset.

Arriving at the beach (later than he liked), Carlos focused his attention on the shimmering red orb, already making its descent into the pink ocean. Subconsciously, however, he could not forget the girl's comment. It stayed with him as he watched from a bench as the sun disappeared. He was a heavy man, with small capacity for physical endurance. Invariably, his thoughts turned to his philosophical explications. "Life is just a sequence of choices. It's that young girl's choice to be homeless. She made her choice. As we all must."

Rising, self-satisfied in his assumptions, he saw an elderly Mexican man pass on the boardwalk selling the last of his paletas from a wheeled freezer-cart. Magnanimously, he bought a strawberry paleta, all the while thinking of one of his father's favorite lectures. "I had thirty-five years when I arrive at U.S., only myself, no one here ever help me. I work, mijo. Work hard. Mexicans not waste time, food, money. Nada."

His mother, Ethel, was of a different philosophy. His father regularly accused her of being a typical wasteful American: throwing out uneaten food not to her taste, buying overpriced clothes or gaudy jewelry she rarely wore. Even expensive Chanel no. 5 perfume, which she overused on their one-evening-a-week dinner out at Denny's. And the worst thing for Jesus, was her insistence on maintaining her classic, gas-guzzling 1961 blue Pontiac Bonneville convertible she'd inherited from her parents and refused to sell. As a show of affection, Carlos washed and waxed it every Saturday in preparation for their Sunday drive to the beach post-mass at St. Mark's.

Every Sunday, invariably, the family would head for the beach with a packed cooler of bologna sandwiches, bags of chips, and several RC Colas on ice in the trunk. Only Ethel drove the car—Jesús refused, and Carlos had no driver's license.

One of Ethel's great pastimes was suntanning. She'd sit in her special beach chair, eating chips, sipping RCs, and reading magazines in her one-piece aqua bathing suit that exposed her grossly obese legs, while Jesús, in khaki pants, white T-shirt, and a Dodgers baseball cap, combed the beach with his metal detector.

Carlos spent his time building elaborate sandcastles. But sometimes, he would agree to walk beside his father. When the detector beeped, they'd both drop to the sand and dig together. "Mijo, no money should be waste. Even a penny ees money you not have before, entiendes?"

More often than not, the contraption found scrap metal. But once they found a 14K gold plated pendent with the initial "L" spelled out in quartz crystals. Jesús gave it to Ethel on her birthday, telling her it stood for love.

But whenever he asked his son if he'd like to use the detector, Carlos refused.

"Bueno. Go build your castles," Jesús would say. "But someday I find gold watch, or a diamond ring maybe. There's treasure to be found in sand. De veras. If you work to find it."

Sunset over, making his way back toward Rose Avenue, Carlos considered whether the homeless girl would still be on the sidewalk where he left her. He thought of going another way, so as not to be disturbed again by the young lady "sin casa, sin comer, sin Díos," as his father would say.

Approaching Rose via the Boardwalk, he passed the area of Venice Beach where he'd spent most of his childhood Sundays. His thoughts turned again to his parents, having long buried them both at Woodlawn Cemetery in Santa Monica. He thought it strange that his mother and father never slept together. Each night, they retired to separate bedrooms in their three-bedroom house, keeping mostly to themselves. He rarely heard them laugh together, nor speak at the dinner table. But then, he never heard them argue either.

He thought their coupling a strange agreement—a partnership for the business of cleaning clothes at Ethel's Dry Cleaners, a business she took over after her parents were killed in a bus accident on a gambling trip to Las Vegas. Heavy and unattractive, Ethel remained single after inheriting the house she grew up in. She inherited as well, the cleaners, the Bonneville, and a huge insurance settlement check. She worked the business alone for many years. But as she grew older, alone and exhausted, she finally posted a sign in the window seeking help. Jesús applied. She hired him on the spot.

But as can happen between two lonely humans thrown together, Ethel got pregnant. By traditional standards, at forty-four, she was too old to have a child. But she was a strict Catholic. And though Jesús looked older, their courthouse marriage certificate indicated he was thirty-nine.

Doctors warned there might be complications for the child.

Still, even with their premature deaths, Carlos regarded himself a lucky person. He had a mortgage-free home to return to, financial security from his mother's insurance and savings. And he had philosophy. Granted, none of those choices were his own. Everything in his life was inherited—even his philosophic study of Schopenhauer was a serendipitous event.

He'd gone into his high school's library. "I need a book by a famous philosopher to give a presentation," he told the librarian.

The woman behind the desk looked up with a critical eye. Lowering her glasses hooked to a bead chain she said, "For Ms. Bartlett's tenth-grade English class, right?"

"Yes."

"Well, unfortunately, you've come too late. All the best philosophers have been picked over already." She got up. "Follow me." She led him to a bookshelf. "Schopenhauer's all we got left," pulling out *The World as Will and Idea*. "Pretty tough reading though. He's very dark and horribly pessimistic. I don't think the man had a happy bone in his body."

"Guess it's him then," Carlos said with a sigh.

She would never know how much that book would change Carlos's life.

When Carlos reached the intersection of Rose and Main, he realized from his musings that his happiest times were his teenage years working in the dry cleaners. He hated sports and belonged to no social clubs or afterschool activities.

During high school, Carlos had one good friend. Khalib. He was an Egyptian boy who transferred to his high school at the beginning of eleventh grade. He had a mild case of cerebral palsy and was slightly cross-eyed. One particular episode cemented their friendship. After gym class, which for Carlos was one long series of insults, several boys had taken his clothes, shoes, and white towel while he was in the shower and threw them outside the locker room. Khalib, who couldn't participate in gym, was outside when it happened. Seeing the boys toss the clothes, he picked them up off the ground and limped into the locker room. Carlos was sitting on a bench, shivering. "You looking for these?" he said, holding up a blue polo shirt, khaki pants, and his soiled towel.

"Where were they?"

"Brady and some others threw them outside. You should tell Mr. Dornan."

"Why? Then they'd never leave me alone," he said, putting on his clothes. "No, there isn't any trouble that an hour's reading can't assuage." He was quoting Schopenhauer already.

Together, they hurried off to class: Carlos, lumbering with his chubby legs, Khalib, limping alongside his new friend.

But what Carlos enjoyed most after school was going to help out at the cleaners. He loved seeing how clothes became clean. Learning how to de-stain shirts and pants that came in soiled. After treatment, he'd wash, dry and fold the garments like his father taught him, then hand them to his mother smelling fresh and clean to give to customers. That's how he remembers his family—working together in the laundry—and after his parents passed, they both remained with him through the scent of bleach and soap, and, of course, his mother through Channel No. 5.

And even though Carlos had the highest GPA of his graduating class, he was not chosen valedictorian. "Way too arrogant," a faculty member on the panel declared. "It's Schopenhauer this and Kant that, with Epictetus and Spinoza thrown in. He even tries explaining to me their philosophy."

Actually, those who voted against Carlos didn't believe a Mexican boy could be so smart.

To no one's surprise, he was accepted as a philosophy major to every university he'd sent an application: Berkeley, Stanford, Columbia. Each offered him hefty minority student scholarships. But in the end, he chose Loyola Marymount in LA, not for their excellent philosophy department and Jesuit education, but because he wanted to stay close to home, most especially, close to the Pacific Ocean, which was as much home for him as the grass in his front yard.

At LMU, he focused his studies on Schopenhauer and Kant, investigating their oppositional theories regarding fate, or God.

"Call it what you will," Schopenhauer quipped one night, breaking Carlos's concentration. "Whatever the name, it's that which is formless and always noncommunicative, the maker who appears indifferent to his product—leaving us poor humans to fend for ourselves—to act as we must according to some fated individual nature (regardless of the nurture)."

He began comparing Schopenhauer's thoughts to Kant's, who was diametrically opposed in their vigorous debate. "It's God, my son," Kant would rebut. "You best believe that. Don't listen to that depressing, pessimistic fool. God is the author and moral ruler of the world; holy, just, omniscient and omnipotent. Count on that."

As fate dictated, Jesús died of prostate cancer at the end of Carlos's junior year at LMU. The young man's reaction was severe. He didn't return to finish his degree. He retreated into his home with his mother, having decided to carry on his philosophical studies on his own.

Ethel at sixty-five retired and sold the cleaners. Their reclusive habits functioned harmoniously. They festered together. No friends. No family. They stopped going to mass, and to the beach. They carried on in seclusion until Ethel died of a stroke as the two were watching *Princess Bride*—a bowl of popcorn balanced on her lap. She regularly fell asleep in the middle of their movies, so Carlos had no idea she had died until after the credits.

He buried Ethel next to Jesús. And standing over their grave sites at the cemetery, he realized, "They're lying closer in death than they did in life. No, I never want to get married," he'd reaffirm. "After all, Schopenhauer never married," he took comfort in the thought.

"That's right, my boy," Schopenhauer would whisper into his ear. "A solitary life is best for a philosopher."

Reaching Rose and 2nd, Carlos could see in the distance the girl still sitting in the same spot at 3rd Street. Seeing this, Schopenhauer poked him in the arm and said, "You see her there? Look at her, my boy. You know, as children, we are like lambs in a field, disporting ourselves under the eye of the butcher, who chooses out first one and then another for his prey. So it is that in our good days we are all unconscious of the evil Fate may have presently in store for us."

With this, Carlos chose to cross the street and walk on the other side farthest from her location.

Schopenhauer, keeping pace, added most approvingly, "Yes, that's the idea. Let her be. It's not your business to interfere in another's destiny. It's where she's chosen to be. You understand that now, don't you?"

"Yes," Carlos half-heartedly agreed. "What business is it of mine to interfere in her life. The sidewalk is littered with lots of people who've made this choice, lying in tents, surrounded by garbage. The debris of homeless humanity all up and down the street." This last phrase he gave voice to, so loud that he looked about him to see if anyone beside Schopenhauer had overheard.

Carlos shivered. It had begun to turn cold, and hastening up Rose Avenue, face down to avert any intrusion, he saw a field mouse skitter out of the ivy and pass near his feet. It disappeared into the gutter. Something about the sight disturbed Carlos. This rodent scrounging through the streets to survive—to find something to eat.

Carlos could not rationalize what he next did. Almost unconsciously, he turned back toward 2nd St. and entered the Rose Café. He felt awkward in doing so, for he'd never been inside the popular eatery—though he'd passed it almost every day.

Schopenhauer followed him in right on his heels, whispering into his ear, "My boy, what are you doing? You're making a mistake." But Kant showed up behind the counter to rebut: "Son, never second-guess the instinct to be generous. That's all I have to say."

For Carlos—something stronger than himself was at play. He ordered a takeout meal that he would never have ordered for himself: Mediterranean chicken with a Dijon sauce, quinoa, steamed vegetables, and a berry cream tart for dessert.

While waiting for the meal to arrive, he couldn't stop imagining how the girl might look if she were clean.

He walked the meal to 3rd and Rose. Approaching, she looked up at Carlos as he handed her the bag. "Here," he said, "I brought you something to eat."

She didn't hesitate to reach up and grab the bag. "Thanks, mister."

She lifted out the container, opened it, and began to eat with her fingers, ignoring the restaurant's plastic utensils.

Carlos whiffed the strong odor of pee and vomit she was sitting in. She had pulled her dirty blonde hair away from her mouth exposing a large bruise on her cheek. He saw in more detail the tattoos on her arms. The left arm was covered with an elaborate angel, the right, a large black and red devil. Her inner elbows had Band-Aids.

Becoming uncomfortable with her voracious eating sounds, Carlos began to back away.

"Hey, mister," she called out. Carlos stopped. "You can have that towel if you want it," she said as she chewed. "It ain't mine anyways. The guy who slept here last night left it. Tried getting fresh, the little punk. Left quick when he saw who he was dealing with," and she showed him a large hunting knife with a wooden handle lying near her hip.

She continued eating greedily, making slurping sounds. But what disturbed Carlos most was the knife. Is that what happens to humans surviving on the street, he wondered? Was she sending some kind of street warning?

Still, as she ate, he couldn't help seeing—beyond the knife, the tattoos, the hoarse voice, the sunburnt and bruised face, the vomit smell, the dirty hair and soiled clothes—a frightened kid sitting on a piece of pavement, hungry, cold, alone. And again, he imagined her clean—just an innocent child looking through the window, waiting for Santa Claus to arrive. This image often occurred to him whenever he passed a young homeless person scrounging through barrels or passed out on the sidewalk.

"No, that's okay," Carlos answered. "But . . . if you don't mind me asking, why are you out here, sleeping on the sidewalk?"

He thought he heard, "Left home," or maybe "hated home."

"But why?" His philosophic nature forced him to inquire.

She looked up at him with cautious, probing eyes. "Well, mister, if you really want to know, I wasn't what they wanted. And they didn't like what they got; someone they couldn't control. So, they told me to get out. I just walked out to the highway and hitch-hiked to LA, that's what I did. Heard it was the best place to live. And I always wanted to see the ocean."

Her last reason touched Carlos. "Do you mind me asking how old you are?"

She stopped eating and looked up at him. She could tell by his heavy build, he was definitely not a cop. But her street survival instincts were already honed. "Eighteen."

With her face opening up in conversation, Carlos could see she was lying. He saw traces of innocence in her face. He guessed her to be fifteen, sixteen tops.

She stood up, walked the carton to the trash bin on the corner. He liked that. "Thanks, mister."

"My name's Carlos. What's yours?"

Again, she looked at him, circumspect. Always deciding danger or advantage. "Lookin' for one actually. Didn't like the one they gave me. So, I dumped it. Got any suggestions?" she quipped.

Carlos smiled with a chuckle. "Not really."

"Yeah, well, this time, I'm going to pick one of those one-word names, like Cher, Madonna, or Lady Gaga. No more last names for me." And she smirked, "Brandi . . . more like branded. No different from one of my father's cattle. Nope. No one gets to own me anymore. That's what I told that guy last night before I walloped him."

As she walked back to her spot and sat down, Carlos, without considering whether it was wise or a stupid thing to do, said,

"Listen, I'm not like that guy who got fresh with you last night, so don't take this the wrong way."

"I know you ain't, mister. I can tell."

"I live eight blocks up Rose Ave. I own a house. I'm not a rapist or anything like that, which I know sounds like something a rapist would say, but I'm not. If you want, we can walk up to my house and you can take a shower, wash your hair, get cleaned up. I don't want anything from you. I'm just giving you a chance to get cleaned up."

Carlos waited. The girl never took her eyes off of him. He began to feel uncomfortable—unsure what he was doing. "I can even take your clothes and what you got in those bags and wash them. You can rest on my couch. Watch TV if you like, while they're in the machine. Getting clean and wearing clean clothes does something to a person. Who knows. Maybe tomorrow you'll feel like finding a job or go to a shelter, anything besides sleeping out on the street."

At the end of his proposition, she lowered her eyes. "I lied. That guy last night, he's sort of my boyfriend." She looked back at Carlos in earnest. "He said he's looking for a place for us to crash, and then he's coming back for me tomorrow. Only, I found out last night he's a lowlife criminal piece of shit. The mean kind you know. So, I gotta be here." She searched up and down Rose Avenue with nervous eyes. "You're close, huh?"

Carlos said, "Yes, only a few blocks away."

She grabbed her backpack and the two shopping bags next to her feet and stood up. "Alright."

Carlos left the towel hanging on the fence.

No-name emerged from the bathroom wrapped in Anonymous. Carlos looked up from the dining table, where he was reading Kant, and was amazed. She looked younger—definitely fifteen. Her hair glistened from the special shampoo and conditioner, and she was smiling for the first time since they met. He felt a sense of rapture. Knew he would debate Schopenhauer the next time he showed up. He was more with

Kant now, in his belief that one should never second-guess one's instinct for generosity.

On the table among his books, he'd placed one of his extra-large Loyola T-shirts. Pointing to it he said, "That should fit you like a dress while your clothes are drying."

She approached the table but didn't pick up the shirt. For the first time, she began acting like a teenager. "That really felt nice, Carlos. Hey, I really like your house. You own this?"

Carlos nodded. "Yes. I grew up in it. My parents left it to me."

"Oh. So, they're dead, huh?"

"Yes."

"I wish mine were." She re-tucked the towel around her small breasts. "I've never felt a towel so soft."

"That's because it's 100 percent cotton," he said with a sense of pride. "The best towels are made in India or Turkey, but that one was made special in Bangladesh. No doubt by underpaid laborers." He could never dismiss his father's opinions about hardworking immigrants everywhere slaving in sweat shops.

"Special, huh?" she said. "Wow, Carlos, you must be rich or something to afford a towel like this."

Carlos smiled. "No, not really. Where are you from?"

"Does it matter?" She'd reclaimed her wild look, the one she gave him out on the street. Although this time, the hard stare seemed out of place. Her deep brown eyes peered out from a clean cherub face with clean hair—her body wrapped in a freshly laundered towel.

"No, it doesn't."

After a beat she said, "What's that book you're reading?"

"It's a book of philosophy by Immanuel Kant."

"Oh. Is it any good? Like does it have a good story that makes you feel happy?"

"It's not a story kind of book. It's more a book on the way some people think about life. But if any book of philosophy made people happy, this one would. You might say the author sees more good and happiness in life than pain and misery." And he knew his dismissal of Schopenhauer would not pass without further conflict.

"Yeah? I like that. I should read him." She sat down on the table and picked up another book flipping through the pages as if she were looking for pictures. "I'm from Wyoming by the way. Outside Laramie. Just stuck my thumb out on 80 going west. It was easy, once I decided to go. But like they say on the street: easy leaving, but harder finding your way back."

"How long ago was that?"

She put the book down and thought a moment. "What is it now, April?

"May."

"About seven months."

"Aren't you a little young to be out on the streets, lost?"

"I ain't lost, mister." She stood up from the table. "Like I said, my boyfriend's coming back for me." Carlos noticed she'd gone back to calling him mister. And for a second, he felt frightened—maybe it was a mistake asking her here.

"Well, good. I'm glad. He'll find you clean."

No-name said nothing. She grabbed the LMU T-shirt and went back into the bathroom. When she emerged, she could have passed for a college student. She sat down on the couch, reached into her bag for her knife, and said, "That bath was really relaxing. I'm feelin' a bit sleepy, Carlos. Mind if I lay down and close my eyes a spell before I leave."

"Please do. Your clothes won't be ready for about another hour." And tucking her knife beneath her body, she turned onto her side. Within a minute she was asleep, looking like the child she was—everything short of sticking a thumb in her mouth.

As No-name slept, Carlos continued reading at the table.

As he expected, Schopenhauer showed up and began pacing the floor behind him. "You're making a mistake, my boy," he said. "You don't understand? Listen to me. When we're in our youth contemplating our coming life, we are like restless children in a theater, waiting for the curtain to rise, sitting there in high spirits, eagerly waiting for the play to begin. But it's a blessing we don't know what is really going to happen. Could we foresee it, we'd feel more like innocent prisoners, condemned, not to death, but to life."

Carlos closed *Studies in Pessimism* and got up. He was in no mood to debate such darkness tonight, not now, not with all the joy he was feeling in his heart, with the new feelings he was just now beginning to feel. He went to his room (which used to be his mother's) to get a throw blanket for No-name. Stopping before the armoire, he opened the doors and touched several of the towels in his stacked collection. Ethel's Chanel scent was strong and imposing. He wondered what his mother would think of him bringing a dirty homeless girl into the house. He picked up his journal from the shelf and carried it, with the blanket, into the living room. He covered No-name, gently, so as not to disturb her. She turned restlessly on to her other side uncovering the knife. Despite the weapon, Carlos could see how all that toughness in her had disappeared from her clean innocent face deep in the bosom of sleep.

Back at the dining table, Carlos opened his journal and began a new page after the section listing his towels. He wrote—No-name, white, Wyoming, U.S.A.

He looked over at her cleanliness and he was pleased.

No-name slept until the early hours of morning. Carlos had fallen asleep reading at the table, feeling it best to maintain a vigil.

When he heard her stirring, saw her open her eyes, he said, "Good morning."

She appeared a bit startled, sat up abruptly, and felt for her knife.

Seeing Carlos sitting at the table, she said, "Oh, yeah. Good mornin'."

"You really needed that sleep," he said, smiling. "There's cereal and a bowl on the kitchen counter. Help yourself."

"Thanks, mister. I haven't slept like that in a long time."

"Carlos. Remember?"

"Look, Carlos, I'm not feeling so good. I can't eat right now. I need to go and get something."

Carlos wasn't sure what she meant. "Look, I was thinking while you were sleeping, that, if you want, you could stay here for a few more days while you make some decisions. I mean, getting rid of the dirt feels pretty good, doesn't it?"

She immediately lay back down.

No-name spent six days with Carlos. The first three days, she lay mostly sick on the couch, moaning. She slept on and off. Took numerous hot baths (always using Anonymous). Shivered. Perspired. Moaned, Shivered some more. Drank tons of water. Finally, she began eating whatever Carlos made for her, who let her alone to fight through her unknown malady, for he knew nothing of what she was dealing with. On the fourth day, she felt good enough to watch a few of Carlos's movies. Her favorite was *Princess Bride*. She laughed at "My name is Inigo Montoya. You killed my father. Prepare to die." She asked him to play it again and again. Carlos felt pleased.

At night, as No-name slept, Carlos returned to his studies, but now with a different perspective.

Schopenhauer, with a scowl, showed up dressed in his usual black dress coat and high white collar. "It's a mistake, my boy, don't you understand? To think people can be happy in this world. Happiness is no more than a transient illusion. Everything about life proclaims that earthly happiness is destined to be frustrated. Life is not about attaining happiness. The aim should be simply how to sustain a bearable life."

But then Kant showed up to weigh in. "Arthur, you're wrong. With all due respect, suffering isn't the direct and immediate object of life. It is attaining happiness through simple acts of charity and goodness."

"I think I agree," Carlos interjected, which really pissed Schopenhauer off.

"Precisely, Arthur," Kant added, wearing his most spiffy and colorful waistcoat. "All humans should have the right to common dignity and respect. We should never treat others merely as a means to an end, to be used for personal gain, but as ends in themselves. Most people have good intentions in their affairs with others as long as morality forms the basis of their interactions."

"Well, aren't you two just two peas in the same pod," Schopenhauer said. "I'm sorry if you think my view of life as being comfortless is without basis in obvious evidential fact. I'm only speaking the truth about the society all about us, even though most people have been brainwashed by religion to be assured everything the Lord has made is good. Especially those who like building castles in the air." And he looked directly at Carlos.

"Well, I agree with Mr. Kant." Carlos reaffirmed. "If you expect good from people that's what you will get. If you expect they are out to harm you, well then, that's just what you'll get."

"Yes, young man, well said," Kant interposed. "Although I didn't say that. But I do have faith in humans and their capacity for reason. Most humans act in accordance with the rules they hold for themselves, and for everyone."

"Poppycock! Immanuel, you're a fool. As I now see you are too, my boy, and I wash my hands of you. People are dumb, selfish, out to harm you, and, therefore, should never be trusted. Putting yourself in the company of others is dangerous. One has to constantly be careful and cunning to avoid being hurt. I fear the day you finally discover this to be true."

Carlos saw No-name stir in her sleep and closed Kant, shutting both his mentors up. When No-name sat up, they watched *My Fair Lady* for the third time.

On the sixth day, Carlos asked if she'd like to take a walk with him to Venice Beach. She refused. Carlos thought she might fear her boyfriend was looking for her along Rose Avenue. He himself had not taken his regular walk to see the sunset since he brought her to the house, and he was missing the ocean.

Abruptly, No-name announced, "I decided I'm going to return to Wyoming, give home another try."

Carlos felt a strange stab of pain, similar to the one he felt when Khalib's family moved to Portland during his senior year. He hadn't had a close friend since—that is, until No-name arrived. But he wanted to help somehow. "I'm glad. At least you'll be home, protected, and safe."

No-name remained silent on the couch.

But he didn't want her to hitchhike. Carlos called Greyhound and found out the price of a ticket. He grabbed one of his mother's carry-on suitcases out of the garage and placed No-name's cleaned clothes inside, along with Anonymous—folded precisely in thirds. He felt good that his generosity had a little something to do with that. Yes, No-name from Wyoming was one of the redeemable ones.

Just as she was about to leave, Carlos went into his bedroom and returned with some cash—he never used credit cards. Carlos gave her the money for a ticket, adding more than he should for some food, saying, "I don't drive, or I'd take you to the station myself."

"No. That's okay. Got some things I need to do before I go. I can get a Lyft."

"If by chance, someday, you return to LA . . . well, you know where I live. You can come by anytime."

She looked down for a moment, then, back into his eyes. "Nope. I ain't never comin' back here, Carlos. You can count on that."

They didn't shake hands or hug. Nothing. She simply thanked him for the suitcase, everything inside clean and professionally folded, and walked out the front door.

As she reached the sidewalk, on impulse, Carlos raced into the front yard, and shouted, "Hey, I could call you a cab?"

"No. I'm fine," she said without stopping, briskly walking on. She never looked back.

Carlos watched her arrive at Lincoln Boulevard. But instead of heading north toward the station, she crossed the street and continued walking toward the beach—toward 3rd Street.

A deep sigh blew through the hole in his heart.

Nevertheless, a permanent change had been made in Carlos. From that day forward, he felt the joy of a new purpose. He was determined now to continue searching, every day, to find the redeemable ones, and perhaps alter destinies. Initially, he began by giving a few dollars, then five. After a time, he raised it to ten, the amount always rising. And like a missionary, he regularly bought meals at the Rose Café to distribute to the homeless sleeping on the sidewalks around the Public Storage facility—always keeping an eye out for No-name.

Kant was now Carlos's constant companion. They shared the "giving back" philosophy, and, as such, Schopenhauer no longer showed up for discussions. The last time he showed, they'd gotten into a heated argument over the philosopher's belief that the object of life, regardless of one's generosity, is pain and suffering. "I just hope I'm around when you learn your lesson, my boy," Schopenhauer concluded, before disappearing for good.

Three months later, Carlos was found stabbed several times in his home. Searching the house after the homicide, detectives found a metal box in his bedroom that had been broken open. They discovered, as well, in an antique armoire a collection of white towels. They were puzzled by the detailed record Carlos kept in his journal of their existence. One detective noted a towel marked Anonymous was missing. What was even more curious to the detectives was the record he kept on the following pages, names of friends, as detectives first assumed they were. But after a thorough investigation, they discovered that most on the list could not be tracked to a specific address—that many were false names and were homeless.

They found no sign of forced entry. Then, a few days later, Anonymous was found lying next to a dumpster on 3rd and Rose with Carlos's blood on it.

That's the Schopenhauer ending.

As Kant told it, Carlos died at the age of fifty-seven from the same prostate cancer that killed his father. A story appeared on the front page of the *Free Venice Beachhead* announcing the date of the service at St. Mark's. It sung the praises of a man everyone knew only as Big Carlos (no last name needed), beloved throughout the Venice community. The article told how, over a period of thirty-some years, Carlos befriended hundreds of homeless, made them clean, gave them food, even shelter when needed, while never asking for anything in return.

Throughout the Venice homeless population, Carlos was spoken of as a saint, and his reputation continued over several generations. Whenever this very large man was spotted walking down Rose Avenue toward the ocean, in his later years with a cane, the young homeless learned from the veterans that they could count on him for a few dollars or something to eat.

On the day of Carlos's memorial service, St. Mark's church was filled to capacity—Carlos, it seemed, had many friends—though no blood relatives were in attendance. One local woman stepped forward and handled all the cost: the flowers, the food, the church service, though she wished to remain anonymous. She cited Kant as her reason, how all acts of generosity should be "an act of duty, not of benevolence—lest the flattered heart swell with generosity making benevolence the sole rule of his conduct."

She was a striking woman, but with a face that showed life's struggles. Her husband sat with her and their two teenage children during the service.

Outside, she took off her jacket and rolled up her sleeves to supervise the serving of meals to the homeless, who all commented on the tattoos on her arms—one was of a black and red devil. The other, an angel.

Borders

Ellen Francese

You know—

It is not the surge
of brine and breath of
lace-shawled waves
that shuts your heart
Nor is it the way
the water pulls and releases,
the hidden undertow,
a hand around the throat
Your bare feet repel the
infinite stretch of soft, hot sand,
panicked by the cloying grains

Daddy

I can only guess—

The photographs from World War II
scatter on your oceanic bedspread,
the one Mommy had chosen with care
You climbing a coconut tree
smiling like a naughty, victorious child
Brown faces of dark-eyed women
unafraid of the camera

And your stories of how
you shared your meals with children
and braved the Japanese sweep of Manila
to find a lost Filipina friend
I ask you then if you once killed.
My words hang heavily,
a worn, weighted curtain
dividing you from me
Silence follows us
mutely revealing your
reluctance to visit the beach,
your refusal to speak
Your tension wraps 'round us like a rope
I have no knife to cut us free

You feel the disappointment
in Mommy's gaze,
fragile, hardening to stone
The ocean is a part of her,
her first love
Yes, you try to walk
hand in hand,
feeling the heartbeat of
something larger,
something that
enfolds all hearts.

But to utter the truth will taint
her cherished paradise
You an invisible martyr
lashed by her displeasure,
Your secret sacrifice
not enough
instead

her words punish you,
build a cold loneliness
in our house as we each
live behind closed doors,
hide our love,
and anger, too,
grip our secrets tightly,
at times the house's unbearable silence
punctuated by your fist
punching walls,
your hand
shattering glass

And your children, Daddy—

Only our voices lure you into the cold water,
feeling our hot skin and
watching our mouths open,
rounded in joy and wonder
How I cherish the heat of your flesh,
the tickle of your curling hair as
I press my face against your chest,
your arms enfolding me,
waves slapping against us,
voices and landscape disappearing
Until only we remain,
Here I am safe,
misreading your quickened heartbeat
as only
your love
for
me

A child's shriek
Gulls sharply slicing sky
Rogue waves fiercely rearing
The sickening suck of damp sand

And you are back—

Trudging through rough water
Your pack heavy upon you
Gunfire and flames
Seaweed and corpses
Crimson sea and sand
Your friend's cry
and fading light
eyes looking into yours
your hand holding his
as it stills, cools
And you breathing in
the rawness of blood
and the dying—both
uncleansed by
the stinging sea.

Never have you spoken of this
Your refusal the first words uttered
to your sister upon
your return home
A vow made to your
wounded heart
to forget and
begin
again

Until now

Here we sit
at opposite ends
of the long kitchen table,
your grandchildren nearby at play
You describe the magazine cover
in the doctor's waiting room,
the beach you have carried
for half a century
Waves of memory
rise and crest
Never have I seen you
cry until this moment
beneath the soft lamplight
Silent tears
No shame
in the surrendering
Together we enter
those seas
The truth telling
A kind of love
between you and me
Slowly, you reach
deep into your wallet,
pulling out a photograph.
A young Japanese woman
stares at me,
still waiting for
her lover, father, or brother
to return home from war
I listen and understand
my inheritance,
my own silent dedication to the
guardianship of your penitence
and hope

for
redemption

Perhaps we are now less alone
You in death
and I—
still often live the
then of my childhood
and your grief
borders blurring
into a
vastness
greater
than
sea
and
sky

This Morning

Joseph J. Ridgway

felt like
the cold was
coming directly
from the moon,

high and bright,
indifferently fixed
in the dark sky
of the early day.

Shivering while
retrieving my
morning newspaper,
I wondered.

One million
years from now,
what would the
headlines say?

Would we all
be ensconced
in heaven
or hell,

or maybe in
the "Limbo" of
my grade-school nuns'
ominous teachings?

What of our good deeds,
or
our horrific
ones?

Would there be
a cost
or
a reward?

Where would
the god(s) be,
if ever there
were any?

One more glance
at the sky,
my coffee is waiting,
among other things.

The Midnight Special

Hayden Park

I guess it started in the Thunderdome. The Atkins Elementary School had a dome-shaped monkey bar set, and our gang agreed to call it the Thunderdome after a movie only Jim had seen.

In fifth grade, the hour we had recess after lunch, was mostly spent talking to our friends. We sat in the Thunderdome, inside the bars, and talked, mostly about movies or TV shows we liked, or sometimes we became literary and discussed comic books.

Fridays, however, were a little different.

We still did the same thing, but Friday afternoons outside were the best, because it was like Christmas Eve every week, when the anticipation of the weekend became an unwrapped gift, sweeter than actually having it. Anticipation was intangible and it never disappointed. You never needed to wait to hold anticipation because it was already there.

That Friday afternoon, we discussed scary movies we liked. *Jurassic Park* worked. It had come out a few years before we were in fifth grade, but we still shared books on dinosaurs and agreed we should all have a healthy interest in cloning.

Jim finally stopped talking about how *The Lost World* was not as good as the first movie, and then Elliot spoke the words that started it all:

"Y'all want to hear about something really scary?"

We all said yes, because being scared was our favorite pastime. When you are ten years old, you still get scared by monsters, because you don't know that life will be much worse than ghouls and slimy things from a video cassette.

Jim cocked an eyebrow. "Yeah, what is it?"

"They call it the Midnight Special." Elliot had heard it from his dad, who had heard it when he was our age from another kid, just as these things go.

Turns out, the northern border of Atkins, Texas, was where the old railroad tracks that kept the produce and cattle moving in the east in Georgia all the way out to Southern California crossed on their way west. Sometime in the '40s, which I imagine had something to do with World War II, they outfitted the trains to take prisoners out west in the evening shifts. So, during the midnight hour, you might hear the train roll through and tap the outskirts of the town. And if you listened hard, you might hear the cries of lonely men being taken to prison, many of whom might be taken to the gas chambers really quick after that.

At least, that was the story, but I wasn't sure what it had to do with what came next. Fast-forward a couple dozen years and these particular tracks don't carry trains out west. Not with produce, not with cattle, not with men of any kind.

Now nothing crosses the tracks but green weeds, choking the lines and delivering the area back to Mother Nature as best as it can. The tracks remain, the wood cracked and looking like a ladder that was never set up right. Nothing goes down the line, at least not officially.

Some say, as all these stories tend to promise, that if you go out to the tracks around midnight and you look to the tunnel that feeds out the tracks, you'll see a train. It's blue, but it also isn't. You can see it, but you can also see right through it. The locomotive has a conductor just like you saw in the cartoons; he wears a big hat, and his skin is shrink-wrapped around the bones of his face. If he sees you watching, he points at you and opens his mouth, and there are bugs and light inside, begging to be freed. Then he laughs at you for as long as the train rolls by you.

The train is empty, just a long line of flat pallets with no cars on top except for one. Right in the middle of the length of the train, there's a storage car and the doors are wide open. You can see in. You can look right inside and what you'll see is the future, your future. Right there, in blue and nothing, is your future. And you'll know the rest of your life because the Midnight Special rolled through and looked right back at you. And you'll hear the laugh of the conductor the entire snaking length of the train and for the rest of your life.

"Maybe, but only one way to find out."

Christopher was eating a Payday, but when Elliot began the story, he had been eating a Kit-Kat. He kept his legs crisscross applesauce, and his knees didn't reach the end of his shorts, so he looked like nothing but ankles and shins. He shrunk. "You mean going there at midnight?"

Elliot nodded, grinning. "That's just what I mean. I say we go out there at midnight and see the train for ourselves."

"My dad won't take me," Christopher said. "He never lets us stay out past nine. Even when he and my mom go out, they always come back by night. He hates being out late."

Elliot tossed a stick of gum. "We're not going with our dads, dummy. We'll sneak out by ourselves."

"I don't want to sneak out! My dad will kill me. My mom might kill me too, which means I'll be double dead. You don't come back from that, Elliot."

"Don't be caught, then. Come on, do they check your room every night?"

We all shrugged.

Atkins was a homey sort of town. We were all pretty cozy in our southern suburb lives. All of us still had our parents. Most of us had siblings. We all thought we didn't lack for much, and we were still too young to go around feeling our oats.

"You guys suck. My dad snuck out to see it when he was our age. This could be so much fun. Come on." Elliot kept casting, but none of us were biting.

Elliot must have been ready to go against his parents' wishes, but in fifth grade, the rest of us weren't. No, we weren't sneaking out to see a ghost train.

The ironic part about the whole thing was that the ghost train wasn't what ended up scaring me.

It took a couple years, but we reached the end of middle school, and since it felt like we might never see each other again, Elliot convinced us we were ready. "It's now or never, guys. Let's go."

Recess and a playground had been replaced by bleacher seats in the gymnasium during lunch hour. Jim had hot pockets, which always grossed me out. Chris, who'd dropped the "topher" along with about fifty pounds, pawed at a salad. I was working on a cold turkey sandwich I'd brought from home while Elliot worked us over. He stood while the rest of us sat, moving his hands around like Nixon making his own case.

We waited for Friday. We met at the gas station and headed out of town around eleven at night. I told my parents I was headed to bed early, around ten. They believed me because most nights I spent in my room around eight to ten anyway, working on my short stories. I'd been sending them out and even received my first rejection letters. I was becoming a better writer and I enjoyed it, so I kept working even when nothing was being published. I just kept telling myself, this is just the way it is now. The rejection slips made me feel like I was in the game at a young age, so I never felt too bad about it. I carried a paperback in my back pocket as I did everywhere I went and still do. *Testament* by David Morel. Good book, but a downer.

Jim told us he'd left home around nine and told his parents he was going to stay with Chris. Jim ended up at Chris's house, dropped his bag in the bedroom upstairs, and they snuck out together down the pipe outside of the second story. My parents had gone to bed at ten so all I had to do was not make any noise headed out our front door. Elliot never talked about home much anymore since his stepdad moved in. So to hear that his parents weren't home and he went out the front door was the most we'd known about his home life in a couple of years.

We walked out to the edge of town and came to the tracks a half hour before midnight. Jim had a pocket full of Slim Jims. I liked those.

Chris had the first candy bar any of us had seen him with since the fifth grade. He said simply, "What? It's Friday. I like to treat myself."

We all thought that was a good idea. For some reason, it made us feel better about the whole thing.

I sat with Elliot over at a tree, a few feet from the tracks. The tracks only came around one corner on the northeast part of Atkins. A tunnel on the right that came through Rook Hill, spit out the tracks that curved around the border of Atkins and lasted for another half mile, before another tunnel took the tracks into Grover's Pass, near Silver Lake, and past the Carter County boundary.

We were all about halfway between the two tunnels, so the train would pass right by us, and give us plenty of time to see it coming and going.

The night sky looked like a satin sheet pulled taut, the stars bright like pinpricks in the fabric. The stars, like everywhere I guess, went dimmer as the years went by in the town. But out near the edge of Carter County, they've always been bright as that night. When I look at the stars now, I often think back to the night when we finally learned that we would grow old.

I talked to Elliot under the tree while Jim and Chris competed to see who could throw rocks the farthest. I still wasn't satisfied with his answers on why the midnight special was so important to him. Why, after years of moving from adolescence to our early teenage years, he never gave up hope to go see it.

He recited the same stuff he'd said at that lunch hour, but it didn't convince me so well. He never did give me an answer I liked, but I think I figured it out after he was gone.

Chris's digital timer went off at 11:50, enough time for us to be ready. They put down their rocks. Elliot and I stood up, myself knocking off the leaves still clinging to my 505 blue jeans.

We gathered around the center of the tracks, where it came closest to the town in the parabola between tunnels. We stood there and no one said a word. No one dared to.

Out of the corner of my eye, I saw Chris check his watch. "Five minutes late, boys."

"Not all trains run on time," Elliot said. He was looking down at the center of the tracks, not at either tunnel.

As if on cue, we felt it.

I remember the rumble in my toes, working its way through my shins and up to my shoulders, slowly, like resin creeping backwards into a tree.

The ground shook for a minute or more before I heard anything, but then I did, coming from my right. I still had doubts about the Midnight Special until I heard the faint sound of a train whistle.

Suddenly, the tunnel was so bright I would have believed it if you told me there was a bonfire inside. But it was blue.

The light poured out of the tunnel and the face of a large train appeared. It didn't look like a modern train, but like one I had seen in this movie, *The Train Robbers*, where John Wayne takes gold off a black locomotive for Ann Margaret.

This train was not black, but blue, but only where the outlines of the train would have been. The rest was there, but it also wasn't.

I couldn't quite see through the train, but I couldn't quite see the whole thing either. The wheels turned and it came right toward us.

I looked over at Jim and Chris, but they didn't see me. They just kept looking at the train.

I looked at Elliot and he looked back at me for just a second, and then we both turned our attention back to the train. By now it was within fifty yards of us, and I started to make out the conductor. Elliot had been right.

The conductor saw us watching him, and I swear he made eye contact only with me. But the rest of the guys would probably tell you the same thing. His hat was comically large, with vertical stripes of blue and nothing. His skin was pulled tight around his skull, as though another person was behind it and it grabbed the excess fat, pulling as hard as they could.

What I had not heard was that he would not have eyes, but just sunken caves where they should have been, with dark caverns where the pupils might be hiding. The caverns looked right at us if they could look.

And then the conductor pulled up his hand and pointed. He dropped back the top of his head, while his bottom jaw stayed stock still, and in his mouth lived the only genuine light around. I did not see bugs, but I heard the most terrifying laugh crawl out of his mouth like a man rising out of quicksand.

I still hear the laugh.

The conductor's car pulled past us, and we all stood watching it as it moved from our right to our left. Suddenly, we were looking at nothing as the empty flat cars moved into our view. I shook my head, tried without success to clear it, and looked to my right, seeing only the blue-and-nothing flats coming out of the tunnel. Then a new car came out and clambered down towards us, followed by nothing but more flat cars. At this point, I don't remember what I was thinking. I simply waited until the storage car pulled in front of me.

Once the open storage doors were directly in front of me, I lost all sense of the universe.

I was overtaken by a swarm of blue light and no longer stood on green grass covered by night. Instead, I was standing on a wooden panel floor, looking at a brown chestnut desk. On the bureau was a computer screen, where words were being typed. I could see them being typed: the end.

I panned my vision over to the left and a stack of thick hardcover books with my name along the spine in different vibrant colors, like a rainbow that only moved vertically.

To the right was a framed photograph of a man, a woman, and beautiful children. The man looked a little like my father, but that wasn't my mother, and none of those kids—three boys, two girls—were me.

I only had a glimpse at the room with the desk, with the books and with the photograph, but I desperately wanted to live there. Never having considered before what my future life might look like, I knew instantly that this was what I wanted. But as soon as the thought crossed my mind that I would never want to leave, I was sucked back into reality, or what passed for reality that night.

I was looking at the car headed to the left now, and the doors closed by themselves as it departed from view. The train kept rolling until it finally disappeared into the tunnel with a final flash of light and the final echoes of the conductor's laugh echoing off the walls of my head.

We stood for a while, no one saying anything. I kicked dirt in front of me, not because I wanted to, but because I felt compelled to do something.

Elliot was the first to speak. "Let's go home, guys."

We did.

I first learned Elliot passed away from Jim.

After middle school ended that summer, Jim and I stayed at Atkins High School. Chris was taken out to go to a school his parents had hoped might end with a football scholarship, and it did.

Elliot's stepdad moved them away when he lost his job at the aluminum chair factory. We lost touch, the way old friends always seemed to do.

The funeral was light in attendance. It was in Dallas, ten or twelve miles from the Galleria where he jumped off. Jim said he saw pictures from the scene, and they made him cry.

I didn't need the photos to cry. I did it all by myself, before I even made it into the funeral parlor. The only family there was a half-sister.

Jim told me that he caught up with Elliot a couple years back on Facebook, and Elliot shared pictures of a daughter that was in Phoenix. He showed me the pictures because she didn't make the funeral.

It was a cremation, and Jim got the ashes.

Chris wasn't able to make the funeral because he was coaching a college team. The playoffs. They lost, and he was free the next weekend to meet us in Atkins. He told us when he arrived that he would have come anyway, win, lose, or draw. We believed him.

We all met at Pat's Pub. This was the first drink we had ever shared together. We purchased a fourth that went untouched and talked about recent successes.

Chris had his team and a new contract in negotiations to secure him for the next five seasons. Jim had his law practice, and it kept him shaking hands with all sorts of men and women. He seemed to know everyone and have more money than he knew what to do with, so he was venturing out to other enterprises.

I shared news of my latest book deal. I had finally been accepted a year after college for the second novel I wrote. The first was utter nonsense. And the next five books were all published and sold well, too. Pay was good, and I could write full-time.

I still received rejections on my short stories, but I didn't tell them that.

I also told them that Rachel had just found out she was pregnant again and we would be expecting our fourth child soon, our first girl.

We made it out to the tracks thirty minutes before midnight. I was carrying the urn. It wasn't really an urn. It was just a cardboard box with a plastic bag of ashes inside.

I walked over to the tree I had sat with Elliot under. I took a copy of *First Blood* with me, mostly for nostalgia.

Jim and Chris tossed rocks.

We hung out until Chris's phone alarm went off, five minutes before midnight. We stood in the same spot we had stood in as kids and waited.

No train.

We waited until two in the morning, maybe because we thought there might be a time delay issue.

Eventually, I turned to Chris and Jim and asked them what I never had before. "So, what did y'all see that night?"

"You mean, other than a ghost train?"

"Yeah, you know what I mean."

Chris looked at Jim and went first. "I saw myself on a football field. Lights were shining down on me, and people filled the stands cheering. I saw myself doing what I loved. Sports in some way or the other."

I looked at Jim. "You?"

"I saw myself making movies."

I shook my head. "What?"

"Yeah, I saw myself making movies, like directing them and stuff."

I continued to shake my head like a bobblehead with a loose spring. "That's impossible. You're not directing movies now, right?"

"No." Jim squinted at me, the cotton of his navy polo shirt being gently pushed in the wind.

"I saw myself writing books and having a wife and five kids and stuff. Now, I'm doing it. I saw my future, and so did Chris, right?"

"Well," said Jim. "I don't know if I saw my future. I just saw what I loved. Like, what made me happiest at the time. Yeah, I like to think I direct all the time, in front of the jury. I tell them stories and direct them in my cases. That's why I always liked watching movies. I feel like I use that now, telling a good story."

None of it made much sense to me. "Did any of you guys ask Elliot what he saw that night?" I asked slowly.

Chris looked at Jim.

Jim swallowed. "Yeah." He took a deep breath, let it out slowly. I think he knew the longer he stalled, the longer until he had to tell us. "I asked him a couple weeks ago. He brought it off. He told me he never cared much about the story until his dad passed, and it felt like a way to honor his memory. He said he was never happier than walking with us to see the Midnight Special, but when the car pulled in front of him, he said he didn't see anything. Like, he saw the train, he saw the storage car, but inside was just nothing. And when we walked back, he went home and cried. He figured he just would never have anything to look forward to. Didn't help that his stepdad caught him sneaking in, drunk again, and whipped him with a telephone. I think all those things in one night really did a number on him."

I didn't say anything for a while. I nodded along with Chris as Jim told his story.

We all looked at each other and eventually decided it was time to spread the ashes. Jim did the honors, spreading them under the tree and across the tracks.

I cried again, thinking that Elliot had the short end of the stick. I had heard more from Jim that past week, about the stepdad that hurt him, and it apparently was even worse when they moved away from Atkins for a new job that he lost within a month.

He drank, and then so did Elliot. He never kept work down, and neither did Elliot, and Elliot's marriage went the same as his stepdad's did, a bitter divorce and custody battle that Elliot couldn't afford. Apparently, this was the real reason they linked up again. Jim just hadn't wanted to tell us they reconnected over legal services he did for free.

We walked back to town, where they were all invited to stay at my house for the weekend. Saturday and Sunday were good, but that Friday night walking back from the railroad tracks, I thought about the Midnight Special.

I thought about how it was supposed to show you your future, but maybe it didn't, and how dangerous it was to believe the lie that someone knew everything about you. To believe in someone else's solution for you.

Maybe I never wanted to be a writer. Maybe I never wanted five kids. Maybe Elliot was more than nothing. No, I knew that was true. Elliot was more than nothing. He was an old friend, and those are hard to come by. You can't make old friends.

On the way back, I heard laughter, faint but sharp, following me. It still does.

For Jim

Karen Quickley

In this image
there's this beautiful
man (you), and a wife,
probably, who looks
something like me
(or at least like who
I once could have been).
There are children—
the daughter, in a bright
red wool coat, carrying
her toddler brother who
is all bundled up
for this cool spring
day.
Lightly, it's raining,
and I'm carrying fresh,
cut daffodils in my basket.
You've got the umbrella
and are keeping both of us
dry.
I'll always remember
your corduroy pants (a
funny little detail) and
these spring petals
falling like snow
here and there because
of the rain and wind.
If I'd really made it here
(there), surely it would

have been in the midst
of a bit
of weather.
And it still seems
like it could have
happened like this—
somehow; some way.
If only this—if only
that.
How far away
and out of reach
you are (and certainly
our children, now that
I'm perimenopausal).
How I want the shape
of no other man on top
of me in my bed. How
I'll probably never
have you there (here).
I'm 49 now, and the time
to stop waiting has come,
but thank you
for your great, brown
beard; thank you
for your kindness.
Thank you for
being the best
and for imbuing
my consciousness
with my favorite dream
manifested in this
digital painting,
artist unknown.

Because

Pat McCutcheon

Because that first long ago night when I came
to your bed fully clothed, you didn't laugh,
just gently pulled off my jeans, sweater, blouse—
though you've told me since you were thinking
"I don't know how to do this with a woman."

Because when we moved in together to a rental,
we stared in terror as neighbors burned crosses on lawns
of couples like us.

Because creating a family with your spirited boy, cheerleader
daughter, and my wisecracking son, we scaled terrain both
perilous and precious.
Despite how much it hurt when that only daughter transitioned,
we cried, grieved,
but now rejoice at the fine son who has emerged.

When I came home one day to our forever home in a new,
accepting town, you blew me away:
you had mown the giant word JOY into our lawn.

You grew a garden of fluttering scarlet poppies, sketched
their intricate leaves and drooping oval pods, then
watercolor washed their crimson petals.

Because you always stream water from the red kettle
onto rich dark roast to make coffee for two,
avidly read the daily papers, *The New Yorker*, Facebook,
and share only the good parts while
I write out checks to pay the bills.
You wash our clothes, I fold the laundry,
and together we chop veggies for stir fry—
the scent of onions rewarding us with their sharp identity
in the warm twilight.

Because you used your art frame to create a goal post
for our grandson's soccer ball.
And you are always your best preschool teacher self
should he throw a tantrum.

Because when we massage one another with our favorite
rain-scented oil, we know each brown mole and freckle
on our beloved's back.

Because after thirty-nine years now, I still knead your calloused
toes while we watch TV,
you rub my shoulders, stroke my graying hair before we sleep,
both find each other's hands in the night.

www.ingramcontent.com/pod-product-compliance
Lightning Source LLC
Chambersburg PA
CBHW070922180626
46817CB00003B/1170